I0628761

Sign up for our newsletter to hear
about new and upcoming releases.

www.ylva-publishing.com

FINDING MS. WRITE

JAE & JOVE BELLE (ED.)

TABLE OF CONTENTS

INTRODUCTION

EVERY TIME WE GO TO a book fair or a literary conference, we again realize what a special bunch "book people" are. When talking about books, even the most introverted readers and writers step outside themselves and become very passionate.

While some of them leave their non-reading spouses at home, many share the love of reading, writing, or publishing with their partners—and some even met their significant others through books. One of them is Ylva Publishing's very own Lois Cloarec Hart, who fell in love with her editor and is now married to her.

So we thought why not put together an anthology full of stories about book people—writers, editors, bookstore owners, librarians, journalists, beta readers, and readers finding love with each other. We had a lot of submissions, and we think we selected a wonderful mix of stories from established and first-time authors from all over the world.

We hope you enjoy this glimpse into the publishing world!

Jove Belle & Jae

CONSIGNMENT
BY ELAINE BURNES

PATRICIA SCANNED THE IMAGES FROM the various security cameras, keeping an eye out for shoplifters. A woman sat by the window in the café, nursing a cup of coffee and typing on her laptop. Again. She spent hours every day in the store, with her one cup, pretending she wasn't there just for the free Wi-Fi. But from the outside, she made the place look busy, so that was good. Patricia moved on to the next screen. A couple of women read to their toddlers in the kids' section. At the new-releases table, Jean chatted with Sally while they unpacked books and stacked them carefully.

Done procrastinating, Patricia turned to her computer and called up the distributor's online order site. When did bookselling become so tedious? Twenty-five years ago, she reminded herself, when she bought the place. Seemed like a good idea at the time, right? Her only competitors were chain stores she could outmaneuver with good customer service. Then came the World Wide Web. And Amazon. But she was surviving. Putting in the café a decade ago helped. Now if she could just find the time to take a vacation. Maybe meet someone. She couldn't remember the last time she had a date.

An incoming e-mail pinged. Patricia switched programs. She stared at the new message in disbelief. She read it again. Three times. Rhonda Fernly would come to her store for a book signing. *The* Rhonda Fernly. Patricia gasped. Rhonda Fernly was the hottest lesbian romance writer...ever. Hot both in looks and in popularity. Even straight women wanted her books. Wanted her. Rhonda almost never went on book tours. Patricia had been trying for years to get her to come. It wasn't as if The Bookmark was a tiny shop in the middle of nowhere. This was trendy, hip Cambridge, Massachusetts. Okay, so the shop was in a strip mall on Mass. Ave., almost in Arlington. Not in the Square, any square. Not Harvard, Central, or even nerdy Kendall Square. Still.

Patricia focused on the details. Next month. Thursday, the fifteenth. Good. Plenty of time to prepare. Maybe the *Globe* would list it in "Bookings." Plan. Come up with a plan. She raced out of the back room to tell her staff. Everyone squealed appropriately. The woman at the window looked up, furrowed her brow, and then went back to typing.

Midweek, Patricia sat alone at the cash register while Sally ate lunch. That woman, the Wi-Fi freeloader, stepped up to the counter holding a book. "Could I speak to the manager, please?" she asked.

Patricia eyed her. She wasn't as young as she had appeared, sitting by the window. About Patricia's age, maybe forties. She didn't recognize the book. "I'm the owner. Will that do?"

The woman's eyes widened, and she inhaled audibly. "I'm sorry. I mean, yes, of course." She wouldn't make eye contact. "I was wondering... I didn't see this on the shelf...

Would you ever consider...?" Her blush deepened with each stammer.

Patricia waited. It wasn't as if there was a line forming.

The woman cleared her throat, made eye contact, and took a deep breath. "I wrote this book. A novel. Could... Would you consider carrying it on consignment?" Those last words came out in a rush.

Patricia mentally rolled her eyes. *One of those.* "So you are," she looked at the cover, "Julie Bower?"

"Brower. With an R. Julia Brower."

"Julia?" She squinted. Time to consider glasses? "Yes, Julia. Brower. Congratulations. That's quite an accomplishment." Which any Tom, Dickhead, or Harriet could achieve with a laptop and CreateSpace.

Julia smiled and held the book like an offering.

Patricia leaned back ever so slightly. *Don't touch it. Once you touch it, you've lost.* "What's it about?"

Julia's face lit up. "Oh. Well. It's a multigenerational family saga about a woman, adopted as an infant, who..."

Patricia's mind wandered. How many bottles of water will Rhonda need? What brand did her agent's e-mail say she preferred?

"...then after the fire, once she realizes all she's lost, she goes in search of herself. Metaphorically, really."

"Really."

"I can leave you this copy. See if you like it." She still held the book. Patricia didn't take it.

What did this make? The tenth this month? At least she was a regular customer. "Sure. Leave it, and I or one of my staff will take a look. I can't promise anything, though."

Julia beamed. "Oh, thank you." She placed the book on the counter and stepped back, nearly colliding with Sally, who had an armful of books. She apologized with a stammer and left the store.

Sally shook her head. "Another one, eh?"

Patricia sighed. "I wonder what her story is."

"I'm sure she'd be happy to tell you. She looks like she has a crush."

"She does not. She only wants me to carry her book. She and a gazillion others."

"I'm surprised you let her leave it."

Patricia shoved the book toward Sally. "You could read it."

Sally backed away. "No way. I can't keep up with the mainstream stuff."

Patricia picked it up and flipped to the copyright page. "It's not self-published. Small press. Lesbian."

"Definitely your genre," Sally said with a wink.

Patricia looked around to see if any customers were in view and then flipped the bird at Sally, who chuckled and disappeared behind a bookcase.

The problem with accepting the book at all was seeing Julia every day. Now that they'd spoken, Patricia feared there was some contract between them, that she should let her know about the book, but she hadn't had time to even think about it. Thankfully, Julia mostly hung out in the café, and Patricia left that to Roberto. Really just Bob, but he said Roberto sounded better for business. No, she had a real contract with Rhonda Fernly, whose agent had a list of demands two pages long.

Patricia updated her website and Facebook page to feature the upcoming reading, sent the notice to her e-mail list and all print and online media she could think of, and put Jean in charge of posters for the stores in the mall. Then she put together the shopping list for the reading—a rug for Rhonda to stand on, a specific brand of bottled water, a snack of select organic fruits and nuts. Endless. But so worth it. Rhonda Fernly! Just to meet her. She'd be the biggest name Patricia had ever had in her store. Would she have room for everyone? As it was, she pushed bookcases out of the way in the reference section to set up chairs. She had to be sure to order enough copies of Rhonda's latest, *Plunging to the Falls.*

The night before the reading, Patricia made sure the cleaners waxed the floor. The day of, she harassed her staff endlessly to keep the store straightened. Nervous as a gnat, she steered clear of the café at the front and the table where Julia sat. She'd deal with her after Rhonda's reading.

As evening approached, Patricia hovered near the door, waiting for Rhonda to arrive. Julia, she noticed, had left. Business usually slowed after dinner, but not tonight. Customers streamed in. All for Rhonda. But no Rhonda. Patricia waited. And, well, waited.

With only minutes to spare, Rhonda arrived with a flash of chartreuse scarf, scarlet lipstick, and an expression that reminded Patricia of Norma Desmond. Not the Gloria Swanson version. Carol Burnett's. Bright scarf, flowing dress, lots of makeup. Her author photo must have been taken decades ago. And her perfume. Floral. Was that Chanel? Patricia wrinkled her nose. Her mother used to wear that.

Patricia had hoped to have time to chat with Rhonda, perhaps show her the store. She tried not to gush as she introduced herself and her staff, impressed Rhonda came alone and not with an entourage.

"Lovely to meet you, Patty," Rhonda said with a glance around the store. "It is rather smaller than I expected."

"It's Patricia, actually."

Rhonda smiled. Cheshire cat–like.

Then Rhonda spent another thirty minutes in the back room—getting ready, she said. What does one have to do other than pull out the book and find the page to read from? Patricia appeased the audience by letting them know Rhonda was in the building. Latecomers were filling the aisles around the chairs.

Finally, Rhonda made her entrance. Wild applause broke out. Patricia breathed a sigh of relief. This would be good. Very good indeed. She introduced Rhonda to a rapt audience of a few men but mostly women, with an age range from college girls to grannies. Pleased, Patricia stepped aside, and Rhonda took the podium. More wild applause.

As it died down, Rhonda glared at the bottle of water. "It's too cold," she said. "I need room temperature." It had been at room temperature since Patricia bought it two days ago, but she switched it out for another one.

The mic was bothersome. "I never use them," Rhonda said. She began reading in a soft voice. The room stilled except for the customers at the front ordering cappuccinos and the boy in the children's section who decided to melt down.

"Could you speak up," someone from the back called out.

Rhonda paused, glared, and then resumed at the same volume. She read in a dreary monotone, plodding through sentences meant to be energetic, erotic. She gestured wildly with ring-bedecked hands, bracelets clanging. That, everyone could hear. Patricia cringed. Rhonda complained she was hot. Patricia's staff set up a fan, but then Rhonda complained it blew her hair. Plus, the fan drowned her out. Then her sheaf of papers flew off the podium. Those in the front row scurried to collect them, and Rhonda spent the next fifteen minutes reordering them. It seemed she hadn't numbered the pages. She resumed reading, but the next page made no sense. She stopped, reordered some more, and continued. People started chatting to each other. Some checked their phones. Those standing wandered away. Others eased out of their seats and left. Patricia wanted to leave too.

By the time Rhonda finished reading—twice as long as Patricia had allotted—half the crowd had left. Instead of taking questions, Rhonda lectured. Romance, she griped, was the miserable stepchild of literature. Ignored, left to fend for itself. Not the brilliant literary fiction prize judges fawned over, or that spoiled brat, mysteries. Patricia wanted to raise her hand and argue that, regardless, romance was her bestselling category. She wouldn't be in business but for the likes of Rhonda's many books. But Rhonda took no questions, barely looked at the audience. She exhorted, "Don't ever let me hear you call my books *lesbian* fiction."

Patricia gasped. The audience, what was left of them, was ninety percent dykes. Rhonda wrote some of the hottest lesbian sex scenes found anywhere. Her books fairly steamed off the shelves.

"Don't belittle yourselves," Rhonda continued, "by labeling me a lesbian writer. We are beyond labels."

Except, Patricia mused, for the ones on the shelves specifically categorizing all books. Labels aren't about the writer, she grumbled to herself because Rhonda sure wasn't going to let her have her say. Labels are for the reader. No one complains when science fiction is off by itself, or mystery. Patricia prided herself on The Bookmark's extensive LGBT section.

The audience, Patricia noticed with concern, glared back at Rhonda. Her staff, now an hour into overtime, gave her pleading glances. Time to shut this down while there were still people left to buy books.

Patricia strode to the podium and declared decisively, "Thank you, Ms. Fernly!" She clapped, hoping the audience would pick up on the cue. One or two did. She escorted Rhonda to the table, with the special Mont Blanc pen Patricia had to purchase for her to sign with, and urged those left to come forward.

Alas, Rhonda sat at the table, piles of her books like a wall around her, but no one lined up. Some mingled and chatted, but no one bought a single fucking book.

"Patty," Rhonda called out, "this water is too warm. I need some ice."

"Patricia," Patricia said.

"Excuse me?"

"My name is Patricia." She fought the urge to bellow.

Rhonda smiled and held up her glass. "Ice?"

Bitch.

Thank God dinner hadn't been part of the deal. Patricia ushered the few remaining customers out, told her staff to leave the chairs set up, and sent them home to get some rest. She ignored Rhonda until she switched off the lights and had time to cool off.

"Thank you for coming, Rhonda," she said as she escorted her to the door.

"Well, that was a bust, as they say in showbiz," Rhonda said. "Not one book signed."

"Maybe they already owned all your books," Patricia said, dodging the truth.

"But even those who brought books didn't ask for them to be signed." Rhonda didn't sound hurt. More peeved. As if it was the customers' fault.

Patricia considered the potential consequences of being blunt. The reading was over. She didn't care if Rhonda ever came back. What could Rhonda do to her? She certainly wasn't going to pull her books from the store.

"I hope you don't mind if I'm brutally honest..." Patricia paused, but Rhonda didn't stop her. "I think you turned them off with that speech. Half had already left because they couldn't hear you read."

Rhonda narrowed her eyes and looked Patricia up and down. "No need to get defensive, my dear." She waved a bejeweled hand around the dim store, lit only by security lights. "This is hardly a venue commensurate with my stature. Forgive me for being 'brutally honest,' as you say, but I think it's more likely my agent confused your little shop for another, more appropriate, establishment."

With that Rhonda pushed through the door and disappeared into the night.

"Fucking bitch," Patricia muttered as she locked the door.

For the next hour, Patricia folded and stacked chairs as a form of therapy. Swoosh, click, thunk. Over and over. What a disaster. She cringed, imagining what would go around Facebook and Twitter by morning, if not already.

It was past midnight when she crawled into bed and lay awake another hour. She reached over a pile of books to click on the light. For the hell of it, she grabbed the one on top and started reading. Didn't even look at the cover or blurb.

The next morning, Patricia staggered around the store, both sleep deprived and hung over. Not from booze, however. She stood in a daze by the front window, at the empty table where Julia should be sitting but wasn't. Nor did she come in over the weekend.

Monday, still feeling stuck between alternate universes, Patricia spotted her, back in her usual seat. She nearly wept with relief. She made two cups of coffee and went over to Julia.

She held out a coffee. "For you."

Julia looked up from her computer and blinked as though waking from a dream. "Oh." She took the coffee. "Thank you."

"May I? I won't stay long." Patricia gestured to the empty seat.

"Of course."

"I loved your book."

"What?"

"Your book. I read it Thursday night. The whole thing. In one big gulp. I didn't want it to end, but I couldn't wait to find out what happened." Patricia didn't usually gush. She'd had time to formulate her feelings, but it still came out in a rush.

"Oh my God. Really?"

"Oh, really. So tell me, the cigarette ash, the house ashes—all those references were metaphors for the ash of her life, right?"

Julia stared at her. She closed her computer. "Yes. You saw that?"

A warmth spread through Patricia, like those tiny tsunami waves that looked harmless but kept flowing ever farther inland. They talked for an hour. Turned out Julia didn't come to the shop for the Wi-Fi. She liked the sunlight in the window, the soft chatter in the background. It made her feel settled to see Patricia and her staff straighten shelves.

"I love how you can pass a table of books and, without appearing to be conscious of it, you fix the piles, move misplaced books, make sense of things. It helps me believe there is an order to the universe. That it isn't just chaos. You may have noticed I'm pretty shy."

No kidding. Julia's gaze dropped to her hands, over to the books, and then out the window, only briefly making eye contact.

"This is a way for me to be out there while still in my own world."

Patricia understood. She knew talking about books was one of the best ice breakers at parties. "I'm really honored you chose my shop. Look, I'll carry your book. I'll order it from the distributor. You don't need to worry about consignment."

Julia looked stunned. "Thank you." It came out in a whisper.

Patricia stood. "I should let you get back to your writing." She started to leave but stopped. Considering the Rhonda Fernly disaster, she surprised herself by asking, "Would you be willing to give a reading?"

Julia's expression switched from stunned to fearful. "I'm not sure..."

"It doesn't have to be right away. Let's get your book in here and selling. As a local author, you'll have a ready audience, I'd think. Plus, the book is damn good! Think about it."

"I will." Julia nodded. "Thank you. I'm so glad you liked it."

Patricia fairly hummed through the rest of the day. Her mood had improved so much that Sally confronted her in the office after closing.

"I saw you talking to that woman. Did you eviscerate her? Is that why you're so happy?"

"Eviscer—?" She picked up Julia's book and thrust it at Sally. "Read this, and tell me it isn't the best thing you've read all year. We're going to carry it, feature it on the front table, and I've asked her to do a reading."

It was Sally's turn to look stunned. "A reading? We don't even know her. She could be worse than Rhonda. Probably would be if she's a newbie. Are you sure?"

"Read it, and then we can discuss."

Sally loved it. Jean loved it. Even the part-time stock boy loved it. They placed piles by the door with a *staff-pick* tag from all of them, a first. Sales began slowly, but momentum built until Patricia was reordering every week. Julia signed piles of copies. Patricia took her to lunch, to convince her to do the reading. "Every week, we sell a few more. Signed ones aren't enough for your fans, I'm afraid. People have been asking about you, knowing you're local."

Julia sipped her tea. She nodded, not necessarily in ascent, but clearly thinking. "I don't know. I like my anonymity. I worry about losing my muse."

"It's just one evening. I promise I'll let you go home right after."

It took a few more weeks, a few more lunches, during which Patricia found herself becoming friends with the shy writer who laughed at her jokes. They liked different authors, so they pushed each other to try new ones. Patricia learned Julia did not write full-time. She worked nights at a call center. That was why she could sit in the shop during the day.

"My writing time is precious," Julia said, during one of Patricia's break-down-her-resolve lunches.

Finally, she agreed to a reading. Six months to the day after Rhonda's. Auspicious, Patricia thought. This time, the to-do list was much shorter. Chairs, podium, microphone, Julia. The *Globe* did not list it, but it didn't matter.

The reading was a huge success. Standing room only. Julia read like an actress, giving each character a unique voice and mannerisms. She chose a compelling passage that rendered even the toddlers quiet. She answered questions endlessly. The only bad part was they ran out of her book. But rather than disappoint those who wanted a few words with her, she talked to everyone in line, writing down their name so she could inscribe a copy when more came in. "The benefit of being a local author," she said. "I'm in here all the time." That prompted everyone to prepay, making Patricia even happier.

Like Rhonda's reading, it went long past closing, but this time Patricia wasn't upset. She still sent her staff home to rest, but Julia insisted on helping her pack up the chairs. How many diva writers do that?

"So, it went well?" Julia asked. They were in the back room while Patricia put the bank deposit together.

Patricia grinned. "Oh, yes, it went very well."

"I'm so relieved."

"Don't you know how good your book is?"

"Not really. My publisher loves it, and obviously that's an objective opinion. They're not going to take on a money loser out of sentimentality. But you still wonder. I got some good reviews online, but not a ton. I'm an unknown with a first book. I have no 'brand,' I've been told."

"I think brands are overrated," Patricia said, thinking of Rhonda.

Julia shrugged. She sat in a quiet stillness. Patricia zipped up the deposit bag. They could leave now. Instead she said, "I'm kind of wired. Any chance you'd be up for some decaf and day-old scones? I know this café..." She nodded toward the front of the store.

"Sounds lovely." Julia's face brightened.

Patricia tossed the deposit in the safe and made coffee. They were about to settle on the couch in the LGBT section when her phone buzzed. She scowled. "The security company." She took the call and explained she was still in the store—that was why the alarm hadn't been set.

Julia looked around. "Are there cameras here?"

"Yes, each section." Damn, the realization hit her. They were being recorded even now.

"It's late," Julia said. "I should probably go, but I walked here, not thinking I'd be going home after midnight."

Patricia tried not to sound disappointed. "Say no more. I'll give you a ride. I just need to drop the deposit off. I shouldn't have kept you so long."

"It's not that. In fact, bring the picnic. We can eat at my place."

Patricia's stomach jumped a bit. She felt warm all over. "I'd like that."

14

They chatted as they walked to the bank a couple doors down, then drove to Julia's. Patricia had to admit, she liked her. A lot.

Julia lived on the third floor of a Victorian over the line in Arlington. Her cat greeted them with a hungry meow. Julia poured her some food, and then they settled on her couch.

Patricia couldn't say either of them started it. Once they'd finished eating, they seemed to move closer simultaneously. They kissed. Both were startled, but only for a fraction of a moment. A tiny hesitation, as though to reassure each other, before ardor replaced surprise.

A good kiss, Patricia had long ago realized, can make you lose all sense of yourself. Pure sensation, no self-consciousness, almost no consciousness other than blazing joy. This was such a kiss.

Did Julia push her down onto the couch or did she pull Julia on top of her? Either way, she liked the weight of her. They fumbled with each other's clothes, but Julia, after nearly tumbling off, sat up, grabbed Patricia's hand, and led her to the bedroom.

She said only, "Will you stay? After."

Patricia whispered, "Yes," and kissed her throat.

After, Patricia was glad Julia had asked her to stay. She didn't want to leave. She lay awake, cradling Julia, asleep in her arms.

In the morning, they made love again. After breakfast, Patricia left, reluctantly, because she had to get ready for work.

Sally followed her to the back room. "Last night with Julia was great, wasn't it?"

Patricia stopped, suddenly faint. "What?"

"The reading?" Sally snapped her fingers in Patricia's face. "What's wrong? You look like you've seen a ghost. Did she throw a tantrum after we left?"

Was that just last night? "Oh, yeah. Terrific reading. No, no tantrum."

"Can't trust these writers. You sure you're okay? You look pale."

"I'm fine."

What had she done? Her thoughts swirled. She wouldn't mind telling Sally what she'd done. Well, not *everything*, but that she was seeing Julia. She'd have to tell her sooner or later. But not yet.

Her phone beeped with a text. From Julia. *Hi.*

Patricia smiled and typed back, *Hi, too.*

Sally was busy getting the cash drawer out of the safe.

Another text from Julia. *I probably shouldn't fling myself at you next time I'm in the store. But know I want to.* No abbreviations. How writerly.

Patricia responded, *That might be best until I have time to let staff know.* She paused. What, exactly, would she say?

Julia typed back, *Understood.* Then a little heart.

A little heart! Patricia smiled. She looked up to find Sally staring at her.

"You? Texting? What's up with that?"

"Nothing."

Sally's eyes narrowed. "Something's going on."

Not now. Patricia needed time to get used to this. "Don't you have a store to open?"

Because of Julia's night job, they only saw each other on weekends. When Julia came into the store, Patricia avoided even looking in her direction. When she spied her on the security camera, Julia was usually staring out the window. She was having trouble concentrating on her writing but said she didn't mind.

Once they settled into a kind of routine, weekend dates and sleepovers, the occasional morning delight on Patricia's day off, she prepared to tell Sally and then the rest of the staff.

After closing, Patricia and Sally were in the office. Patricia stammered, "So…Julia and I have become…friends. Well, more than friends…"

"Are you making her a partner in the store?" Sally leaned back in her chair and put her feet on Patricia's desk.

"Partner? No…"

"Then what is it?"

"You see…" She stared at the floor.

Sally snorted. Patricia looked up to see her friend grimacing, trying not to smile.

Confused, she asked, "What's going on?"

Sally burst out laughing. "I'm sorry. I couldn't hold it in anymore."

"Hold what in?"

"Do you seriously think no one knows what's going on between you two lovebirds?"

"Lovebirds! You know?"

"Only since the morning after the reading. God, you were disgustingly happy."

Patricia's mind raced. "Does everyone know?"

"The UPS guy might not have made the connection yet. But yeah, pretty much everyone else."

"Oh."

Sally leaned in and squeezed Patricia's hand. "Hey, I'm happy for you. We all are. Just be careful. I don't want you to get hurt. You haven't done this in a while."

"Thanks for the reminder."

A palpable relief lightened Patricia. Like coming out. Now she was free to see Julia, smile at her in the store, talk about their dates the way Sally talked about hers. Life began to feel very complete. Successful business. Successful relationship.

Until Julia started declining dates. She didn't hide why. "I'm not getting any writing done."

"I'm sorry."

Julia pulled her into a hug. "Don't be. I'm happy. Except, well, my editor is on me. I had a nice break after I sent my manuscript in, but I've got the edits back. And now people come up to me in the store all the time. It's hard to concentrate."

"Shit."

"It's just for a few weeks, but I need to pull back."

"A few weeks?" Patricia's insides hollowed out. Crystal clear, she realized she had consigned her heart to Julia. Was it now being handed back? Unwanted?

"I'm sorry."

"Don't be," she said, pretending to be understanding. "This is what you want." *But is it all you want?* She wanted to ask but didn't dare.

Julia stopped coming to the store. They limited their time to one date a week. For Patricia, it meant a harsh withdrawal from a sweet addiction.

"Where's your new pal?" Sally asked.

They were rearranging the remainder table. Books that were once hot sellers got sold off at bargain basement prices after losing their glow. Patricia tried not to see her relationship with Julia as losing its glow.

"She needs time, apart, to get some writing done. I seem to be a distraction."

"It's probably just as well," Sally said.

"How so?"

"Think about it. Married to a writer. Clearly, you'd hardly see her."

"Who said anything about marriage?"

"I'm just saying, a writer can't be monogamous. She'd be cheating on you with every character in her head."

"Thanks for that image." Patricia adjusted the pile of Barbara Kingsolver's latest. "But I like her."

"Does she like you as much?"

"I don't know. I thought so."

"If she does, it'll work out. If not, you're better off without her. Give her time."

"Set her free? And if she loves me, she'll come back?"

"Exactly." Sally leaned close, conspiratorially. "And if she doesn't come back, hunt her down and kill her."

Patricia laughed. "You've been spending too much time in the horror section."

The days without Julia dragged by, reminding Patricia how much better life was with her in it. She shouldn't need Julia to make her happy, but damn it, maybe she was one of those people who operated better when partnered. Julia wanted to quit the call center job and write full-time, and Patricia could offer her that. But it was way too early in their relationship to suggest it. Julia's first love was writing. Patricia had to accept that before she could take any next steps. What if Sally was right?

Two weeks dragged into three and crossed into a fourth before Patricia got a text from Julia that made her heart soar and forget any misgivings.

I finished my edits!

Congratulations! Patricia typed back.

Let's celebrate.

After a sumptuous dinner, they cuddled on Patricia's couch in front of a roaring fire. Life was, once again, good.

Patricia played with a strand of Julia's hair. "I know writers can be funky about this, but can you reveal what the next book is about?"

"I'd rather not." Julia twisted around to look at her. "It's purely superstition. I just get weird about things like that."

"So what should we talk about?"

Julia fingered a button on Patricia's shirt. "I was hoping we didn't need to talk."

"Oh. I'm good with that."

Words are a singular form of communication, common to both writers and booksellers. But there are many ways to communicate without words, and Patricia and Julia explored them all. They went for walks around Fresh Pond, holding hands. They watched movies at the artsy theater in Kendall Square. They danced. They kissed. They touched. They melded together and flowed apart, only to rejoin and rejoice. Patricia's hands made order of chaos. Julia's fingers created ecstasy, elation, bliss. An entire thesaurus of emotion.

One Sunday morning, they lay entwined on Julia's bed, bright sun warming their bodies. Julia slept, spent. Patricia traced words across Julia's back, kissed her shoulder. She had come back.

The next morning, back at her own place, Patricia watched TV while eating breakfast. Rhonda Fernly had a new book coming out and was going to be interviewed on *The Now Show*.

The host, Matt Lager, gushed, "Your hundred and twentieth book! How do you keep it so fresh?"

"Story is everywhere, my dear," Rhonda said.

The low lighting and soft-focus lens made her look thirty years younger than she had at the store.

"So, this new book," Matt burbled, "is it based on a real bookseller?"

Patricia choked on her toast.

Rhonda winked and smiled. "I only tell tales between the covers."

Patricia turned off the set. When she got to the store, she rummaged through her box of advance reader copies. There, in the corner, Rhonda's latest, *Lust Among the Stacks*. She barricaded herself in the office and spent the day reading— and nearly retching.

The main character, Mary Sue, was a world-famous romance author. While on tour, she has hot, throbbing sex with a bookseller in, *gasp*, Cambridge, Massachusetts. Patricia wanted to throw the book out the window but didn't want anyone else to find it. *Dear God.* She had to sell this in her store. In *Cambridge!* She forced herself to read the whole thing. The plot deteriorated into a murder for hire as the bookseller attempts to kill off Mary Sue and take her place on the tour. She's saved by a sexy police detective. *Really, Rhonda? You come up with this?*

Patricia tossed the book into the recycling bin and rubbed her face. It was even worse than she had imagined when she'd told Rhonda off. What could she possibly do? This, unfortunately. What was that saying she always saw on Facebook, "Don't piss off a writer"? Well, shit and a half.

She thought of Julia. Is this what she had to look forward to? Where do writers get their ideas?

Oh God! What have I gotten myself into?

Dazed, she wandered into the stockroom and stared at the piles of boxes of Rhonda's book, embargoed till the official publication day. Tomorrow. Patricia wanted to chuck them into the dumpster. Burn them. Hire someone to mur—

"Hey, boss." Stewie, the stock boy, greeted Patricia as he punched in. "I'll get those unpacked today, so they're ready to go out in the morning." He nodded toward the boxes Patricia stared at, plotted about.

"Sure. Thanks." She retreated to her office.

She couldn't face Julia. She couldn't face anyone, but especially not Julia. What was she writing about? Patricia peered at the security camera image, trying to zoom in on Julia's laptop. Too blurry. She couldn't help but replay their every interaction. Was she merely fodder for Julia's muse? Rather than being distracted, Julia had been writing feverishly. Clearly inspired by something. Patricia didn't want to be anyone's muse. Not if it meant being displayed naked, literarily, for all the world to see.

Patricia fell into a funk. Abruptly, she was too busy to see Julia. Preparing for inventory, she lied. When Julia asked for her, she told her staff to say she was busy with paperwork. When Julia called, Patricia let it go to voice mail. She ignored texts. She needed time to think.

She had positioned Rhonda's book on a table by the romance section, not by the door. It was not going to get prime placement, to hell with publisher demands. Still, it sold out in hours. Then Patricia had to avoid the sales floor altogether. Did that woman look at her funny? Had she read it? Did she know it was about Patricia? Was she picturing Patricia nak—? *Oh God.*

Sally thought it was funny. "I think we should capitalize on it. Advertise—"

Patricia's cold stare stopped her dead.

"I was kidding. I think you're making way too much of this. How many bookstores are there in Cambridge, anyway? Dozens."

"Maybe in Harvard Square, but not in an 'out-of-the-way corner of Cambridge, far from the learned miasma of the Harvard's hallowed halls,'" she said, quoting from *Lust Among the Stacks*. "Miasma. Harvard's hallowed halls. She actually wrote that."

Sally had her feet up on the desk, leaning back. She flipped through a tattered copy of *Lust*. "Maybe it's not you at all. Maybe it's me. Did you ever think of that? She never says Prunella is the owner, just that she works at—what does she call it? The Bookworm."

Patricia glared at her over new reading glasses.

Sally tossed the book on the desk, stood, and stretched. She glanced at the security monitors. "Julia's gone. It's safe for you to leave the cave."

"I'm not avoiding her."

"Yes, you are." Sally didn't stick around to argue.

Patricia flipped the key in the lock and tucked the night deposit under her arm. She turned and almost bumped into Julia. She froze.

Julia looked as if she was about to say something, then stopped. She stepped aside and walked beside Patricia past the darkened hardware store and to the bank just beyond.

After Patricia dropped the bag into the deposit drawer, Julia spoke, the pain in her voice solid and heavy. "I don't know what I did, but I deserve to know why you can't stand to see me or even speak to me."

Patricia closed her eyes and leaned against the brick wall. Traffic roared by on Mass. Ave., as heavy at ten o'clock as at rush hour. "I'm not sure I know how to describe what's happened," she began. "I don't have the way with words that you do."

"Do the best you can."

Patricia looked into Julia's hurt-filled eyes. Sadness filled the night. How had so much happiness turned into so much sadness without either of them saying or doing anything? It wasn't Julia's fault. "Not here," she said. She drove Julia home and turned off the car but didn't get out. "Here's the thing…" Then she told her. All about Rhonda's book, about how betrayed she felt, how scared she was.

"Thanks for telling me," Julia said at the end. "What do we do with this?"

"I'm not sure."

"Let's think about it." Then she got out of the car and went inside. She didn't wait for Patricia. She shut her door.

That was it. Done. Finished. Patricia thought she should feel better, but of course she didn't.

The next weekend, Julia again waited for her at the store.

"I've been thinking," Julia said.

"So have I," Patricia said. She hadn't been able to come up with a way around the hurt. But seeing Julia, so wan and sad, she longed to reach out and touch her hair. To hold her.

They walked to the bank and then sat in Patricia's car. She was too nervous to drive. The lot, packed during the day, was mostly empty except for a few cars scattered about.

"I'm really pissed at you," Julia said. "But there are things you need to know, at least about me. Writing is part creativity, part business, and there's no room for intimacy in either of those."

Here it comes. "That's what I'm afraid of."

"Wait." Julia's tone softened. "I'm not saying there's no room for intimacy in my heart. That's my point. You wonder why I won't tell you what I'm working on. Thing is, until we kissed, I was about to ask you to read my manuscript."

"Really?"

"I wanted your opinion. But not anymore. Don't worry, you aren't in it. I'm afraid, too, you see. That first kiss meant you weren't just a reader, you were someone special to me, and I won't ask you to comment on my writing. My ego can't handle that. I wouldn't believe you if you said it was terrific—"

"But I've already said your writing is terrific."

"I know. I'm not talking rationally here. I'm speaking as a writer, with a fragile, egocentric inner monster who finds it easier to trust strangers than loved ones."

"Loved ones?"

"Yes, you moron. I've fallen in love with you. And you know damn well you've fallen for me. But the fact that you're willing to let Rhonda Fuck-all destroy us makes me both very sad and very angry."

Patricia cringed to hear the hurt in Julia's voice. "Rhonda humiliated me."

"No one knows that was you."

"I do."

"Did you make the wild passionate love she describes in the book?"

"Of course not! You read it?"

"I had to. I had to see if you were justified in your outrage, if anything I might write could hurt you that much. But that could have been any bookseller in the country. She was on a national tour."

"It takes place in Cambridge."

"So what. Maybe she liked the locale but really had the hots for some chic in Seattle."

Patricia supposed she could be right.

"By the way," Julia continued, "I thought that whole dildo scene was written for straight readers."

Patricia looked at her, incredulous. "You want to get into a literary criticism of a Rhonda Fernly romance? Now?"

Julia shook her head. "Sorry, occupational hazard." She relaxed back into the seat. "Look, I can't promise I'll never write a character who's a bookseller. Just because we writers draw on people we know for our characters doesn't make us paparazzi soul robbers."

Patricia stared at her hands. The cold reality of her idiocy sent a shiver through her. "Have you really fallen in love with me?"

Julia's eyes welled, and she turned toward the window. "God help me, yes."

Patricia looked at her. "Me too. I mean, with you."

Julia let out a shaky breath that fogged the glass. "I had no idea what I'd do if you didn't feel the same way."

"Can you forgive me?"

Julia turned back. "Can you forgive yourself?"

"As long as you know booksellers can have fragile egos, too."

"Noted. I'll also promise never to write about a bookseller. Unless it's a man." She paused, smiling. "A gay man. A really old, gay man."

Patricia laughed and nodded. "That works for me." She took Julia's hand. "I am so very sorry."

"I do forgive you." Julia squeezed back.

They sat quietly, holding hands, watching a bus roar by. *She came back. How lucky am I?*

"Any chance we could recreate that love scene?" Julia asked, her voice low. "It was pretty hot."

"The one with the dildo?" Patricia asked.

"No. The other one."

Patricia thought about that. "I don't think those positions are physically possible. I might dislocate a hip."

"Worth a try?"

"I'm game."

Patricia started the car and drove Julia home.

Scanning the security images, Patricia noted the empty café. A couple of people browsed in the cookbook section. Julia entered, ordered a coffee, sat by the window, and looked right into the camera. She smiled, blew a kiss, and then opened her laptop. Patricia grabbed her cane and hobbled out to greet her.

No, not really.

They'd written a much better love scene.

CHERRY PARK PULP

BY JOVE BELLE

THE EARLY SPRING SUN SPARKLED through the clear glass. The windows, along with the house, still had the shine of something new. Barbara and her husband, Richard, had moved in when they'd married, just after the war, and fallen into a comfortable routine. At seven each morning, Richard drove to the station to take the train into the city, leaving Barb free to do...whatever. He was a money man. A broker that turned nothing into fortunes and fortunes into even bigger fortunes.

"I'm planning a roast for dinner," Barb called out as she ran through her mental checklist for the day. Even though she didn't care for red meat, Richard loved it, making it an appropriate choice for their anniversary. Plus, if he ate enough, perhaps he'd fall asleep right after dinner.

"That sounds great, darling, but I have a late meeting." Richard stepped into the room with three ties draped over his arm, one blue, one black, and one yellow. "Have you seen my red tie?"

"Wear the blue." Barb slipped the tie off his arm, looped it around his neck into a perfect double Windsor, and rose up on her toes to kiss his cheek. He wore the red tie only when he had a date with one of his women. Of course, she wasn't supposed to know that, and it made suggesting the blue all the sweeter. Not that it would stop him from fooling around, but he'd have to work a little harder to hide the lipstick on his collar.

"All right." He smiled his charming smile that showed too many teeth. "The blue it is."

"When will you be home?" Barb took the other ties from his arm. She had to play this just right. She wanted to make him feel guilty enough to buy her a new typewriter, but not so guilty that he canceled his plans. Barb poured him a cup of coffee and slid it into his hand.

He shrugged and sipped the coffee. "It'll be late. At least nine."

"Oh." Barb averted her eyes and did her best do look as if she were sad but trying to hide it. "It's just that..."

"Can we have the roast another time?" Richard slipped his arm around her shoulders and pulled her into a sideways hug. "Tomorrow night?"

Barb sniffed and nodded. "I suppose. But today..." She let her voice fade.

"What?" Richard took a long drink of coffee. If he had any idea what she was referring to, he hid it well.

"It's just that today is the twelfth."

"The twelfth?" Richard's eyes opened wide, betraying the exact moment he realized the significance of the date. "Of April. Oh, Barb, I'm sorry. I've been working so hard on this new account, and I forgot. I'm a terrible husband."

For any other woman, he would have been right, but for Barb, Richard's chronic philandering and absentee status made him just about perfect. "No, your work is important. I understand."

"I should cancel."

"No, no. I would feel just awful if you did that." Barb slipped her apron from around her waist and set it on the counter. "I have plenty to keep me busy here. My book club meets this afternoon, and I promised to make an apple pie."

"Well, now I'm really sorry I won't be here tonight." Richard smoothed his hand over his hair, tidying his beautiful, boyish curls that he kept slicked back with Brylcreem. With his dimpled smile and easy confidence, combined with the war stories he told with swaggering bravado, he was a charming man. Perfect husband material, really, and exactly what Barb needed.

She patted his arm and handed him his briefcase. "It's all right. I'll make the roast tomorrow night, like you said."

"If you're sure." Richard was halfway out the back door when he turned, briefcase extended like a pointer in her direction. "Why don't you take the checkbook downtown and buy yourself something nice. You could do with a new dress or two."

"Well, I do have my eye on something." Not a dress, but that beautiful teal blue Smith-Corona Electric in the window at Woolworth's... She'd give up ten new dresses for that.

"That's decided, then." He patted the doorframe and stepped outside.

Barb waited until she heard the car start, and then she rushed to get her coat and purse. If she hurried, she'd have just enough time to make it downtown and back before the ladies arrived.

"Yoo-hoo!" As usual, Abby from the next street over was the first to arrive. She pushed the door open with her backside and entered without waiting to be invited. To be fair, Barb had propped the screen door open and left the main door slightly ajar. That was as good as an invitation on book club day.

"Hello, Abby." Barb glanced up from her work at the kitchen counter. "I know I promised apple pie, but I just couldn't resist." As much as she loved apple pie—and she loved it a lot—the smell of toasted coconut outside the bakery this morning was simply too much. When she'd finished with her shopping, she headed straight home, her new typewriter swinging at her side as she walked. As soon as she arrived, she started baking.

"Oh, that looks lovely." Abby set a Tupperware snack tray on the table with a heavy sigh. "I know you said not to bring anything." She touched Barb lightly on the shoulder. "But I had some cold cuts and cheese."

Abby had a stout husband and four equally stout boys. It was unlikely she had anything extra just lying around, but that was her way.

"Oh, you didn't have to do that, but thank you. There on the table is just fine." Barb sprinkled toasted coconut over her freshly frosted cake, and Abby dipped a plump finger into the remains of the cream cheese icing.

The screen door squealed and then slammed against the frame.

Barb looked up.

"Oh my. I'm sorry." A stranger stood just inside the door. She shuffled from foot to foot and smiled sheepishly. "I didn't mean to bump it."

Abby hustled over to the newcomer and linked their arms together. "Barb, this is Muriel. She's Caren's oldest."

Barb's mind raced. She had no idea who Caren was or why Abby thought that was a suitable way to clarify who this person—Muriel—was or how it explained why she was standing in Barb's kitchen. Nonetheless, she smiled her best and said, "It's lovely to meet you."

Muriel returned the smile, a dazzling, brilliant display of teeth that made Barb falter even more. Where Abby was short and solidly built, with extra padding attributed to the birth of her four boys, Muriel was tall and slender. Rather than the traditional housewife dress that was the norm in Cherry Park, she wore a button-down dress shirt that fit too well to be a man's, slim-fitting trousers, and sensible, yet highly polished, shoes. Her makeup was straight from the Hollywood rags, and combined with her perfectly coifed curls à la Hollywood glam, she looked like a bona fide movie star.

Back when Barb had been young and more than a little reckless, she'd had a *friend* who looked a great deal like Muriel. No, that wasn't right. They looked nothing alike, but they both carried themselves with the same casual daring, as though they had been miscast as the heroine and were really the dashing hero. Later, that friend had become her roommate, and Barb finally understood what made her different. All it took was the lion's share of a bottle of very fine brandy and an extremely satisfying round of cunnilingus. They'd remained friends—and more—after they'd graduated and gone off to work. Barb worked for the phone company, kept her Victory Garden to do her part to support the boys overseas, and spent her nights not thinking about how perfect it felt when her friend curled up behind her as they slept.

The war ended; she lost her job at the phone company, and Richard, along with the other soldiers, returned from flying bombers over tiny islands in the South Pacific with names Barb couldn't even pronounce. Her friend moved to Manhattan, and Barb moved to Cherry Park. Now, five years later, she spent her nights trying not to think about how much she missed being held at night. Muriel looked to be about the age Barb had been when she'd married Richard.

Barb reflexively brushed her hands over her hair, patting it gently to tame the frazzled mess.

"...and so she'll be with us through the summer at a minimum. Possibly longer, depending upon how her job search goes."

Barb missed a good part of Abby's explanation but smiled and nodded along in the appropriate places. She stared at Muriel, captivated by the teasing glint in her eyes that promised more trouble than Barb could afford. It was the same look that always led to a lot of fun followed by a lot of consequences when she'd been younger—a look she'd never figured out how to say no to.

The conversation droned, a low buzz with the occasional shrill note mixed in as Abby and Harper argued over the emotional impact of their latest read. Barb half listened. It was rude, but truth be told, she hadn't enjoyed reading the book and cared even less about discussing it. Besides, how could she be expected to concentrate while Muriel sat opposite her, drinking sloe gin and staring at her with those intensely teasing eyes? It was downright distracting. And if the arch of Muriel's eyebrow was anything to go by, she knew exactly what that look was doing to Barb.

"…think, Barb?" Abby's voice barely broke through her mental haze.

Muriel took another sip, her glass unable to fully hide her smirk.

"Barb? Are you with us?" Abby patted her on the knee. "Everything okay, sugar?"

Muriel looked pointedly down the hall toward the bedrooms, and Barb gulped for air. "What?" She forced her gaze away from Muriel and to Abby. "What's that, now?"

"The book, silly. What did you think?"

Barb considered her words. It was always so tricky, finding the balance between polite society and the absolute truth. "Well, it wasn't my favorite book we've read."

"What didn't you like about it?" Muriel asked, her voice low and teasing to match her eyes. How had her blatant flirtation gone unnoticed by the other women?

"It was boring." Betty jumped in, answering first for a change and smiling at Muriel in a way that made it clear her flirtation hadn't gone as unnoticed as Barb thought.

Leave it to that harlot to pick up on the subtle difference in Muriel's attention. Wasn't it enough that she had an ongoing affair with Richard? Did she have to hone in on the most interesting person to walk through Barb's back door since…well, since she'd said "I do"?

"Boring?" Muriel gave Betty a fleeting glance. She returned her focus to Barb with a lazy, borderline predatory smile. "Did you find the book boring, Barb?"

"I suppose that's one way to describe it."

Muriel nodded and leaned forward, elbow braced against her knee, chin propped on her closed fist, her movements liquid and smooth and downright feline. "What would you find…not boring?"

"You mean interesting?" Abby interrupted. "This book *was* interesting. What a silly question."

"Aunt Abby, what about the new style of book you found? Tell them about it," Muriel said.

Aunt? With that one word, Barb connected the dots. Caren was Abby's sister-in-law. Muriel was her niece.

Abby's cheeks flared red, and she stammered, "Well… yes…you see."

Barb patted her on the back, and Betty said, "Come now, it can't be that bad." She sounded interested, which made sense. Anything that embarrassed Abby that much had to be interesting by Betty's standards.

Harper nodded. "Just tell us. I'm intrigued."

"Remember I told you about my old college mate who went to work for that publisher? Well, we met for lunch the other day, and she told me about this new style of book that features…women…" Abby's voice faded away, and she drew her brow together in concentration. "And these women… fall in love."

Betty flopped back in her seat with a sigh. "That's exactly what we've been reading. Boring."

"That does sound much the same, Abby." Barb hated to agree with Betty, but sometimes it was unavoidable.

"Go on. Tell them the rest." Muriel rose like a goddess from the settee and went to pour herself another drink. On her way past, she plucked Barb's glass from her hands, her touch lingering on Barb's fingers far too long.

"Yes, well, you see…" Abby spoke in stops and starts, and Barb's attention switched to Muriel long before she reached the point.

Muriel met Barb's gaze in the mirror above the serving station. She poured herself another glass of sloe gin and Barb bourbon over ice. She did it all without looking away from Barb. When Muriel licked her lips languidly, Barb found herself mirroring the motion. An understanding passed between them in that moment. Muriel's actions were more than a flirtation. She was making a clear offer, a promise to follow through on the implied intimacy she offered with each casual movement. And as Barb stared at the moisture that clung to Muriel's lower lip, every dirty intention that she had swallowed down with her marriage vows flared to life.

"Ooh, that does sound interesting." Betty's voice cut through the haze Muriel cast over her.

She had no idea what Abby had said, but if Betty approved, Barb disapproved on principle.

"I don't know," Harper said, decidedly less enthusiastic. "What do you think, Barb?"

Muriel pressed Barb's drink into her hand and then continued to the settee. She answered instead of Barb. "Well, it definitely won't be boring."

"But it seems...distasteful," Harper continued. "Two women should not do those things together. It's not God's way."

Betty scoffed. "Since when do you care about God?"

It was a fair question. Sure, Harper went to church on Sunday. They all did. Harper also spent Sunday afternoons playing poker, smoking cigarettes from the pack her lover— not husband—kept rolled into the sleeve of his white T-shirt, and drinking indecent amounts of whiskey.

Harper didn't even blush at the implication of Betty's accusation. "Even a heathen like me knows God doesn't approve of two women carrying on like that."

"So what? He doesn't approve of a lot of things. That's never stopped you."

Harper glared at Betty as she took a long draw from her glass. The ice shifted and clanked against the sides as she drained the remains of her Jim Beam. She didn't respond.

Somewhere in the middle of their argument, Barb realized *exactly* what type of book Abby was suggesting. Her brain battled against itself, half embracing the idea of their book club discussing the pulp fiction she loved so much, the other half panicking at the thought of them discovering how familiar she was with the genre. Not that she'd bought any herself, but why would she do that when her publisher would supply them for free? Abby wasn't the only one with an old college friend in the industry; only Barb suspected her relationship with hers was more complicated as Abby was unlikely to have slept with her friend or published a book with her.

Barb followed Harper's example and drained her glass.

"I vote yes." Betty smiled at the group, a sparkle of keen interest in her eyes. For the first time, someone had suggested a book she wouldn't find boring. "Obviously, Abby is a yes since she suggested it. Harper is a clear no. What about you, Barb? It's two to one now. Want to make it a clear majority?"

Barb stared at her glass, wishing it would magically refill itself. She took a deep breath and tried to calm her thoughts. It didn't help, but the rest of the group was staring at her, so she had to say something. She opened her mouth. Closed it. Took a sip of the melted ice gathered at the bottom of her glass.

Muriel laughed, a dark, low chuckle that stirred things deep inside Barb. She rose from her seat and crossed the room. "Let me help with that." She took Barb's empty tumbler and refilled it once again.

The brief reprieve should have given Barb an opportunity to collect herself. Instead, she spent the few moments fixated on the easy, controlled way Muriel moved from place to place.

"Don't keep us in suspense, Barb! Yes or no. Let's have it."

"Yes, well…" She sipped her drink. "Abby, could I see the book?" She asked the question before she considered the full weight of it. What if Abby pulled one of Barb's books from her oversized black purse? Not that they had any way of knowing their unassuming suburban friend Barbara Wilson né Lewis and the scandalous, worldly author B.B. Lewis were one and the same. Logically, she knew that, but the swell of panic in her chest demanded that she ready herself to run. Where to, she didn't know. But fleeing was her only clear option if one of B.B.'s bawdy adventures found its way into her parlor.

Abby blushed as she rooted around in her bag. Despite her obvious discomfort, she eventually produced the book and held it out to Barb. Her cheeks grew redder with every passing moment.

Barb took it from her carefully and flipped it over. *The Women of West Hollywood*. The hard, repetitive *kerwoosh* of her blood flooding through her head receded. It wasn't her book. It wasn't even her publisher. She took a deep breath, and this time, it helped to settle her thoughts.

"You know, Abby, a friend of mine from Vassar also works in publishing. She mentioned this new trend as well." Barb left out the part where that same friend had shared her bed through most of college and had encouraged her to write her own book at the beginning of the trend several years ago. Barb had released one a year, starting her senior year at Vassar. The publishing royalties were tucked away in a rainy-day fund, along with half of each week's budget for household expenses and any other bit of change she could secret away from Richard. She didn't know what she'd do with it all, but she imagined she'd grow tired of his philandering at some point. Not that she was jealous, but he wasn't as discreet as she would have liked. Eventually, word would get back to her friends and family, if it hadn't already, and she wanted to have options when that day came. "I understand Harper's hesitation, but I also think it wouldn't hurt for us to expand our options a bit."

Harper, who had been visibly stiff for most of the debate, relaxed incrementally. "I suppose we could try just this one."

Betty released a hearty whoop that wasn't very ladylike.

Barb smiled despite herself. Very few women embraced their inner harlot as readily and easily as Betty. It was refreshing, if not entirely charming.

Abby pulled two more copies of the book from her purse and handed one each to Betty and Harper. "Now that that's decided, I need to get going. The children will be home any time now." She pulled herself out of the lounge chair with a loud huff. "Muriel will share my copy, but the rest of you owe me a dime each."

And with that, the meeting was over. Muriel gave her a secret smile as Barb made her way out the door.

They finished *The Women of West Hollywood*, and even Harper had to admit it had been exciting to read about the forbidden nature of the story. They read and discussed two more and were reviewing the third today. They still hadn't stumbled across any of Barb's titles, and she was thankful for that. She had no idea how she would react to reading and discussing something she wrote without actually letting anyone know she was the author. It was all far too complicated.

Muriel continued to attend with Abby, and with each visit her flirtation grew bolder. The glances lasted longer, the smiles grew more heated, and the casual touches became increasingly less casual. As dangerous as it was, Barb couldn't bring herself to put a stop to it.

Last week the meeting had been held at Betty's house, and Muriel had slipped down the hall after Barb when she excused herself to powder her nose. Somewhere between Barb flushing the toilet and opening her makeup case, Muriel knocked lightly on the door. Bemused, Barb opened the door, and without preamble, Muriel had pulled Barb into her arms and kissed her. And Barb hadn't been able to think of anything else since. At the moment, she couldn't even remember the name of the book they were supposed to discuss today.

Once again the reading group was meeting at Barb's house, and she was about halfway through a double batch of chocolate chip cookies.

"No coconut cake this time?" Muriel leaned casually against the backdoor frame, her legs crossed at the ankles and her arms folded over her chest. She looked Barb up and down, her gaze lingering on Barb's hips and breasts.

Barb blushed harder than a mere glance should ever warrant. To distract herself, she turned and opened the oven. "Not today."

Muriel apparently took the open oven as an invitation to come into the kitchen. She stood far too close, placed her hand lightly on the small of Barb's back, and bent to look in the oven with her. "Mmm, looks good."

Her touch ignited a fire in Barb that radiated out from the point of contact. Barb closed her eyes and forced herself to take a long, slow breath. This was neither the time nor the place for her libido to remind her exactly how long it had been since she'd felt that kind of heat low in her belly. A shudder ran through her, despite her best effort to contain it. She sidestepped away from Muriel and closed the oven.

"You're here alone? Where's Abby?" Barb's brain was flooded with too much...everything. She wanted to do too many contradictory things all at once, and it was a miracle that she managed to even say those few short sentences.

Muriel smiled, one eyebrow arched. "One of her boys is home sick from school. I thought she called."

"Oh, that's right." Barb remembered now. That left her alone with Muriel for the next—she glanced at the wall clock—nuts, twenty minutes at least. Muriel was early, and Harper and Betty were almost always late. "Well, it's nice that you could make it."

"Yes, it certainly is."

She stepped closer again, and Barb took a step back. "How's the job search?"

Muriel took another step toward Barb, close enough that she could brush the back of her knuckles softly over Barb's cheek.

Barb's eyes slipped shut, and she sighed. This was far too dangerous, and, God help her, she was too overcome to stop it.

"It's not going well at all. It's been over five years since the war ended, and employers still use the excuse of putting 'the boys' back to work. It's infuriating."

Barb turned her face ever so slightly and pressed a kiss to Muriel's palm. She was tired of pretending and, just for a moment, allowed herself to enjoy the nearness of Muriel's body to her own. "What will you do?"

They'd had this conversation before. Muriel resented that she might have to settle for something well beneath her education, and Barb encouraged her to take any job she could find. There wasn't a lot to choose from for young women these days.

"I may expand my search, look at other areas."

This was news to Barb. Until now, Muriel had been unwilling to discuss anywhere that wasn't New York City.

"Other cities?"

Muriel nodded and took another step forward. "Other cities, other states, even other countries if I have to."

Two more steps and Muriel was pressed flush against her front with the cabinets to her back. Muriel placed her hand easily on Barb's waist, and Barb reached behind herself to grip the counter. The heat of Muriel's body against hers burned every thought right out of her head. All she could concentrate on was the perfect fit of their curves and the warm puff of Muriel's breath on her cheek.

"Is this okay?" Muriel asked as she leaned in close enough to brush her lips against Barb's.

Barb nodded and let her eyes close. Muriel's mouth was soft and delicate as she kissed Barb, and they continued like that long enough for Barb to lose track of time. She stayed wrapped up in Muriel and surrendered herself to the press of her lips and the faint mint flavor when she slipped her tongue into Barb's mouth. It was wonderful…overwhelming…

Muriel cupped the back of Barb's neck, her fingers smooth and firm as she held Barb still and deepened the kiss.

A moan rose from somewhere deep inside her, sounding wanton even to Barb's own ears.

"God, you are amazing," Muriel murmured without fully breaking the kiss.

The oven timer dinged, loud and impossible to ignore. For the life of her, Barb couldn't remember why the oven was on in the first place.

Muriel loosened her grip and took a step back.

Barb felt the loss acutely. She reached out to Muriel, eager to renew their embrace.

"The cookies." Muriel smiled. Her perfect lipstick was smudged, visible evidence of what had just happened between them.

While Barb removed the cooking sheet from the oven, Muriel slipped out of the room. When she returned, her makeup was pin-up perfect again. The flush of heat in Barb had settled to a low, easy simmer—still there, but not overwhelming. Barb excused herself to check her own makeup in the mirror. As she suspected, she was a bigger wreck than Muriel. Her lipstick had smeared, along with Muriel's shade at her temple, a bit on her jaw, lower still on her neck, and a perfect lip mark in the open V between her lapels, just above her cleavage.

The next week, Barb picked up a new magazine while standing in the checkout line at the grocer. This one featured tips on home decorating, along with a few recipes. Not that she needed help in the kitchen. She'd learned all she wanted, plus a whole lot more from her mother.

But, between the articles, this magazine contained information about new housing developments, some as far away as California. The homes she could afford were nothing as nice as the one she lived in with Richard, but they all held the universal appeal of not including him.

She settled on the couch with the magazine, a thick black marker, and a sandwich. Richard said he planned to "work" late tonight, so she didn't see any reason to bother with a big meal when a sandwich would do the trick.

Headlights cast a zigzag slash of light through the front window as a car pulled into the drive, followed by the low rumble of the garage door opener. Richard was home, and it was only half past seven. Odd.

He entered the house a few minutes later and dropped his briefcase, overcoat, and hat in the arm chair adjacent to Barb.

"You're home early." She started to rise. "Hungry?"

"No, no. I already ate. You don't need to get up." He loosened his tie as he spoke. "I have another meeting tonight, but I wanted to stop by and see how you're keeping yourself."

Barb eased back into her seat. Since when did Richard care what she did with her time? "Really? How interesting." She spoke softly, fighting hard to keep sarcasm out of her tone.

He nodded earnestly. "Lately, it seems as though I only see you for a few minutes before work, and you're already sound asleep by the time I get home."

Richard said "lately" as if he just realized the pattern, and Barb choked back a snort of disbelief. He'd just described their routine of the past year, possibly longer.

"That's sweet of you to check in like that."

Richard smiled, too sure of his own worth to guess that Barb was anything less than thrilled to be granted audience with him for ten minutes between dalliances.

"What are you looking at?" He sat next to her on the couch and put his arm around her. "Anything interesting?"

She sat rigidly still, resisting the urge to push his arm right back off. "Just some recipes and decorating tips." She flipped lazily through the pages, hoping that he wouldn't notice the black circles around a few of the ads.

Of course, he did. "Whoa, what's that?" He took the magazine from her and found the page advertising the new houses in Florida.

"Oh, just dreaming."

He drew his brows together and nodded slowly. "About what?"

"These places just sound so exotic and exciting. I found a listing once for a development in Paris, France. Can you imagine?" She did her best to sound vapid and fanciful. The last thing she needed was for Richard to join her when she made her big move.

"I had no idea you were interested in these places."

"Well, I'm not. Not really. I'm happy here with you, but sometimes it's nice to imagine, you know?"

"Sure. That's great. Maybe we could take a vacation and explore? What do you think? Europe? Florida? Hawaii? You name it."

It was sweet of him to try so hard to please her, but she couldn't help wondering how he would explain the time away to the other women in his life. Still, she smiled and agreed that it would be lovely.

"That's decided, then." He pressed a kiss to her temple and stood. "Now I must get going if I want to be on time to my meeting."

She brushed her fingers over the spot where he kissed her. She felt none of the spark that Muriel sent racing through her body. It was time for her to stop planning and start doing. She had the money. Soon, she decided.

Another week and another dime novel from the rack, this one featuring two women who, in a misguided fit of patriotism, had joined the army and now lived together in the barracks. If the inevitable outcome hadn't been that their relationship would implode, followed by one, or both, rushing to marry the nearest man—much as Barb herself had done after the war—she might have enjoyed the story. As it was, she was quite done reading and discussing books that she not only wrote in her spare time, but that also mirrored her own life and surrender to expectations.

She arrived at Abby's house right on time, perfect Jell-O mold in her hand. She set it on the table and slipped her coat off. Then she noticed that the conversation around her had stopped abruptly when she walked in. The others stared at her, various shades of pink staining their cheeks. Except Muriel. For once, she didn't greet Barb with her patented lazy, flirtatious smile. Her brows were drawn down, and her hands were clenched in tight fists at her side.

"What's going on?" Barb asked. As she untied her headscarf, she tried to keep her tone light but couldn't judge if she'd succeeded.

"Oh nothing." Abby, Betty, and Harper answered in unison, their voices strained. None of them looked at her.

"Oh come on. Clearly, there's something."

"You should tell her." Muriel's voice was low and firm, with a hard, dangerous edge. Despite the situation, it sent a thrill down Barb's spine.

"Tell me what?"

"It's just that…" Abby started but petered out like a half-inflated balloon.

"Barb," Muriel touched her arm gently, "Betty was just telling us that Richard has been having an affair."

Barb stared at her, trying to decide how to react. An affair was hardly news to Barb since Richard had been sleeping with Betty off and on since Betty and her husband had moved to Cherry Park.

Barb decided to let this play out a little more before she reacted. "Betty? Care to explain?"

Betty shuffled, and her gaze flittered between the floor and Barb's kneecaps. "I…"

"She said he's been seeing his secretary." Muriel glared at Betty.

"Ah." Again, this wasn't news to Barb, but it obviously was to Betty. Was she really surprised that a man who ran around with her would also run around with other women? It seemed very naive, especially for a woman who claimed to be as worldly as Betty did. Carefully, Barb said, "I see."

Everyone stared at her, waiting for something. She had no idea what. How did other women react when faced with this type of revelation? Should she cry out and pound her chest about the lying, cheating bastard? Or maybe she should lift her chin and dab politely at the corners of her eyes? She couldn't muster the energy for either.

"Are you okay?" Abby finally found her voice, followed rapidly by Harper asking the same.

"Yes, I'm..." Barb glanced at the ring of Jell-O with its bits of floating fruit, then at Muriel and her barely contained anger, and finally at her own feet. She needed to get out of here. Her only reason for staying, the charade of respectability, was officially shattered. "I'm going to go."

No one, not even Muriel, followed as she made her way out the front door and down the steps. By the time she reached the sidewalk, she was smiling and her steps were lighter than they had been in years. A weight had been lifted.

The next morning, Barb rose, fixed breakfast as usual, and kissed Richard on his way out the door.

Then she started to pack. She filled two large suitcases and a travel bag and stuffed her purse with the cash she'd tucked away in an envelope behind the hall mirror. There were many other things she'd have liked to take, but not enough to delay her departure. After calling for a cab, she removed her portable typewriter from the shelf in the study and set it on her bags.

This was it. She took a deep breath and dialed one last number.

"Hello?" Muriel answered, her voice clear and strong and a touch confused.

Barb didn't blame her. It was a bit early for the phone to ring. Nobody used the telephone before eight unless it was an emergency. Barb didn't know if this truly qualified, but she had a deep, urgent longing to invite Muriel, and for once she was taking a chance and asking for what she wanted.

"Muriel, so glad you're the one who answered..."

BOOKS, RENOVATIONS, AND A VESPA
BY MELISSA GRACE

GINNY POUNDED AWAY ON THE keyboard. The deadline for her next round of edits loomed over her like the branches of the large oak that threatened the roof of her home. Maybe the guys she had hired to remodel her kitchen could cut back the sagging lower limbs. One more item on her ever-growing list of renovations.

She examined the empty wall across from her bed, where a large clock used to rhythmically tick her into a deep sleep. The substantial round timepiece had struck its last beat just days after her grandmother's recent passing.

Ginny pinched the bridge of her nose. The hammering and snapping of the timeworn cabinets in the connecting room made it hard for her to focus, even through a closed door and her noise reduction headphones. She thought the guys she'd hired to renovate her grandmother's old kitchen would have completed the demolition by now. They had been there since breakfast, and now Ginny's tummy rumbled for a late dinner.

Two knocks came at her bedroom door. "Miss Wolf?"

Am I ever going to get these edits done? Ginny growled quietly as she tossed her laptop on the pillow, marched over to the door, and opened it. "Yes?" She stuck her head through the cracked opening.

"Almost done knockin' the cabinets down. The guys and I'll be headed out in the next half hour, and we'll be back tomorrow for the delivery. Once we install those upgrades, we can get the template for your new countertops."

She wanted to slam the door shut to muffle the hammering still coming from the kitchen. Instead, she said, "Thank you for the update, Stanley."

"Not a problem. And hey…"

She had started to shut the door. "Yeah?"

"A van just pulled up. Says somethin' about *Jo the Pro* or somethin' like that. Don't know what they're doin', but I woulda cut you a deal." When he smiled, the puff of air between his nicotine-stained teeth smelled of coffee and a hint of Bailey's Irish Cream liquor.

Ginny exhaled so quickly she could have squelched a bundle of burning candles. What made her decide to rush in so many home updates, all at the same time? She could've just saved the money her grandmother had left her and used it to buy books instead. Of course, those books needed a lovely built-in bookshelf on which to reside.

The doorbell rang. She opened the bedroom door just enough to step out and quickly shut it behind her. Stanley craned his neck to get a peek of what was inside. When she saw her kitchen, her knees went weak. She steadied herself by clinching the doorknob. "Oh my!"

"Don't you worry," another contractor said. "There's always a storm before the calm."

Ginny shot him a look. Either he was joking or he had some sort of dyslexia for sayings. More than likely it was the latter. "I just wasn't expecting..." She couldn't find the right words to complete the sentence.

"We'll clear some of the debris, and then we'll be on our way," Stanley said. "Don't you worry about nothin'. This ain't our first rodeo."

Ginny turned her back to the chaos and made her way to the front door. She took a deep breath before opening it.

"Hello, I'm Jo. I'm here to speak with Miss Virginia Wolf about building some bookshelves."

She was not at all what Ginny expected. First, she was... well, a *she*. Second, she had a slight British accent. Not that Ginny had ever been to the United Kingdom. And third, she wore knee-high brown leather boots, a white button-down shirt, a dark suit jacket, and a pair of stretchy tan trousers. If she had worn a velvety cap to cover up her lengthy reddish-brown hair or carried a riding crop, she could have passed for an equestrian.

"Please call me Ginny." They shook hands. "Come in." She stepped aside to allow Jo entry.

"I'm a day early, but if it's not too much trouble, I thought I would take some measurements of your space." Jo reached into her leather messenger bag and pulled out a tape measure. She held it up, flashing a brilliant white smile between deep-set dimples.

When Ginny turned toward the kitchen, she realized just how quiet it had become the moment Jo walked in. The guys stood there, gawking at her.

Jo leaned forward and looked at the crew standing in the newly made pile of rubble. "Hello, gentlemen." She gave a quick one-handed wave.

"Hi," the men stammered in unison.

Ginny refrained from huffing. "Jo, this is Stanley, Matt, and Jamal. They're here to renovate the kitchen. Guys, this is Jo. She's here to build a bookshelf in my master bedroom."

"Pleased to meet you," Jo said.

They continued to stare, their jaws agape.

"Okay…" Ginny rolled her eyes and turned back toward Jo. "They're just about finished for the evening. How about I take you into my bedroom?" She blinked twice. "You know, to where I would like the shelves built."

"Perfect. Lead the way."

Ginny escorted her to the room and shut the door behind them.

The guys snickered and gave a few quiet whistles.

"What a lovely room," Jo said.

Ginny followed Jo's gaze up at the ceiling. An upper row of windows and a thick layer of crown molding outlined the soaring ceilings. Large dark-stained wooden beams gave the windows a shelf that Ginny had decorated with a handful of stained-glass panels.

"I bet those look even more spectacular when the sun hits them directly," Jo said. "Did you make them yourself?"

"My grandfather made them for my grandmother many years ago."

"Well, they are absolutely brilliant." Jo crossed to the French doors that led out to the patio. "And what a beautiful sitting area you have outside." She turned with a bright smile. "I bet that oak out there gives you a lovely canopy."

"It does. My grandparents planted it when they bought this home over seventy years ago. It grew with them, protecting them and their loved ones."

"How lovely."

"And over here is where I would like the bookshelf." She indicated the blank wall.

Jo set her messenger bag on the bed and approached with the tape measure in hand. "How large were you thinking?" She stretched the tape out to begin taking measurements.

"The entire wall. I have quite the book collection."

"Wonderful." She measured the wall's length and then up to the height of the beam that encircled the room.

Even with the impending deadline of edits, Ginny waited patiently. Jo moved so elegantly that she found it easy to ignore her laptop.

"Got it." Jo let the tape spin back into its housing. "I can see why you have asked for a dark distressed wood for your shelves. They're going to look incredible against the white walls and textiles in here. You have exceptional taste, Ginny. What time can I get started tomorrow?"

A crash came from the other room, and Ginny held up her index finger before running out of the bedroom. "What happened?"

Jo walked up beside her.

"This vase fell off the shelf over here," Matt said.

"Grammy!" Ginny ran to the broken pieces of porcelain and kneeled. Tears welled up in her eyes.

"Grammy?" Stanley walked over to the tiny fragments while scratching his head.

"My grandmother was cremated. These are her ashes."

"You burned your grandma and stuck her in a vase?"

Ginny's jaw dropped. How could she answer such a ridiculous question? She tightened her jaw and balled her hands into fists.

"It's okay, Ginny." Jo placed her hand on her shoulder. "I'll help you get your grandmother back safely into a functional container." She looked over at Stanley. "I'm sure Stanley here will be more than willing to foot the bill for a new urn."

"Yeah, we can do that," Stanley said. "It was just a mistake, but we'll make it right."

Ginny remained on the floor. She covered her eyes with her hands.

"We'll be back in the mornin' to get the cabinets in. The truck should be here first thing."

Matt and Jamal followed Stanley out the door.

Jo kneeled next to Ginny. "Since I'll be spending the night parked out in your driveway, I'll help watch for that delivery."

Ginny nodded. She pulled her hands away from her eyes.

"I've got something in my van that will help you out here. If you'll give me a moment, I'll be right back."

Ginny stopped crying and wiped the tears from her cheeks. Her lips quivered. "Thanks," she said quietly.

Jo came around the side of the house and joined Ginny on the patio. She held two cups of steaming coffee. "Good morning! I thought I might find you back here." She sat down. "Don't feel obligated to drink it." She slid the mug in front of Ginny.

"How sweet, thank you." Ginny nearly burned her tongue as she took a sip. "So you fit a bed and a kitchen along with all your tools in that van of yours?"

"Absolutely. It's a home away from home, but I do have to use a makeshift outdoor shower to bathe." She looked at the street. "I see the guys haven't made it back yet."

"No. And they haven't returned any of my texts. Feel free to use the shower inside whenever you'd like."

"That's very kind of you." Jo smiled. "Well, if it's okay with you, I would like to set up my shop out here under the tree. It'll give me shade as I make cuts, and it should be far enough to prevent sawdust from entering your home."

"Under the oak sounds good."

"So, is it all right that I work throughout most the day, or do you have other plans for your bedroom?" Jo raised an eyebrow.

Ginny laughed. "No special plans yet, but I'm sure the bookshelves will remedy that."

"Right." Jo smiled.

"As long as the day remains beautiful, I plan to work out here on the patio. Feel free to come and go as you please."

"Do you work from home every day?"

Ginny nodded. "I work for several publishers and directly with a handful of authors. I edit their manuscripts for them."

"Well, Miss Wolf, a significant bookshelf in your master bedroom it is." She smiled. "Perhaps you are the most avid reader I have ever met."

"I absolutely *love* reading! Although," she sighed, "some of these deadlines stress me out to no end. I enjoy the work, but keeping up with the demands can be quite a feat."

"I bet."

"But it helps pay the bills."

"With all these renovations you have going, it must."

"Oh, well…my salary fluctuates. It's more like feast or famine, but when my grandmother passed away a couple weeks ago, she left me this beautiful home and cash enough to make some essential updates." Ginny giggled. "I won't even tell you about the blue countertops that matched the carpet in the kitchen."

"Carpet in the kitchen?" Jo laughed. "Oh my, that must have been a sight." Their gazes connected for a moment before Jo looked away. "Well, I picked up materials as soon as the lumber yard opened this morning, and I think I have everything I need to get started."

"You certainly don't waste any time."

"I much prefer to be efficient. Besides, I don't want to keep you from a restful night's sleep in your cozy bed. The sooner I complete this project, the sooner I can get out of your hair."

Ginny nodded, and the faint rumble of a truck pulling into the driveway drew her attention. "That must be the guys." She stood up. "Let me know if you need any help getting your tool thingies ready."

"Tool thingies?" Jo's chin dropped to her chest, her smile still prominent across her cheeks.

"You know what I mean, the wood-cutting equipment."

"I think I've got it under control, but if I need you, I will certainly let you know. Holler if you need me as well."

Ginny sighed. "Just send good vibes that things will go much better today than they did yesterday."

Jo winked. "You've got it."

Ginny found herself chewing on the cap of her red pen, staring as Jo measured and cut pieces of wood in the distance. The air smelled of fresh sawdust and coffee, and Jo had removed her denim button-up shirt. She wore a sleeveless top with a collar and buttons. Her strong shoulders and long arms distracted Ginny from her manuscript.

"Am I making too much noise?" Jo yelled from under the tree.

Ginny quickly looked away from Jo's biceps and blushed at the thought of being caught ogling. "Not at all. Just zoning out. I'd better get back to these edits." Out of the corner of her eye she could see Jo approaching.

"I think I may take a quick break for some lemonade." She walked up the steps to the patio. "Can I fetch you some as well?" Sweat beaded on her skin above the open buttons of her shirt and glistened in the sun.

Ginny gulped. "Lemonade sounds fantastic, but I should be fixing you some. I am merely sitting, making minimal markups with my handy red pen." She raised it in the air before realizing it was full of teeth marks. She quickly set it down and hid it beneath her hand.

"Well, I think my van may be more suitable for mixing up some drinks than your kitchen at the moment."

The sound of drilling came from inside the house.

"True." Ginny looked at her watch. "I guess it's still too early to break out a bottle of wine."

"I would love to share some wine with you when I've finished for the evening. It's best I don't drink and cut."

"Will you join me for dinner?" Ginny wrinkled her eyebrows. "I mean, if you're okay with delivery. I still don't have a working oven."

"I'll tell you what...I have lasagna that I need to warm up. Do you eat meat?"

"Absolutely. You have an oven in your van as well?"

"No, my roommate—Kimberly—made it the other night. She gave me a large enough slab to feed a classroom of hungry preschoolers. All I need to do is throw it in the microwave. It would mean a lot to me if you'd share it with me. Seriously, there's plenty, and Kimberly is an outstanding cook."

"Sounds great." She blinked twice. "I have some Cabernet Sauvignon that would pair well with a meaty lasagna."

"Perfect, so a late dinner on the patio?"

"Absolutely."

"Fantastic, I'll go fetch us some lemonade."

Ginny tried not to pay too much attention to the form-fitting pockets on the back of Jo's jeans as she descended the patio steps and disappeared around the corner. "A roommate named Kimberly?" she whispered.

"Great, you're here. I was about to send Jamal to get you," Stanley said. "We have a problem."

"A problem? What problem?" Ginny asked.

Stanley waved for her to follow him. "Your plumbing."

"My plumbing?"

"After we install the granite and then attach the under-mount sink, everything's gonna be off by an inch or two. We need to get all new pipes. It's gonna be expensive."

"How expensive?"

"Two thousand, maybe three thousand dollars."

"Three grand?"

"We gotta buy all new stuff and cut everything to fit. It's all gotta be customized. Customization is expensive."

"But the plumbing, electricity, time, and materials…I thought all that was covered in the initial bid."

Matt's gaze darted over to Stanley.

"I'll tell you what," Stanley said as he patted his pocket. "I'll work you out a deal because I like you. How's that sound?"

She scowled.

"I'll drop the price a whole fifty percent. I got a friend who has a friend who can get me the materials at a discounted price. I'll pass those savings on to you. Capisce? How's fifteen-hundred dollars tops sound?"

"I need to think about it."

"There ain't nothin' to think about. We'll save you hundreds, get the best quality materials, and build it up right. You have my word."

She took a deep breath. "I need to think about it."

He shrugged. "All righty, but it's a good deal." He snatched the cigarette he had tucked behind his right ear and stuck it to his bottom lip. "I'm gonna go grab a quick smoke."

"Ginny speaking," she answered her cell phone without looking to see who was calling.

"Hey, Gin, it's Fiona. How are those edits coming?"

She was at least a day behind. "I've got my red pen out and manuscript lying in front of me as we speak." She lifted the remaining pages she had left to edit and tapped them against the patio table in an attempt to line them up. The untouched pile felt even thicker than what she had started with days earlier.

"Great, I can't wait to see your notes. Any chance I'll get them a day early?"

Ginny's eyes bulged at the request, just as Jo walked up the steps and set a glass of iced lemonade on the table in front of her.

"I'll see what I can do, but I'm still planning on e-mailing the updates to you Friday." She gave a half smile to Jo.

Jo winked and walked back to her workspace beneath the oak tree. She took long, confident strides toward the table saw.

"I understand. Can't blame me for trying." Fiona snorted. "What do you think so far?"

Ginny looked at the pile of pages she had completed. She certainly had to ramp things up to have it done on time. The amount of markings in red ink didn't seem to be too overwhelming, but for the life of her, she couldn't even recall what she had read. "You'll have to wait until I have completed all my edits."

"Oh, come on. Throw me a bone here. I'm dying to know what you think so far."

She pinched the skin at the bridge of her nose and closed her eyes. "Fiona…"

"All right, all right. I'll wait and read what you think tomorrow." She snickered.

"Friday," Ginny corrected. "I can't promise any earlier."

Stanley yelled something in the background, but she had no idea what he was saying.

"Okay, I'll let you get back to it, then."

Ginny opened her eyes and blinked several times to regain her focus. "Have a good rest of your day."

"You too, sweets."

The cell phone went silent as Ginny watched Jo slice a thick board in two.

She slipped her red pen between her teeth, picked up the manuscript and lemonade, and then headed into her room. She hoped working from her bed would provide fewer distractions.

"They quoted you how much?" Jo shook her head no, her chin sunk to her chest. "They are definitely taking advantage of you."

"I just don't know what to do. I know what they initially quoted is pretty competitive after getting similar quotes from other contractors." She looked at Jo. "These excessive upcharges are going to drain what I have set aside for other home projects."

Jo pushed her plate to the side and grabbed her wineglass. She leaned on the table and rested her fingers on Ginny's wrist. "Let me take care of the plumbing for you. You just have them bring the materials, and *I'll* do the customization, free of charge." She withdrew her hand. "It frustrates me when people try to take advantage of others."

"I can't have you do that."

"Of course you can. It's a very simple task, really. I want to do it for you." Her eyes darkened.

Ginny smiled and gave a tentative nod. "I'm going to have them complete what they started, and if they ask for more money, I am going to say hell-to-the no." She blushed from using such language, but after drinking more Cabernet than she had intended, she felt recklessly uninhibited.

"That's my girl." Jo's dimples looked even more recessed in the dark.

"Speaking of girl, who is Kimberly?"

Jo chuckled. "Kimberly…as in my roommate Kimberly?"

Ginny squinted. "Define roommate." She didn't care; she would allow the Cabernet to help her speak her mind, even if it meant she would need to play the alcohol-induced forgetfulness card in the morning.

"Well, she is one of my three roommates. I make number four. There's Kimberly, who made the incredible lasagna we just scarfed down. Jack, who happens to be one of the most excellent hairdressers I know." She flipped her hair for effect. "And last but not least, there's Johanna. She works in retail, but the housewife styles don't suit me, so I have to regretfully refrain from shopping her boutique."

Ginny leaned back in her seat. The glow of the battery-operated lantern illuminated the patio table. "So, you're all just friends?"

"Friends who save each other money by sharing a lease on a four-bedroom home. We all have our own bedroom." She paused as if to let the words sink in. "I fix things when I'm there, but for the most part, I go from place to place, living out of my van."

Ginny took another swig of wine before smiling down at the now empty glass.

"Now I want to know something about you." Jo swirled the wine in her glass. "Tell me how you acquired the name Virginia Wolf…Wolf with only a slight variation of spelling to the British modernist author herself. As you can tell, I am a big fan."

"Well, I'm named after my late grandmother, Miss Virginia Ida Carroll. Since she helped raise me and we had the same first name, I acquired the nickname—Ginny—and it stuck."

Jo's probing stare sent heat flashes through Ginny's body.

"Wolf came from my mom and dad. They married just after I was conceived."

"But they didn't raise you?"

"From what my grandmother told me, their marriage lasted less than a year. They divorced and went their separate ways—from me as well as my grandparents—so my grandparents raised me here in this very house." She flung her hands up in the air. "And here I shall stay." She almost slid off the edge of her chair before grabbing the table for support.

Jo was quick to get up and help her back into the center of her seat. "I take it you're feeling the wine."

"I have something to confess." She shook her head. "I don't drink very often."

Jo chuckled. "It's no problem. I'll make sure you make it into bed safe and sound, and then I'll clean up here." Jo wrapped Ginny in her arms and lifted her to her feet.

"You are quite strong." She placed her hand over Jo's and held it as she steadied herself.

"And a tad inebriated myself," Jo admitted. "But not enough to where I can't get you into bed."

Ginny's shoe caught on the threshold, making her trip. "Oh?" Her smile widened as the floor beneath her seemed to move of its own free will. "You're not looking to take advantage of me too, are you?" She licked the essence of wine from her lips.

"The thought had crossed my mind." She sat Ginny on the bed. "But no, I promise to behave myself." She lifted

Ginny's legs so that she would slowly fall back onto her pillow. "How's that? Are you comfy?"

Ginny reached for Jo's arm and gave it a firm squeeze before pulling her down, closer to her mouth. She stared at her lips as she tried to rise to meet them.

Jo gently rested her hand on Ginny's chest to push her back onto the pillow. Her eyes were intense and her smile caring. "I better go clean up."

Ginny frowned. She'd overstepped her boundaries. How had she misread what she thought was a bout of mutual teasing? The soft blankets on her bed would have to suffice for the rock she wanted to crawl under.

"I'll bring you some water shortly." Jo stood and pulled the covers on top of Ginny. "Be right back."

Ginny closed her eyes to pretend she was on the verge of sleep. Anything to spare her the embarrassment of rejection would be ideal. She wanted to roll over on her side and cover her face, but she feared the sudden movement would make the room spin even quicker.

Jo sat on the edge of the bed, and the mattress dipped beneath her weight. "I have some water right here. Let me help you sit up so you can nip some."

Ginny rolled over more groggily than she truly felt. She gulped some water before lying back onto her pillow.

"Skootch over. I hope you don't mind."

Ginny's eyes widened. Maybe she hadn't misread their friendly banter after all. She folded her hands over her stomach and waited for Jo's next move.

Jo wriggled beside her, sticking her butt up against Ginny's side as she pulled the covers over both of them. "Let me know if you need me to get you anything," she whispered.

"I'll be right here if you need help to the bathroom or more water. We both could use a little sobering up."

A hint of moonlight passed through the stained glass in the windows above, casting a psychedelic swirl on the ceiling. Only day number two and her contractor—a very attractive contractor—lay in her bed with her. This was something story-worthy, exciting, and frightening. She smiled herself to sleep.

As daylight crept in through the windows, Ginny opened her eyes. Jo was still lying next to her, her back up against Ginny's side, and her hair fanned out across the pillow. She held still so as not to disturb her rest but equally yearned to snuggle her.

This happened oh so fast. She would never again tell a writer their characters moved too quickly into lust. Her sudden affection for Jo—as well as how quickly she acted on it—must have broken some sort of speed record. She inhaled a lock of Jo's hair that had been lodged under her cheek. The faint smell of shampoo, wine, and sawdust made her smile. It would be too easy to drop her pending edits and get sucked up into the unfamiliar world of this stunning woman, for Jo's world was certainly one she wanted to explore. More so, Jo was a woman she desperately wanted to pursue. She hoped Jo would feel the same way.

The sound of a drill whirring in the kitchen caused her to jump. She never heard the guys come in.

"What time is it?" Jo asked groggily.

"I'm assuming early." She looked at her watch. "It's noon." She shot up and leaned on her elbow. "Holy crap! It's noon!"

Jo turned over to face Ginny. "I don't think I have slept this well in ages." She lightly brushed the tip of Ginny's nose with her fingertip. It was an innocent and sweet gesture, yet once again, it made an achy heat rise through Ginny's body.

Jo turned onto her back. "My next task is to begin assembling the wood pieces I cut yesterday, into shelves." She stared at the blank wall for a moment before turning her head back toward Ginny. Her eyes darkened once again. "I hope it's okay that I went ahead and just stayed in your bed with you." She climbed out from under the covers and stretched. At some point during the night her pants had ended up on the floor, and now she bent to pull them on.

Ginny shot out of bed. She was already too far behind with her edits. "I can't believe it's noon. I've got to get my work done."

Jo buttoned her jeans before tucking in her shirt. "I'll tell you what, it's a beautiful day. How about you get started on those edits, and I'll fix you something to eat before I start assembling your shelves. I'll also keep track of those men in there. I'll see to it they're doing what you paid them for while you play catch-up."

Ginny grabbed the manuscript and red pen. "That would be fantastic." As she spoke, the offensive taste that had been building up in her mouth from the night before made her stop in her tracks. She grimaced. "I better go brush my teeth first." She tossed the pen and manuscript onto the bed and ran to the bathroom.

The few and far between moments Ginny took her attention away from her edits, she glanced at Jo passing by with an armful of stained wood.

"Need any help?" Ginny asked.

"I much prefer to surprise you," Jo answered from inside. "Everything should be installed today, and I can complete any touch-ups tomorrow."

Tomorrow. Friday. The day the edits were due. "So I don't get to peek?"

Jo squeezed her shoulders from behind, and Ginny jumped.

"Absolutely not." She gently rubbed the tension from Ginny's shoulders and leaned in. "I don't normally touch my clients," she spoke quietly.

"Or sleep with them?" Ginny made a red mark on the page before her, acting as if the conversation were like any other.

"It's not normally part of my job duties, no." She chuckled. "I just wanted to."

Ginny looked over her shoulder and brushed her cheek in a light caress against Jo's hand. "I'm not complaining that you did."

"So, you don't see me as being too forward?"

"Well, I wouldn't say that…" She chuckled.

Jo let go of her shoulders. "Well, I guess I just won't know unless you tell me I've gone too far."

Ginny made another red mark in the manuscript. "I guess you'll just have to try a little harder to see what I may deem unacceptable."

Jo walked to the edge of the patio. "That can be arranged." She sauntered toward the oak tree.

Ginny took another deep breath. "Back to these edits," she tried to convince herself.

Stanley set a sample piece of granite on the table and used the pad of his middle finger to rub its surface back and forth. "Nice choice in materials. It's gonna look good with the cabinets."

Ginny nodded. "I'm looking forward to seeing it all put together."

"We're makin' good progress. The template's ready. We just need to get it to the cutter. Shouldn't take long to get it back."

"How long roughly?"

He shrugged. "I'll check with the cutter guy and let you know." He twirled a cigarette between his fingertips before tucking it back behind his ear. "Now about that broken vase...where can I get one like it?"

"I'm thinking of choosing something less vulnerable. How about you knock the renovation costs down one hundred dollars, I'll pick out what I want, and we'll just call it even?"

"One hundred dollars? For a vase?"

"It's an urn."

Stanley rubbed the bald spot on top of his head. "Okay, I'll see what I can do about saving on materials to offset the cost."

Ginny's breath caught. "What?"

"Look, lady. I'm not made of money here."

"Are you kidding me?" This was the first time she had raised her voice. "You break something dear to me—that wasn't even close to where you guys were working, mind you—and you want to cut back on *my* materials to offset the cost?"

"What's going on?" Jo entered the kitchen. She had a drill in her hand and a tool belt hugging her hips.

Ginny pressed the palm of her hand into her forehead.

Stanley spoke up first. "I was just askin' about replacing the urn thing, and she's sayin' it'll cost me a hundred dollars. No way am I paying a hundred bucks for a fancy vase."

"Seriously?" Ginny pointed her finger toward the door. "You can get the hell out of my house!"

"We have a contract," Stanley said.

"Screw your contract," she shouted. "You are the most unprofessional, nitwitted idiot—"

"Hold a sec." Jo strode up to Stanley with the drill clenched in her hand and the thumb of her free hand tucked in her tool belt. It resembled a scene from an old western. "First of all, Stanley, one hundred dollars for an urn is quite a deal."

Ginny nodded.

"Secondly, I have been keeping track of your shoddy work, trying to make sure you guys do your job right for Miss Wolf here. And in doing so, I am a tad behind on my own project."

"We never asked for your help," he said.

"More importantly, I have a city inspector on speed dial." She pointed the drill toward the kitchen. "I wonder if they'll have the same concerns as I have about what's up to code in here, not to mention quality assurance."

"You're bluffing."

She lifted her cell phone from her pocket and pointed it at him. "Tell me, before I place this call, how genuine is that pink piece of paper hanging on the door out there? You know, the one with the word 'permit' bolded across the top?"

"The...the permit?"

Ginny looked at Stanley and then back to Jo. "Is the permit fake?"

Jo squinted at Stanley, her teeth clenched, knuckles white with tension. "I think it best you guys quit while you're ahead. I'll personally see to it Miss Wolf has everything she needs to complete her renovations. I suggest you pack your things and leave."

Stanley grabbed his paperwork on the shelf. "We *will* get paid for the materials and labor completed."

"No more and no less."

The guys followed him out of the house.

"How did you know the permit was fake?" Ginny asked.

"I didn't. It was a hunch."

"Some hunch." She looked at the half-completed kitchen. "I think I need to sit down."

"I think you need to step out for a bit."

"To the patio?"

"Farther, actually. I was thinking more along the lines of a coffee shop with Wi-Fi."

"I think you're right. Will you join me?"

"Do you mind driving? I've got the van all pulled apart to access my tools," Jo said.

"Meet me out front in ten minutes."

"Perfect. I'll go wash up."

As Jo stepped out the front door, she couldn't resist a giggle. "What's this?"

"This is my Vespa." Ginny sat on the mint-green machine, wearing a matching helmet. She raised a second helmet up in the air. "Here, put this on."

Jo took the helmet and placed it on her head. "Don't mind if I do." She buckled it before swinging her long leg up and around the seat to straddle it. She raised her feet up and onto the pegs.

"Hold on," Ginny said as she pressed the starter button. The engine could barely be heard over a flock of geese flying overhead.

Jo slid her hands around Ginny's stomach and leaned in. "This is a wonderful surprise. I had no idea you were a biker babe."

"Stick around and you'll see I have even more surprises up my sleeve." She rolled the throttle as they left the driveway and headed toward the main road.

"Oh, I plan to stick around. I'm quite looking forward to it."

"So, you're going to help me fix the mess I have at home?"

"If you'll have me."

"I would love to have you." Ginny peered over her cup of iced coffee to observe Jo's reaction.

"The feeling is mutual." She gave Ginny that same look she had been giving her since that morning; the one that made Ginny feel it would be more than okay to lean in and kiss her, unlike the rejection she had received the night before. "First, you need to focus on those edits."

Ginny sighed. "True."

"When we get back to your place, I'll begin working on the kitchen so you can have your room to yourself. Also, I'll get a proper permit. Looks like I'll be spending quite a few more nights with you."

Ginny smiled.

"Do you think you'll have the manuscript completed in time?"

"I feel I can get it done. At least I hope."

"If there's anything I can do to help, I will."

"You're already a tremendous help, Jo. I don't know what I would have done without you."

"It's been my pleasure, really."

"Well, one way or another, I certainly plan to make it up to you."

"I may have some suggestions in mind."

Ginny narrowed her eyes. "Anything."

"Really now, are you sure about that?"

"I keep my word." She winked at Jo. "Allow me to prove it."

"Are you asleep?" Jo hovered over the bed, looking at a sleepy Ginny.

"I must have fallen asleep." She lifted the manuscript off her chest and examined the pages. "I did get quite a bit completed. What time is it?"

"Midnight."

"Midnight? You've been in the kitchen working this entire time?"

Jo sat on the edge of the bed. "I did install a new battery in my van." She held up her dirty hands. "I promise not to touch anything I shouldn't."

"You work on cars, too?"

"Only the basics. I much prefer to work with wood. My hands are accustomed to calluses, but not all this greasy car muck." She looked at her hands.

"I can't blame you." Ginny sat up and rubbed the sleepiness from her eyes. "Go shower, and I'll make us some tea. I'll be sure to fluff the pillow on your side of the bed."

Jo raised an eyebrow. "Really now? That would be splendid." She went to reach for Ginny but quickly withdrew her soiled hands. "I better go shower first."

"I think that's a good idea."

The steaming cup of tea sat on the bedside table when Jo entered the room. Once again she wore nothing but panties and a T-shirt.

"I hope you'll enjoy your herbal tea. I added honey."

"Smells terrific." She sat on the edge of the bed and leaned over to take a sip. "It's fantastic."

"I'm glad you like it."

Jo set the cup back down on the bedside table and crawled under the covers. "How are those edits coming?"

"By some miracle, I'm just about back on schedule. I've already begun entering them into the computer. If I work all day tomorrow, I should have them e-mailed to the author before sunset. That's the plan, anyway."

"So my strategy to let you work most of the day without interruption was a success?"

"I guess it was."

"Are you planning on working all night?" Jo rolled onto her side.

Ginny shifted her gaze sideways, looking down at Jo. "I've been contemplating whether I should stop. Why?"

Jo rolled back over so she could face the ceiling. "No reason."

Ginny resumed entering edits into the electronic copy of the manuscript.

Jo sat up just enough to reach for her tea and then pressed it to her lips. "It's so smooth." The mug fell from her hand and onto the bed. "Darn, I spilled it." She gave Ginny a wicked smile.

Ginny hit the save button before setting her laptop on a nearby stand. She grabbed a towel from the master bathroom and ran to Jo's side of the bed. "Are you okay? Did it burn you?" She pressed the towel against a wet spot on Jo's shirt.

"Not at all. It's just a little splatter." Jo stood and lifted the shirt over her head. "I better hang this to dry."

When she saw a full frontal of Jo's naked chest, Ginny whirled around. "Ah, let me get a dry shirt for you."

Jo grabbed her shoulder. "That won't be necessary."

She turned to face Jo, the top of her head barely reaching the point of Jo's chin. "It won't?" She allowed Jo to take her hand and rest it on her bare chest. The skin was warm from the liquid, but also a tad sticky. The smell of spearmint tea with a touch of honey mixed well with the soapy scent of her skin.

"If you don't mind, I thought we could both use a little time off from work tonight." Jo lowered her onto the bed and climbed on top of her. "You know what they say about all work and no play. Maybe we should indulge in a little playtime?"

Ginny opened her eyes wide. "We can do that." She tucked her hands behind Jo's neck, and the strands of her reddish-brown hair stretched between her fingers. She pulled Jo down toward her lips.

Their kiss quickly escalated from tentatively curious to intensely passionate. Ginny cupped Jo's breast in her free hand until Jo sat up for air. Her eyes were now like a dark storm of swirling blues, her hair dangling down from her shoulders, draping itself along Ginny's shirt.

Jo's body arched like a stretching cat as she bent to reach Ginny's navel.

Ginny gasped. "My you're flexible."

She tugged at the bottom of Ginny's shirt with her teeth. Biting the edge of the fabric, she raised it up slowly, first past her belly button, then past her breasts.

Ginny yanked her shirt up and over her head. Stray strands of hair tickled her exposed skin until Jo's body pressed into hers, the sticky sweetness from the honey bonding against her skin. She moaned.

Their kissing advanced in another feverish round of exhilaration. They seized each other's lips until the mini bouts of dominance shifted from one to the other. They were both breathing heavy.

Ginny clutched a handful of Jo's tousled hair. She pulled Jo's head back, exposing more of the delicate skin on her neck before leaning in to lick and suck. She reached into Jo's panties in an attempt to slide her fingers against her clit before realizing their bodies were pressed too firmly together for her to gain access. She shoved Jo onto her side as the stickiness between their bodies gently peeled apart. The unique sensation made her shiver. This time she easily reached Jo's clit. She massaged the sensitive skin with the pads of her fingers until she sank a finger inside and hurried her hand in and out, thrusting harder and quicker at Jo's encouraging moans.

Jo rolled onto her back and then spread her long legs across the bed. She reached up to caress Ginny's hair with her fingers. Her hot breath tickled Ginny's ear as she whispered inaudibly.

Ginny shifted so her mouth hovered over Jo's. As she quickened her pace, Jo's hips crashed into her hand. Her body was strong. Unrelenting.

Ginny leaned in to give Jo a firm kiss on the lips before making her way down her body with her tongue, the taste of the spilled tea still potent on Jo's sweet skin.

"I didn't peg you for being the take-charge type," Jo said.

When Ginny sucked hard on her nipple, Jo arched her back, stretching her arms up and over her head until she grasped on to the headboard.

Ginny dropped her head down the length of Jo's body, tracing her tongue along the defined crevices of her abs. When she reached her navel, she used the stiff tip of her tongue to draw a circle around its shallow recess before gently dipping in once and then back out.

Jo's chest heaved. She pulled at the edge of the headboard with the tips of her fingers.

Ginny shifted so that her mouth joined her hand at the center of Jo's body. She used as much of her mouth as she could against Jo's labia, taking careful aim at her clit when she flicked the swollen flesh with the tip of her tongue. When Jo's hips would rise off the bed, Ginny grasped them and pulled her back down to where her mouth could easily reach.

Jo pressed her feet into Ginny's sides, her toes curled, gently pinching her skin. "Oh," she whispered.

Ginny slid her hands along the length of Jo's body, as far as she could reach. Jo's definition and responsiveness were so damn sexy.

Jo's body swayed beneath Ginny's tongue as she continued to hang on to the headboard. Her breathing grew heavier.

When her feet, still clenching Ginny's sides, rocked her body faster and with more vigor against Ginny's thickened tongue, Ginny knew Jo's climax was coming. She held on tighter, refusing to lose her position.

Jo dug her feet harder into Ginny's sides and then stopped rocking.

When Ginny looked up, Jo's chest was heaving in delight. Proud of herself, Ginny gently drew her lips across the warm, soaked skin until Jo constricted against them.

"Fucking incredible." Jo recovered quickly and pulled Ginny up her body. After urging Ginny onto her back, she kissed her. "Now it's my turn." Jo's hand rose up and down with rhythmic caresses, her fingers pressed against her clit.

Ginny held her breath, focusing on what Jo was doing to her. "Yes," she whispered, allowing the single word to finally escape.

"Yes, please make noise," Jo said under muffled speech. "Tell me what you want me to do to you."

Ginny moaned and gripped the sheets that wrinkled beneath her twisting body. "I want you to make me orgasm."

"How do you want me to make you orgasm?"

"Fingers," she said faintly. "And tongue."

Jo crawled down between her legs and used her thumb and index finger to gently part the folds of skin covering her clit. "There she is," she said and pressed the tip of her tongue into the flesh.

"Yes," she urged Jo on. "Go inside."

Jo gently sucked the skin surrounding Ginny's clit as she slid a finger inside her.

Ginny bent her legs to expose more of her center to Jo. She grasped her knees and used her arms to gently press her thighs down and deeper into the sheets. "Faster."

Jo quickened her pace, now licking the length of the labia.

Ginny's hand shot up to her mouth, and she bit her knuckle. She started to sway against Jo's tongue, feeling the gentle pressure of Jo's long finger sliding in and out of her. Her swaying became more intense, and the pressure of her orgasm started to explode. "Yes," she cried out. "Yes."

Jo knew exactly how to touch her. Her orgasm came quickly and with such intensity. She grabbed on to the back of Jo's head to hold her still as she relished the aftershocks. "Well, that happened much quicker than I had anticipated," she said after she caught her breath.

"No worries," Jo answered. "There's more to come."

Ginny awoke to the gentle ticking of the large round clock hanging on the wall across from her bed. She looked over at her laptop to read the last paragraph of her new story. When she read Jo's name, she smiled. Today would be the day she would inquire about contractors to help update her late grandmother's house. With any luck, maybe she could find the right female contractor to help make her new story come true.

KINDRED SPIRITS
BY LEA DALEY

I was alphabetizing books at Literary Lesbians when I noticed a stranger browsing through a copy of *How We Die*. She was average everything—height, weight, build. Her thick, silver-streaked hair was ragged, as if she normally wore it very short but had missed more than one appointment at the salon. I could only see her profile. Still I'd bet my house that she'd suffered a recent loss, because the newly bereaved all looked alike. Pained. Shrunken. Bruised. After a moment, I decided to step closer. "I found that book incredibly helpful when I lost my partner."

The woman snapped the cover shut, raised wounded eyes. In a voice that sounded rusty from disuse she said, "Excuse me?"

I gestured at the section on death and mourning. "There's a lot of repetitive information here, but that particular book really mattered to me."

"Thank you. I'm so sorry."

I knew what she meant. She was sorry about my beloved Erin. Sorry I was already traveling a path that she'd just set foot on.

"I've had five years to get used to it," I replied. "Not that it's ever over. Or easy."

She shook her head. "Hardest thing in the world."

I gestured at the tiny café in a far corner of the shop. "Want to talk about it?"

She looked hesitant, then nodded. "Let me check out first. I'll meet you over there."

As I lounged against a wall in the café waiting for my order, I watched her at the register. What in hell did I think I could do for that woman? But I knew firsthand how isolating loss was. A compassionate encounter, no matter how brief, could sometimes ease the unrelenting loneliness of early grief. The server shoved a tray toward me, and I carried it to a booth.

Moments later, the stranger slid in across from me and set a Styrofoam cup of plain black coffee on the table. No surprise—even a modest menu could overwhelm a new mourner. She didn't meet my eyes as she smoothed a paper napkin over her sweats. Maybe she was sorry she'd agreed to chat with me, yet was too honorable to duck out.

Hoping my small frame and rapidly graying hair made me look like the harmless dyke I was, I offered a hand. "Natalie Schneider."

She countered with, "Meg Vickerson." Her grip was firm and hinted at normalcy, but this wasn't my first rodeo. I could guess she was trying to deflect pity. After an awkward pause, she asked, "Have we met?"

I stirred my chai, trying to remember. "Depending on how long you've shopped here, you might have seen me around. I was part of the co-op that founded Literary Lesbians. Five years ago, I stepped back to simplify my life. Now I'm thinking I might be ready to return—I'm finally missing it. I stopped in today for a trial run."

"That would explain why you seem familiar."

Since she was rapidly reducing that napkin to shreds, I smiled reassuringly. "I almost never pick up women in bookstores—not even ones I helped establish. But since I've read virtually everything in print about death, I might be able to save you time and money."

"I appreciate that," Meg replied, glancing at my ring— the ring I still couldn't remove. "You lost your wife?"

I swallowed my distaste for the label, an artifact of the patriarchy that neither Erin nor I had embraced. "A car crash. Drunk driver. Dead at the scene. You?"

"My wife, as well—four months ago. Leukemia. Beyond brutal."

I shoved my plate of biscotti toward Meg, motioning for her to eat a slice. "What are you doing to take care of yourself?"

"Writing. Marathon journaling. And I'm just beginning to read about grief."

She and Barbara had been partners for twenty-five years. They'd traveled to Boston to marry in 2004, right after Massachusetts legalized same-sex unions. Like Erin and me, they'd expected to grow old together, to die naturally— preferably in one another's arms. Barbara's death was the first in Meg's social group, and none of her well-intentioned friends understood the depth of her distress. And her boss was like most people, nominally sympathetic, but sending a clear message to buck up. Because there *was* work to be done at the law firm. At my prompting, Meg confessed that she'd taken a pass on the support group at Barbara's hospital and hadn't pursued individual grief counseling.

"It's not too late," I said. "For either."

Staring into her cup, she muttered, "Seems like I should be able to handle this solo."

Ah, a stalwart butch type, an island unto herself. But going it alone wouldn't serve her well.

As if she'd read my mind, Meg lifted her head defiantly. "I just want to be done with this mess—and the sooner, the better."

"Good luck," I said. "Personally, I belong to the Robert Frost school of mourning."

"Meaning?"

"After losing two children, Frost famously wrote, 'The best way out is always through.'"

"You believe that?"

"Let's say there were no shortcuts for me. And over time, I found a lot to value in group meetings, although my first attempt was a nightmare."

"How so?"

I moaned. "When I entered the room, it felt like I'd stumbled into a jolly cocktail party—lots of lively conversation and laughter—at a time when I couldn't imagine ever laughing again. I fled and didn't return for a year. But then the process worked for me. Still, I've known people who are determined to leapfrog over loss. I guess the key words in the Frost quote are 'best' and 'always.' Some might settle for less in an effort to travel faster."

Meg thrust a hand through her shaggy hair. "What's the point of spending a single extra second in this swamp?"

After tossing a crumpled napkin on my plate, I reached for my jacket. "I guess I thought of mourning as my last chance to spend time with Erin—to totally understand what she meant to me and why. To extract every bit of insight from the grieving process. But maybe that's not for everyone."

"It sounds exhausting."

"So is suppressing your feelings."

By the time Meg and I parted that afternoon, we'd exchanged cautious hugs and e-mail addresses. Still I wondered whether I'd hear from her again. I tried, with limited success, to put those sorrow-filled eyes out of my mind. I knew their light wouldn't return for a very long time.

When I'd almost forgotten our conversation, Meg e-mailed me.

> *You were right about that book. It explained so much about the decisions Barb's doctors made and why they couldn't save her. Thanks for the recommendation.*

I meant to pound out a quick reply, but instead launched into a literary review.

> *You might try Joan Didion's memoir about her husband. And some people get a lot out of C. S. Lewis's* A Grief Observed. *But fair warning: those books only describe the first year of widowhood. Which reinforces the popular delusion that mourning's a short-term process, while leaving readers ignorant about later challenges. Also, in order for Lewis to recover his Christian faith in such a short time frame, he had to twist himself into a pretzel—not pleasant to witness. I suppose piety was his default setting. Still I got some benefit from reading his reflections. When he wrote about the way his wife's death consumed*

his every waking thought, I knew exactly what he meant.

Meg responded immediately, saying she'd gladly try both of my suggestions.

I could use targeted material right now, rather than more general discussions about loss.

Then she suggested meeting at a local park the following weekend.

Maybe we could walk our dogs while we talk?

On the designated morning, the air was soft; the sky was cloudless, and the trees were just going green. In short, it was exactly the kind of day that felt like a violent assault on the tender sensibilities of the recently bereaved. I'd despised my first springtime without Erin and resented everyone's rising spirits, their cheery greetings, and their inexcusable cluelessness. The sun should have gone dark with Erin's death. The flowers should have failed. The season should have reverted to endless, bitter winter.

In the park, Meg was waiting by the bandstand just as we'd planned, her golden retriever dozing in new grass. I dropped down beside her on the bench and reined in Alpha, my opinionated little Westie. "Hey. How's it going?"

Her obligatory smile looked more like a grimace. "About like you'd expect—lousy. But it's such a relief to be able to tell the truth to someone. Thanks for agreeing to see me."

I nodded. "I always hated pretending to feel better than I did. It was like wearing a mask. Worse, it felt like a betrayal."

"Yeah. It's not five months since Barb died, but even our best friends think I should be back to normal."

"It's a far longer process than they realize. And, to quote Shakespeare, himself, 'Everyone can master a grief but he that has it.'"

"Bingo!" Meg said. "I'm fed up with unsolicited counsel from people who've never suffered a major loss. I don't understand why they feel qualified to advise me."

"This is the moment where I'm supposed to point out that you probably made the same mistake with someone else before Barb's death—"

"Tell me you won't!"

"Nope. Because even if it's true—and it was for me—it's not helpful."

"Is anything?"

I sighed. "That's a personal matter. The first thing I did after Erin's death was scatter photos around our house so her face was everywhere. Yet I've met dozens of people who can't bear to look at snapshots of the person they lost. And grief books saved my life, but lots of mourners can't concentrate on reading long enough to discover they have kindred spirits the world over."

"You're saying it's an inside job?"

"The ultimate one—though some people really profit from a bit of therapy."

"Not my kind of thing." Meg rose, so I followed suit. Pointing to her dog, she said, "This is Brinx, by the way."

We let our critters work through the usual canine greeting rituals before we began to stroll under those burgeoning trees.

But I knew Meg wasn't really with me in that lovely setting. She was in some hellish hospital room, replaying scenes from the final, fatal period of Barb's life, revisiting them again and again, as mourners must. Because only through tireless repetition would she grasp the unthinkable—Barbara was truly gone. Forever beyond her reach.

We were leaving the park, saying our farewells, when I caught Meg's eye. "Grief sucks," I said.

"Grief sucks big time," she agreed. And I swear she almost smiled.

After that day, Meg and I fell into a pattern of meeting for weekly walks where we talked about life, love, loss, and books. The way books could take you away from yourself, shielding you from despair. The way books could connect you with others mired in the same deep pit. The way books could assure you that your reactions to death are normal—even when the most primitive impulses rose up, shocking you to your core.

Though I realized Meg Vickerson was an attractive woman, I wasn't attracted to her. At least, not in the beginning. Grief had stripped away all her individuality, and it was hard to tell whether we had anything in common beyond shared trauma. For me, those excursions were just paying kindness forward, something I would have done with nearly any mourner. I hardly noticed when our walks morphed from an obligation to a pleasure, to the highlight of my week. July was advancing—the park teeming with carefree children, the lotus ponds riotous with blooms—before I realized that Meg had helped me as much as I'd meant to help her. Because, while I'd long since escaped the leaden gravity of grief, I'd merely slipped into undifferentiated boredom, mistaking melancholy for normal life. But that summer, in her presence, I began to reclaim the skies.

When I first invited Meg to my house for lunch, the trees had dropped most of their leaves. The graying landscape was a reminder that long, grim months stretched ahead. Which made me wonder how Meg planned to survive the coming holidays. Over bowls of chicken chili, I said, "The first Thanksgiving without Barb will be tough, you know. What are you doing that day?"

"Taking to my bed and pulling up the covers?"

I put a friendly arm around her shoulders. "I recognize the impulse."

"God, Nat! I can't imagine getting through the holidays without Barbara. She loved all the fuss. Our house was the hub for our social group, but I damn well don't have the energy—or the skills—to replicate the extravaganza."

Certain that my sister Jana would understand if I bailed on our annual gathering, I said, "If you like, we could huddle together on the dreaded day. I know my way around a turkey, and I bake a mean pumpkin pie. We'd keep everything very quiet and low-key. Maybe watch a few movies after dinner?"

"Perfect! That would be such a relief! I could tell everyone that I've accepted another invitation this year."

"Then we're on. And don't hesitate to bring Brinx—you know Alpha adores her."

"I owe you, Nat. More than I can say."

"We'll get through it, my friend. Trust me."

Nodding solemnly, Meg said, "From first to last."

That night, sleep eluded me. Perhaps our conversation had stirred up too many poignant memories. Finally, hours after lying down, I fell into a troubled dream. *I'm in my living room, one hand on the doorknob, the other dragging an unwieldy suitcase behind. Adventure awaits but I'm paralyzed by a heaviness of spirit—almost a dead weight. I want to take off; I'm reluctant to go. My departure feels premature. Besides, I have a nagging sense that I'm abandoning something vital. Just what, I can't say...*

Even though there would only be two of us at Thanksgiving dinner, Meg insisted on providing wine and a vegetable tray. I suggested that she bring family photos as well. She arrived in early afternoon, laden with grocery bags. Then she and Brinx hung out in my kitchen while the turkey roasted, the potatoes simmered, and the pie cooled. Meg ate sparingly at dinner but agreed to take a plate of leftovers home.

"And half of the remaining pie," I insisted. "You can't leave me alone with that many calories!"

After we loaded the dishwasher, I struck a match to kindling and blew hopefully. We made ourselves comfortable near the struggling fire, dogs lounging at our ankles, before I said, "Tell me more about Barb."

"Words simply can't do her justice, Nat. I could talk myself blue, and you still wouldn't understand Barbara in all her infinite complexity. Knowing that almost silences me."

"Give me five adjectives anyway. Then I'll do the same for Erin."

Meg closed her eyes. In the stillness, she conjured Barb into being again. "Here goes: whimsical, witty, warm, generous, unpredictable. Your turn."

I ticked off a few of Erin's best qualities on my fingers. "Bright, idealistic, uncompromising, patient, empathetic— plus the woman knew how to build a decent fire. But you're right. Words don't come close to capturing her. A lesson you learned long before I did."

The fire finally flared while we pored over cherished snapshots, sharing stories about Barbara and Erin. About lives cut short and futures derailed. Debating an eternal, insoluble question: Was a sudden end like Erin's preferable to a drawn-out death like Barb's? Or was Meg lucky to have had time to say good-bye? There were no good answers; we reached no firm conclusions. The fire was dying when I asked about Meg's plans for Christmas.

"I'm heartsick every time I think about it," she said. "Normally, I'd spend a week in California with my family. But I cringe at the thought of all the noise and chaos at my sister's house. Even buying gifts for her kids seems beyond me."

"Care for my opinion?"

"I'd pay you for your thoughts—and way more than the proverbial penny."

"Internet shopping is your friend. I'd be happy to hold your hand through the process. How many kids are we talking?"

"Three. Two nephews, eight and ten. One niece, fourteen."

"The boys are a piece of cake—they're still young enough to like anything battery-operated. Your real challenge is the teenager."

"You've got that right. She's a real girly-girl. Barb was a femme, so she always chose Ashlyn's gifts, and they were always spot-on."

"Could you consider something like a magazine subscription?"

Meg high-fived me. "She'd love to get *Glamour* or *Teen Vogue* in the mail—even if the thought makes me want to retch. And no doubt she'd appreciate a gift card for some stupid store at the mall."

"Okay. So we can easily manage the presents. Here's a concept about travel: Could you handle two days of festivities?"

"I could probably gut that out…"

"Then tell your sister you'll be there on Christmas Eve and Christmas Day—or whatever the big events are for your family. After that, come back to rend your garments and tear your hair in the privacy of your own home."

"You're a genius, Nat—I'm so glad we met. I just can't think clearly."

"Clarity will return one day. I promise." What I didn't mention was that Meg would feel guilty when it did.

"I live in hope!" She clinked the rim of her goblet against mine. "I suppose we should give thanks that we had Erin and Barb at all."

"If I thought there was a 'someone' up there to thank, I'd be more likely to curse them for ending things prematurely." My tone hardened. "Erin deserved better—and so did Barb. And so do all those kids dying of horrible diseases even as we speak."

"You're not a believer?"

"I didn't get those genes."

Meg actually grinned—a riveting sight. "To tell the truth, neither did I. That was pure formula on my part, though it would be nice to think Barbara's safe and happy somewhere."

But her voice broke as she added, "I guess I just wanted to formally acknowledge our women tonight."

I touched our wineglasses again. "Then here's to time well spent with the ladies we've loved and lost." And the tears sliding down her cheeks were mirrored by my own. I stood abruptly, flattened by weariness. "It's late, Meg. Go get some rest."

"After your turkey, I just might be able to."

"Let's hear it for tryptophan!" I said and went to fetch her leftovers.

Early the next morning, I jerked awake, heart pounding in my chest as the last fragments of a nightmare dissolved: *Erin is trapped in quicksand. Gripping her hand, I pull mightily, but she drags me toward certain doom. Then someone grabs my other wrist. Hauls hard, breaking Erin's grasp. Pulling me toward freedom...*

I bolted upright, shaking uncontrollably. Scooting to the edge of my bed, I fumbled blindly for the tissue box. Black Friday, indeed!

Over time, I began to catch glimpses of the woman Meg had once been. Someone capable of deep love, or she wouldn't be so devastated by her partner's death. Someone capable of great loyalty, or she wouldn't have stuck out Barbara's long decline. Someone determined to conquer this most grueling of life's tests. And a woman who was unfailingly candid about her emotions.

As the seasons passed, we continued to talk about grief. But while we still commiserated with one another, still shared pithy quotes about death and dying, still exchanged books on mourning, other subjects began to creep into our dialogue. We found we each loved travel, politics, and women's sports—though Meg was a soccer buff, while I favored tennis. We were both suckers for complex movies with twisted endings. And we were totally devoted to our ridiculously indulged fur-clad companions. By the anniversary of our first meeting, it occurred to me that we'd become true friends.

One spring Saturday, my cell rang while I was still nestled in bed. Warm and drowsy. Planning to blow off the weekend with a good book, I almost didn't answer. But that was Meg's number on the screen, and maybe she needed help. "Hey, what's up?"

"Hi, Nat. Do you have a bike?"

"Doesn't everybody?" Never mind that my trusty cycle had been gathering cobwebs for years.

"Not Barb," Meg said. "She never learned to ride. But before she got sick, I was a cycling fiend. Anyway, I was wondering if you'd like to ride the Katy Trail for a few hours?"

Gazing ruefully at my comfiest pajamas and my snoozing dog, I kissed the lazy day good-bye. Because this invitation was a milestone—the first major outing Meg had initiated. And even if she was merely trying to outrun heartache for an afternoon, she deserved support. "That sounds great. Where do you want to meet?"

Twenty minutes later, after bribing a neighbor to take Alpha for her afternoon walk, I stepped into the garage, where I stood motionless, staring at a pair of abandoned touring cycles. Erin's Kona Sutra, my Devinci. A quick glance told me both tires on my ride were shot. If I intended to meet Meg on time, I'd have to use Erin's bike. "I'm sorry, babe," I whispered. "I'll take good care of it." I lifted the silver frame from its hooks, balanced its weight on my palms, and indulged myself in a miniature breakdown. Then I turned my attention to essential cleaning, maintenance, and adjustments. Anything to distract me from that futile surge of self-pity. I wanted my woman back. Bad.

And yet I had a fine time that day. Conditions couldn't have been more ideal, and riding Erin's bike reconnected me to a zillion adventures we'd shared. Using my body felt terrific, too—though I'd suffer for it later. Best of all, Meg seemed energized, lighter than at any time since we'd met.

At three, we sat alongside the trail, eating energy bars, watching other cyclists whiz past us. As clouds sailed overhead, Meg's face shifted from dark to bright and back again. A metaphor for her life just then, I thought. Nudging her bike shoe, I said, "What's the latest?"

She turned toward me, shrugging. "You know the drill... Harsh reality just keeps hammering away at my defenses. I feel like it's about bludgeoned me into submission. Now that I've stopped resisting the truth about Barb, there's nothing left but learning to cope with her absence."

I took Meg's hand and hauled her to her feet. "That counts as authentic progress, my friend. Better start homeward soon—the dogs await."

Meg had been in my back pocket for the better part of two years when I had a disturbing dream. *Erin and I are in a hotel room, fighting bitterly. Half-empty luggage gapes on the bed, and clothing's strewn around us. Despite her fury, Erin looks angelically beautiful, and for an instant, I'm waylaid by her stormy eyes. Then, in a crafty dodge, I pluck a book from my lap and pretend to read.*

She snaps, "Don't you dare go silent, Natalie Ann!"

"You're the one who's always quiet as a tomb!"

Enraged, Erin dashes from the room. Just before the door slams behind her, she shouts, "Go back to your bloody books, Nat! They're all you care about now!"

But that wasn't true—not anymore. Because I woke to the certain knowledge that I'd fallen in love with Meg Vickerson. I was captivated by those crinkly eyes, that rare smile, her even temperament, her unswerving commitment to principle. And head-over-heels didn't begin to describe the severity of my condition. The idea felt shocking, unconscionable—especially since my timing was off. Meg wasn't ready for a new relationship. To her, I was only good old Natalie, fellow traveler, favorite confidante. And even if she might someday have a different take on me, I had no right to rush her. Which didn't mean that seeing her was easy. Besides, all at once, I wanted Meg to see me. Standing right in front of her. Alive and eager to rekindle joy. And it was no comfort that I understood precisely why she couldn't respond in kind.

After that epiphany, spending time with Meg was excruciating. Everything that had once brought me pleasure was now a source of pain. I kept stepping over the line with her, retreating, feeling frustrated, feeling ashamed. Each night as the moon cycled through my desolate bedroom, I'd tell myself I was a fool. At last, I took the coward's way out. In an e-mail, I told Meg I had to quit spending time with her. And, choosing my words with exquisite care, I told her why.

Weeks dragged by without a response. In that long silence, depression reasserted itself. Though I slogged through work five days a week and logged a ridiculous number of volunteer hours at Literary Lesbians, I lacked purpose, could scarcely find a reason for rising each day. I mourned Meg's absence nearly as much as I'd mourned Erin's. And I marveled that I'd been so impetuous. So impatient. So selfish. Why had I made this all about me, instead of practicing the restraint I expected others to deploy in the presence of loss?

At last, in the midst of a solitary Sunday breakfast, my cell rang. When I saw Meg's number on the screen, my heart began hammering so violently I hardly heard her say, "Nat, I need to talk with you. Can we meet?"

An hour later, I found her at our usual spot in the park. Meg took my hands in hers and smiled tenderly, but there was anguish at the back of her eyes. Still her words left me weak with mingled hope and relief. "I can't handle a romance yet, Nat. But I know that when I can, you're the woman I'll want. Will you wait a little longer for me to catch up?"

I squeezed her fingers. "I really don't have a choice. But if we're going to spend time together, you'll have to stop me when I overstep my bounds. And you'll have to speak up when—if—anything changes."

Meeting my eyes directly, she said, "You'll be the first to know."

Despite the inevitable awkwardness, Meg and I joined forces again. And if being in her presence while keeping my distance was challenging, it was slightly less difficult than loving her at a remove. Once again, we hiked with our dogs, prowled through museums, attended the occasional book signing at Literary Lesbians. Nearly all of those activities chosen, in large measure, for the attendant calm. Because I'd learned to predict what Meg would say when I snagged tickets to a Cards game or a concert: "I'm sorry—I just can't deal with that much stimulation."

"Not to worry," I'd answer. "I felt exactly the same way in the first two or three years after Erin died." But one day I took the discussion a step further. "Just let me know if you're ever ready for wild and crazy, Meg. In the meantime, maybe we should plan a road trip? Go somewhere super serene and secluded...?"

"That sounds ideal. I'll spring for gas and food if you'll pick the destination and drive."

"Absolutely." I remembered the terrible passivity of grief, the way the smallest action required an extravagant expenditure of energy. I folded my hands behind my head and sorted through possibilities. "If you could take a couple weeks of vacation in early February, I'm thinking Grayton Beach State Park would be ideal."

"Where's that?"

"It's on Florida's gulf coast, very beautiful, very low-key. If we went then, we might get a break from nasty weather here." What I didn't say was that Erin and I had a long-standing tradition of vacationing at Grayton. I hadn't returned since her death, but I'd continued to reserve our customary week in February, throwing away good money each year. Now I was glad I hadn't abandoned the ritual. It felt only a little weird that I was inviting another woman to share a place that held such significance for me. "We could easily make the drive in two days," I said. Then a brilliant thought struck me. "And—!"

"And?"

"There's something in Montgomery I've wanted to see for years. It would add an hour or two to the Alabama leg of the trip."

"I'm up for anything that matters to you. What is it?"

"Do you know about the Southern Poverty Law Center? It's a favorite charity of mine—social justice work done superbly."

"I'm vaguely aware of them. They try to shut down white supremacists?"

"Some of their efforts target those assholes, yeah. But they also support LBGTQ initiatives. They created a civil rights memorial in Montgomery. A while back, I sent money to have Erin's name placed on a Wall of Tolerance there." I choked up but managed to finish: "I'd really, really like to see that."

"I'd like to be there when you do."

"Thanks, Meg! We could keep the drive south simple. PBJs at roadside parks, instead of noisy cafés. And little motels off the beaten path instead of giant chains."

Meg glanced toward Brinx, who—as always—was close at hand. "Can the dogs go?"

"That's the one downside. Pets aren't allowed in the cabins or on the beach. But I know that my sister would gladly watch over our babies. She's done that before. And Brinx would love running free on her farm."

"Call it a plan, then. I'll put in for time off right away."

Something was seriously messed up with my sleep patterns. I couldn't remember a time when I'd been plagued by so many disturbing dreams. Not even after Erin's death. Shortly before Meg and I were due to take off for Florida, I had a corker. *I'm in the process of curbside check-in at an airport, but my suitcase is too heavy. Kneeling before a testy*

skycap, I unzip it, find it's crammed with weighty volumes—grief books, every one. "But I need these!" I wail.

"Keep the books, or board the plane!" the skycap growls. "Your choice!"

I snapped into alertness, then lay rigid in oppressive blackness, breathing heavily. And conjuring the late Sigmund Freud, complete with cigar. "How's that for obvious, Herr Doktor?" I said aloud. But before the great man could respond, I plunged into a deep, untroubled sleep. And when next I opened my eyes, I was oddly at peace. Go figure.

Meg had agreed to stay in my guest room the night before our trip so we could hit the road early. As she helped pack the car at sunrise, I was acutely conscious of exposing my deepest dykely shame. No matter how much I might intend to travel light, I always ended up packing absurd amounts of stuff. And this time was no exception. In the trunk, Meg's lone knapsack was dwarfed by suitcases and grocery sacks and sports equipment and emergency gear. Not to mention pet supplies to drop off at Jana's farm.

Gazing at the jumbled heap, Meg laughed. "Are you sure there's room left for our lunch bags?"

"You'll be happy to have everything when we're at Grayton," I said sheepishly.

We coaxed the dogs into the backseat and drove through snow flurries to my sister's place in the boonies. Meg visibly relaxed when Brinx leaped from the car to bound about the farmyard, sniffing ecstatically, inviting every critter she encountered to play. While she got acclimated, we chatted with Jana, describing each dog's eccentricities. Then we promised to return with a king's ransom in salt-water taffy, hugged my sister good-bye, and climbed back into my Mazda. We headed south, fleeing the dead gray hand of winter in the heartland.

Our first night on the road, we registered at an unassuming motel on the outskirts of Huntsville. Where Meg very nearly unhinged me by stepping from the shower into the bedroom stark naked. Wholly at ease. Totally desirable. She popped a sleep shirt over her head, then sat cross-legged on a bed to towel dry her hair. In a thrilling instant, her body had imprinted itself on my brain. Tantalizing afterimages zinged through me—pale breasts, trim waist, small rear—dredging up impulses too long dormant. Probably I only imagined a wicked glint in her eyes when they met mine. How in hell had I *ever* thought Meg ordinary?

Sitting across the room, watching her run a comb through damp hair, I tried to regain my composure. I'd be lying if I said I could see what lay between her thighs and lying if I said I didn't try.

Wholly unaware of my raging hormones—or at least pretending to be oblivious—Meg asked, "Do you mind if I look for something on cable?"

"Go for it," I said, hoping the distraction would help. "This is your last chance for a while—there are no TVs in the cabins at Grayton."

Her eyebrows shot up. "Ve vill be calm und relaxed or elze?"

"That's the idea."

"Ooo-kay." Meg reached for the remote and powered up the set. "What's your pleasure?"

"Anything but hospital dramas."

She shuddered. "I no longer think of medical shows as entertainment. How about *Jessica Jones*?"

"Works for me."

By the time the credits rolled, Meg was snoring lightly, but I tossed and turned on my lumpy mattress for hours. Fighting off flashbacks of her nude body. Trying to forget how close she was—how beautiful, how tempting. Silently repeating a reluctant refrain: she's totally off-limits, she's totally off-limits...

We arrived in Montgomery before noon the next day. After zigzagging through the inevitable urban construction, we found our target, the spare and beautiful Civil Rights Memorial. Just outside the building was a tiny plaza bordered by a black granite wall that bore one of Dr. King's most inspiring quotes. And at the center of the plaza, a minimalist fountain beckoned us. Its polished top was etched with a tragic timeline—dozens of dates from the modern civil rights era. Beatings. Lynchings. Sit-ins. Bombings. The assassination of Dr. King, himself. Impossible not to touch those inscriptions. Impossible not to weep as the gentle waters rippled around our fingers.

"It's astounding that all this happened so recently," Meg said.

"It's *still* happening. Michael Brown—"

"Tamir Rice—"

"Sandra Bland... What in the world is wrong with this country?"

In that somber mood, we made our way to the entrance. When I asked for directions to the Wall of Tolerance, a guide waved his hand in a just-around-the-corner gesture. We strolled down a corridor, then came to an abrupt halt in a dim chamber. Though Meg released an audible gasp, I was stunned into silence by the spectacle. Clearly, I'd paid insufficient attention to information about the wall's design.

I'd expected bricks and mortar—the conventional donor acknowledgment.

Instead, light, motion, and color animated that space. Glorious. Ethereal. Names—hundreds of luminous names—seemed to hang before a curved wall. Some were floating in the foreground, while others—much smaller—appeared to recede. All were sliding silently downward, then disappearing, only to recur in other locations. I was awed by the sheer beauty of that digital artistry, yet daunted by the prospect of picking out Erin's name from so many others, so many layers, arranged in random order.

Apparently noting my bewilderment, an attendant pointed to a keypad, explaining that I could summon any name on file by typing it there. "Now watch," he said when I finished. Suddenly, a new entry blossomed, pure white light spelling out *Erin Elaine Tanner*. Suspended in mid-air. Drifting slowly toward the floor. Materializing in another spot. I wondered how long her name would remain at the forefront. How soon it would retreat. When it would vanish altogether. *Erin Elaine Tanner. Erin Elaine Tanner. Erin Elaine Tanner.* I couldn't take my eyes off those words. Would anyone ever call up her name again?

"Absolutely breathtaking," Meg whispered. "I wish I could add Barb. She was the most tolerant person ever."

"That's easy," the attendant said. "Just type her name."

Seconds later, we saw it—*Barbara Renee Maddox*—in shimmering coral light.

"Pink! Barb's favorite color!" Meg said. "That's perfect!"

Her hand slipped into mine, and I knew she felt just what I did. We could have stood there forever tracking those names, calling our lovers back into existence. Much too soon we left that sacred place, awed and deeply moved. It was time to get on the road again.

We were closing in on the Florida panhandle before Meg spoke. "You know those completely irrational ideas that seize you in mourning? I'm having one now—the most bizarre sensation. I feel like Barb and Erin are together back there—like they won't ever be alone or lonely again."

I let out a long, slow whistle. "That's one bat-shit crazy idea, Meg. And incredibly comforting. I'll hold the thought."

By five, we'd checked in at the state park and found our assigned cabin, which was nearly hidden amid palms, slash pines, and luxuriant green scrub. Meg stopped unloading our gear long enough to admire the crisp, modern living room, complete with fireplace. "I suppose I was expecting something more rustic."

I opened kitchen cabinets to display dishes and glassware and saucepans. "All the comforts of home."

"Minus a flat screen," Meg reminded me.

"Who needs TV when the ocean's three minutes from our doorstep?"

"You have a point. This place is just what the doctor ordered."

"Let's go for a quick walk on the beach, then. We can still catch the sunset. When we come back, I'll flip you for the queen bed."

"I don't mind the room with twin beds," Meg said. "You've done all the work that made this trip possible."

"That was my pleasure." Opening the door, I pointed down the path. "The water's just beyond those dunes."

Each morning and evening, Meg and I explored the sweeping expanse of shoreline. In between, we spent much of our time snuggled in blankets across from one another on the screened-in porch, listening to the ocean's roar, reading, sharing an occasional passage with one another. I'd returned to *The Poisonwood Bible* with its sensitive descriptions of grief—oh, that wrenching moment when Orleanna Price stands on Georgia sands, gazing toward Africa, where her youngest daughter died! But Meg was seeking pure escape on that trip. She'd loaded the full complement of Stephanie Plum novels onto her Kindle. Each time her laughter punctuated our cozy afternoons, my heart turned over at the sound. She was so near, so dear, so untouchable.

"Too bad Evanovich isn't a dyke," I said. "Her books would be even funnier."

"Yeah—I've often thought Stephanie's confusion about Joe and Ranger would dissolve instantly if she were introduced to the right woman."

"Amen, sister!"

"Maybe we should write a letter to Evanovich suggesting that?"

"I'm in if you are!"

On our fourth night at Grayton, I awoke to a tumultuous storm. Which was why I mistook a muffled knock for booming surf. Then the door to my room eased open, and Meg whispered, "Nat? Are you awake?"

"Yep." I scooted upright, yanked the sheet over my chest, and reached for the bedside lamp. "Is everything okay?"

"It would be more okay if I could join you."

"Scared of being alone in the storm?" I teased.

"Scared of being alone in life—scared of being without you." Meg slipped out of her sleep shirt, into the bed, into my arms.

My skin met hers with a fierce jolt of electricity, but her first kiss was surprisingly shy, gently questing. Entirely unlike Erin's headlong intensity. It couldn't be the same, I thought. Not after all those years with Erin. And it shouldn't be the same.

Maybe Meg felt my hesitancy. "Erin would want this for you," she murmured. "Barb would want it for me."

"You're right, sweetheart," I said. "I know you're right. And God knows I've wanted it for myself. Desperately. For a very long time."

Her lips found mine again, more urgent then, more passionate. Thrusting aside every reservation, I leaned into Meg's kiss, fell into it, lost myself at last in the splendor of her ardent body. And in the ceaseless flash of lightning, the deafening crash of thunder, the world began anew.

BETWEEN THE LINES
BY A.L. BROOKS

MAGGIE SULLIVAN LASTED UNTIL THE afternoon of Nora's second day at Kade Dunn Publishing before asking her out. Nora had been warned about Maggie by some of her new colleagues. She was the office dog. No woman, whether gay or straight, married or single, or anything in between, was safe from her attentions. Absolutely not a person Nora needed to know.

Footsteps approached her desk, and then someone perched on the corner of it.

She swiftly looked up to see who was encroaching so rudely into her space.

"Hi, Nora," Maggie said, her voice practically a purr. Her body was just a little too close, her warmth reaching Nora across the narrow space between them, and Nora's stomach lurched in a not-so-unpleasant way as she breathed in the scent of Maggie's perfume.

"Hello," stuttered Nora, her heart beating a tad faster.

"I was wondering…" Maggie laced her fingers together across one thigh. "What are your plans for Saturday night?"

Out of the corner of her eye, Nora saw David do a little fist pump and reach for a jar containing some cash that sat between the bank of desks. What was going on there?

Slowly turning her focus back to the woman waiting expectantly beside her, she blinked herself out of the sensuous haze Maggie's presence had lulled her into. Had she just heard that correctly? Maggie was asking her out? In front of everyone? Didn't she have any sense of propriety? They hadn't spoken a word to each other since being introduced just the day before. What on earth did the woman think she was playing at?

Blushing, but her response to Maggie hardening by the second, Nora spoke rapidly and quietly. "I have plans, thank you. And if you're asking me out, well, you can save your breath. I am not interested." She knew she was overdoing it on the haughtiness, but really, this woman needed to be put in her place. She could admit that Maggie was extremely attractive. Gorgeous, actually, with that short blonde hair that didn't conform to any particular style, those clear blue eyes, and those soft-looking, slightly pouty lips. But that didn't matter. Nora wasn't going to be led down that path again. No way. Looks would play no part in any decision she made about her next relationship. She needed someone who shared her passion for the finer things in life, such as classic literature, poetry, and walks through the breathtaking countryside. Not someone like her ex, who would stomp all over Nora with her beauty and charm.

As Maggie shrugged and then walked away from the rebuff, Nora took a deep breath and focused on the large screen in front of her. Time to get back to her reading. She'd been tasked with helping out on the Twitter and Facebook campaigns for imminent releases. The digital media team she now worked for was planning to blaze a trail through all social media formats to promote these books.

One of the authors, Jo Green, had completed the long-overdue final part to a murder-mystery trilogy, and the release was eagerly anticipated by her fans. Not Nora's cup of tea at all.

The other book was a new history of the conflict in the Middle East, with emphasis on the relatively recent rise of the Islamic State. The contrast between the two was a challenge in itself—she had to keep the tone and content relevant in each communication she sent out. God help her if she muddled the two up.

Another reason why the shenanigans of Maggie Sullivan hadn't helped—Nora needed to focus, and being pursued by that woman was a distraction. She hoped her put-down had been firm and clear enough for that to be the end of it.

Before the end of that first week, Nora had also been asked out by Peter from the finance department. Although turning him down was easy, he looked crestfallen, and she hurried away from the finance department with alacrity.

On the following Tuesday, Nora came to the rescue of Joanne from editorial when the coffee machine erupted over her shoes. They joked a little as they cleaned up the mess. They discussed what they were both reading at the moment, and Joanne asked some questions about Nora's work that showed a pleasing intelligence. Joanne seemed nice. Safe.

"This might seem a little forward," said Joanne, shuffling her feet and glancing down to the floor and back again. "But would you like to have dinner one night? I'd love to talk more with you about the classics."

Joanne's calm, pleasant manner—so different from the brutish confidence Maggie displayed—definitely appealed to Nora.

"Yes, I'd like that." She smiled as Joanne beamed.

On Monday morning, Maggie strolled in with a grin on her face, a grin that only widened as her colleagues peppered her with questions about her exploits over the weekend.

"So, is the lesbian population of London exhausted and pining this morning?" David asked, and Maggie chuckled.

"Of course, what else do you expect?"

Her salacious tone made Nora's hackles rise, as did the hoots of laughter from everyone else. Nora scowled and returned her gaze to her screen.

Each day Maggie tried to engage Nora in conversation, only for Nora to shut her out.

"So, I heard a rumour about you," Maggie said, one afternoon late in the week.

"What?" Nora's heart raced, much to her annoyance, at the breathtaking smile Maggie sent her way.

"A little bird told me you have a date on Friday."

Maggie's gentle wink caused Nora's cheeks to flame. "If I do, it's none of your business." She turned back to her work. God, the woman was so infuriating! Maggie was boastful and pushy, both traits that set Nora's teeth on edge. At the same time, she displayed a mesmerising confidence in everything she said or did. Her wit and intelligence were captivating and could easily reduce Nora to a heart-fluttering mess. Nora reminded herself of the bragging at the start of the week and steeled her resolve to ignore her body's reactions to Maggie's...charms.

Nora shook off all thoughts of Maggie as she and Joanne walked out of the office on Friday evening. They shared a carafe of red over a light meal at one of the brasseries on the Chiswick High Road. Over dinner they discussed Jane Austen. It was nice. Nothing spectacular, but nice. So when Joanne asked if they could do it again, Nora concurred, and they arranged to meet the following Wednesday. There was no kiss goodnight, for which Nora was grateful. She didn't need any of that nonsense getting in the way right now. And, she supposed, a physical attraction to someone didn't have to be instant, did it? So, the fact that she felt nothing remotely like that for Joanne was neither here nor there. Was it?

The note was waiting for her when she got to work bright and early on Monday morning. There were a handful of people in, including that obnoxious Maggie, who had not stopped smiling at her every opportunity she got since that day Nora had turned her down.

She smiled now, as they stood near each other at the bank of lockers, and Nora found herself returning it, which only made Maggie smile wider, her eyes sparkling.

Nora blushed furiously and looked away. Why did her body keep betraying her like this? She was supposed to be ignoring the woman, not giving her any encouragement. But the smiles from Maggie lately were more friendly than lecherous, and part of her couldn't help responding to them.

She stared at Maggie's face, pondering her predicament. Oh God, she was doing it again! She tore her gaze away, but not before she saw Maggie's wistful expression. What was that about?

She set aside her curiosity and redirected it to the note taped to her locker. The inside of her locker. The locker that required a four-digit combination to open it, the combination code she had not shared with anyone. How had someone got into her locker to leave the note?

And then she read the words on the printed-out note.

> *You looked so beautiful on Friday night, I couldn't take my eyes off you. And hearing you talk so eloquently about Jane Austen made me tingle, as I love her works as much as you do. I would love to share more of this with you, our mutual love of the classics. I can picture us snuggled up on a sofa on a Sunday afternoon, each of us with her nose buried in a book, but with our bodies wrapped around each other, sharing our breath, our warmth.*

The note finished with a quote, one from Austen herself.

> *There is safety in reserve, but no attraction. One cannot love a reserved person.*

Why had Joanne broken into her locker to leave her this note? On the one hand, it was romantic—deeply romantic, she had to admit. On the other, there was something a little disconcerting about how it had been done.

She wandered back to her desk with the note in her hand, and looked up to find David staring at her questioningly. She got on well with him, and they were fast becoming friends. He was a quiet, unassuming geek, with a mop of black hair and small, wire-rimmed glasses that made him look much younger than his thirty years.

"What's up?" he asked.

"I... Someone left a note in my locker. My closed locker." She handed over the piece of paper without thinking—maybe Joanne wouldn't want it shared, but it had perturbed Nora too much not to share it with someone.

"Ooh, a secret admirer?" His tone was playful.

"No, actually, I think it's from Joanne. We went out for supper on Friday, and we talked about Jane Austen a lot. So it must be her."

"Aw, and she left you a cute note afterwards—how romantic!"

"Well, yes, but don't you think it's a bit...creepy? You know, breaking in to my locker?"

David smiled gently. "She probably just saw you enter your combination one day, remembered it, and thought it would be a cute thing to do. She seems nice enough, doesn't she? I mean, not creepy in real life?"

"Of course not. She's very nice in real life."

"Well, there you are, then! So, Friday was nice, yes?"

"Yes, it was. Nice." There was that word again. *Nice*. She glanced down at the note when David handed it back. It wasn't exactly *nice*. The note was emotional, passionate, and romantic. It talked to Nora's soul in a way she wasn't entirely comfortable with, but she couldn't put her finger on why. And why had Joanne included that quote at the end? Was it her way of saying that she, too, thought there was no spark between them? But if this was a romantic note, why put in a quote that suggested they weren't actually attracted to each other? Baffled, she shoved the note into her jacket pocket before taking her seat.

Footsteps made her look up to see Maggie returning from the kitchen with a steaming mug in her hands.

"Oh, God. Here comes Maggie. Presumably we will now have to suffer a retelling of her weekend conquests again." She turned her gaze to her screen to blot out the sight of the approaching woman.

"I doubt it," said David quietly, leaning across the space between their desks. "I heard her talking to Michelle in the kitchen on Friday, saying she was off the market. And that all that bragging last Monday was just to keep everyone happy, but there wasn't a word of truth in it. Seems she's met someone she's crazy about, and all other bets are off."

"Seriously? The serial one-night stander has found someone she can concentrate on for more than five minutes?" Nora's tone was bordering on scathing, but she couldn't help it.

David raised his eyebrows and shrugged. "Apparently. Totally smitten, she said, and determined to prove to this woman that her past is all behind her."

Nora snorted.

When Maggie reached their bank of desks and sat down, David spun in his chair to meet her gaze. "So, lover girl, how many this weekend?"

Maggie smiled. Almost shyly, if that could be believed. She glanced at Nora and then back to David.

"Quiet one for me this weekend. Caught up on stuff at home. Did some research for the Christmas webpage plans. Took Monk out for a lovely long walk in Epping Forest."

"Oh, I bet he loved that." David grinned and turned to Nora, who was eavesdropping but trying to make it look as if she wasn't.

"Have you seen a picture of Monk yet?" he asked her.

She shook her head slowly. "Who or what is Monk?"

Maggie chuckled throatily, and the sound sent inexplicable quivers down Nora's body. "My dog. Here, take a look." She pulled a small photo from her wallet and handed it over.

In the picture was the most adorable little scruff of a dog Nora had ever seen.

"Oh, he's gorgeous!" she exclaimed before she could help herself. Maggie's delighted expression made her breath hitch in her throat.

"Yep, that's my boy." They stared at each other.

"But, seriously," interrupted David, and Nora almost hated him at that moment. "No conquests? At all?"

Maggie's smile seemed forced. "Nope. Like I said, a quiet one." She turned to her workstation, indicating that the conversation was over.

Nora couldn't decide whether she should bring up the note with Joanne before Wednesday or leave it until then, partly because she felt so conflicted about it. Especially the quote. Those two short sentences were on a rolling loop in her brain. What on earth was Joanne trying to tell her? In the end, she decided to wait until Wednesday. Today was the launch of the two campaigns she'd been working on since she first got here, and she needed all her focus on that.

The initial response to both publications had been good, but, of course, the Jo Green one was leaping off the shelves, both physical and electronic. Nora's Twitter feeds were picking up good coverage, and the Facebook splash she'd worked on with David had already achieved over 5,000 likes before ten in the morning. Nora was too young to remember the old days of book promotion but revelled in the possibilities offered by the new digital age for an industry she had loved since she was a small child.

Maggie, despite working on the digital team, didn't seem quite so enamoured. "I can't help it," she said to David. "For me, there is nothing better than opening a fresh book, an actual book made of paper and board, waiting to see where the author will take you in their story."

"Still only buying in hardback, then?"

Nora couldn't help glancing up to hear what Maggie's response would be. This was a side to Maggie she would never have imagined.

"Whenever possible, yes. And no, I don't own a Kindle and never will. I'll buy paperback if I have to, but only as a last resort."

David laughed.

"I remember, as a child, thinking I was in paradise every time I was given a new book by my parents." Nora hadn't planned on joining in the conversation, but something about Maggie's passion for the printed word had lured her in.

Maggie met her eyes, and her smile took Nora's breath away.

"You too, huh?" Maggie's voice was quiet and filled with something Nora couldn't identify.

Nora nodded, unable to look away. "I spent hours huddled up in my bed, absorbed in any book my parents lavished on me. Books were my first true love."

Maggie stared at her with an indecipherable expression and then cleared her throat. "At last, an ally in my battle to educate this team on the sheer power and joy of a book in hand." She smiled warmly.

Nora blushed. She would never have imagined they would have something so profound in common.

By lunchtime, her head was spinning from keeping up with all that was happening out in social media land, and she decided to take a break. She grabbed the volume of Emily Dickinson poems she'd started at the weekend and headed out into the park. It was a beautiful autumn day, the sun surprisingly warm, with only a gentle breeze, so she found a patch of grass overlooking the waterway that flowed through the park and opened her mind to the curious yet compelling stanzas written some one hundred and fifty years ago.

When she returned to her desk, Joanne walked over, asked how she was, and confirmed their date on Wednesday. Their conversation was brief but pleasant. Joanne gave no hint of the note she'd left in the locker, and neither did Nora, determined to leave that conversation for a more private setting.

After Joanne walked away, Maggie caught Nora's gaze. "Got another hot date on Wednesday, huh?" Her smile was teasing, but not maliciously so.

"If I do, I'm quite sure it's nothing to do with you," replied Nora, more sharply than she had intended.

Maggie's eyebrows lifted. After a moment she shrugged and returned to her work.

Nora's conscience immediately nagged her. There had been no reason to be that rude, had there? Maggie was just being friendly. What was it about her that made Nora react so…irrationally? Maggie unsettled her; she could admit that. What she couldn't figure out was why.

"Look, I'm sorry," she said across the space between their desks. "I didn't mean to snap at you."

Maggie looked up, her smile radiant. "No worries." She paused. "I didn't mean to pry."

"It's okay. You weren't really."

They stared at each other for a few moments, and Nora's pulse quickened at being subjected to Maggie's penetrating gaze. She didn't know what to say after that, so she turned back to her workstation, trying to ignore the electric sensations that had erupted all over her body. And trying to understand what was happening between them. Maggie had a girlfriend, apparently, so why did she look at Nora so… tenderly? Did she think she could play around? Nora huffed out a breath. *Not with me.*

Nora dressed up a little on Wednesday for her date later that evening. It was a bit much for work, but easier than carrying a spare outfit in on her commute.

When she reached her desk, David gave her a wolf whistle.

She waved him off. She saw Joanne in passing later in the morning, and she had also dressed up, which made both of them smile. Nora had opted for a teal-green sweater with short sleeves and a V-neck, a pair of tight black jeans, which she tucked into knee-length black boots, and a short leather jacket. Joanne wore a flattering knee-length dress, with a slash neck across the shoulders, in a deep burgundy that complimented her dark hair beautifully. Again, Nora tried to ignore that part of her that didn't register even an ounce of physical attraction to Joanne. She admired how Joanne looked, but it didn't set off any sparks. It didn't matter, she told herself, it was about more than that with them.

When she got back from lunch, she was shocked to find another note, this time in the top of her handbag. With trembling hands, she pulled it out of the bag. After glancing around to make sure no one else was in sight, she opened the sheet of paper and read the words on it.

> *You look stunning today. You have literally left me breathless. And the most wonderful aspect of your beauty is that I don't think you realise just how gorgeous you are. Looking at you makes me ache to be with you. Are you sure you want to go out tonight? I can imagine whisking you off to somewhere private and cosy, where I could simply hold you close—oh, to feel you in my arms, to taste your lips with mine...*

Like the first, this also finished with a quote, the first stanza from one of Emily Dickinson's poems.

> *Wild Nights—Wild Nights!*
> *Were I with thee*
> *Wild Nights should be*
> *Our luxury!*

Nora's breath caught in her throat. The passion in the note sent shivers careening down her spine. Her heartbeat raced; her palms dampened; her face glowed. Good grief, no one had ever made her feel this way with mere words. She would never have known Joanne was so...passionate, so eloquent. She had given her no hints of this yet in their conversations. Perhaps she was shy, and the notes were her way of expressing her innermost thoughts. While it was lovely, Nora couldn't shake off the feeling that they were on different pages if these words spoke of Joanne's true feelings. That lack of physical chemistry was nagging at Nora. Yes, the words she'd just read made her pulse race. But when she read them, she didn't conjure up an image of Joanne in her mind's eye. No, the image that flashed through her brain was of a faceless, yet almost familiar woman, someone whose beauty and presence matched the depth of the words in front of her. Someone who could sweep Nora off her feet with very little protest. She tried very, very hard not to put a face to that person. Because the face she inexplicably kept coming up with was Maggie's.

She was determined to talk to Joanne about the notes. They, and Joanne's intentions, were now officially confusing the hell out of her. She waited until they were seated in the restaurant, this time in Covent Garden, and each had a glass of wine in hand before she broached the subject.

"So," she began, "I have a question."

Joanne leaned forward on her elbows, smiling warmly. "I'm all ears."

To Nora, though, the smile lacked the level of emotion the notes expressed so eloquently.

"Well, it's possibly a little awkward, but I really wanted to talk to you about the notes."

Joanne stared at her blankly. "Notes?"

Nora tilted her head to one side. Why was Joanne playing dumb? "Yes, the notes. I guess I'm just trying to figure out why. I mean, it's very romantic, don't get me wrong, but... Well, it's early days in this"—she motioned between them—"and they speak of something I'm not sure we've become yet."

Joanne sat back in her chair, her brow furrowed in a frown. "Um, Nora, what are you talking about? What notes?"

Now it was Nora's turn to stare. "The notes! The ones you left in my locker on Monday and my handbag at lunchtime today."

Joanne shook her head slowly, as if trying to clear her head of a particularly long sleep. "I have no idea what you are talking about. Someone has left you notes?"

Nora slumped back in her chair. "You mean it really wasn't you?"

"No, I swear, I have no idea what you are talking about."

"Oh God," Nora whispered. "Then who is it?"

And then she told Joanne everything, fishing both notes out of her handbag where they had been burning holes since she'd received the second one. They discussed them rationally, the way two friends would, not like a potential couple. And they both quickly realised that fact, and it led to a very friendly exchange about just what *this* was between them. They laughed when they each admitted that what they felt was purely platonic. And then they both relaxed, ordered more wine, and tried to unravel the mystery of the notes together.

"Okay," said Joanne, after their meal and with her third glass of wine in hand. "The one that really gets me is the first one. The only way they could know about the Jane Austen discussion was if they were sitting near us in the brasserie at the time. So, do you remember seeing anyone from work near us that night?"

Nora sipped at her wine. "I don't recall anyone near us that night. Mind you, I was trying to be very attentive to you as it was our first date, so I didn't check out the room at all."

Joanne giggled. "Me too. Damn, we missed a great opportunity to find out who your secret admirer is!"

Nora laughed. "I'm wondering if 'stalker' is the correct terminology now. I mean, they followed us on the Friday night, they know my locker combination, they know what I'm reading this week, and they know how to get in my handbag without anyone seeing. It's freaking me out a little, if I'm honest."

"Hey, don't worry." Joanne's voice projected calmness. "I think if they meant anything nasty, they'd have done something far worse than this. And they could have easily stolen something from your handbag today and didn't, so I don't think this is anything other than a pretty persistent admirer. I mean, you've got to hand it to them, they've been rather clever so far. And the notes are very romantic, not seedy at all."

"True," mused Nora. "So, what do I do now?"

Nora arrived at work early the next day, determined to talk to David before anyone else appeared. As she'd expected, he was already at his desk, flicking through the Metro newspaper while he sipped his large Starbucks cappuccino.

When she saw he was on his own, she relaxed and threw the second note down on top of his newspaper. "I got another one, yesterday after lunch. And they're not from Joanne."

He stared at her for a moment, then picked up the note and read it.

"Oh my," he murmured, putting a hand on his chest. "She's making *me* tingle, and I haven't even *looked* at a woman in fifteen years."

Nora sighed and dropped into her chair. "What makes you think it's a woman?"

"What?"

Nora's last frightening thought before she went to bed the night before had been to question the gender of whoever had left the messages for her. There was nothing in either note to outright suggest the sex of the author, so why had she assumed it was a woman?

"It could be Peter," Nora whispered, shuddering.

David looked sick. "Oh no. No way. These notes were not written by a forty-something, straight man who looks like he still lives at home with Mummy."

"God, I hope you're right." She sank her head into her hands briefly before looking back up at him. "David, I'm really struggling with all of this."

"In what way? The whole creepy thing, like you said on Monday?"

"Partly." She hesitated.

"But also...?"

"But also... I think they're beautiful. They make me feel things I haven't ever felt. They stir something in me." Her face flushed, but she was, at the same time, glad she'd confided in someone. She hadn't wanted to tell Joanne; it hadn't seemed appropriate to share that element with her.

David smiled and reached across the desk to take one of her hands. Before he could speak, someone made their presence known with a clearing of the throat from just a few steps away. They both glanced in that direction, to find Maggie looking at them quizzically.

"Something you two want to share with the team?" She looked at their joined hands and smiled that little teasing smile again.

David giggled. "Now that *would* be news!" He let go of Nora's hand, but not before giving it a gentle squeeze.

"So, everything okay?" Maggie looked between the pair of them as she moved to her own desk.

"Fine," muttered Nora, switching her gaze away from the stunning sight of Maggie in a form-fitting tailored trouser suit and shirt.

"Well, don't you look all dapper." David smirked. "Hot date tonight?"

Maggie shook her head, looking almost bashful.

Nora was gawping at her again. *God, stop it!*

"No, I'm not... I'm... Never mind. I've got a presentation to give to some of the directors this afternoon, so thought I'd better smarten up."

"Well, I think you look delicious." David gave her a wink.

She blushed ever so slightly before meeting Nora's eyes.

And then it was Nora's turn to blush because she was staring *yet again*. She pulled her gaze away and stared instead at the screen in front of her.

David passed the note back to her from where it was still sitting on his desk.

"Love notes too?" Maggie grinned, although it seemed a little forced.

"Not mine," replied David before Nora could stop him. "Hers."

Maggie met Nora's embarrassed stare but said nothing, which astounded Nora. Surely that was a topic ripe for Maggie to rip into? Instead, she gave Nora a sad half smile and then turned back to her own screen without a word.

Nora spent the day hunched over her screen, determined not to look at Maggie. She was baffled by her continuing reaction to the woman, which was bordering on the ridiculous. They hadn't spoken much, mainly because Nora kept trying to avoid doing just that. But she had to admit to the pleasure she had gained from the few conversations they had shared and everything she'd learned about Maggie from the conversations she'd heard her having with David. Her clear love of literature, her affection for her dog, her love of cooking. Knowledge of all these things, along with Maggie's irrefutable, all-around bloody *hotness*, had led to Nora feeling completely befuddled. She didn't want to like her, especially after her brash display that first week. But everything she had done since then had been anything but brash.

On Friday, the digital team decided on impromptu drinks at the pub after work. Maggie declined, said good-bye as they left the building, and headed off in the direction of the Tube station.

Nora willed herself not to watch her go, much as she willed herself not to be disappointed that Maggie wasn't joining them.

David pinned her down, figuratively, after their first drink.

"Time to spill," he said, out of the blue, as they sipped their second glasses of wine.

Nora stared at him. "Spill what?"

"What's going on in that cute little head of yours?" When she started to protest, he held up a hand. "It is very obvious to me—and no one else, I hasten to add—that you are very preoccupied with something. Or should that be some*one*?" He stared her down until she felt the blush inflame her cheeks. "You know she's involved with someone now. Save yourself the heartache—get past it, find someone else, whatever you need to do. She's got a reputation, even if she is temporarily off the market. And I don't want to see you get hurt."

"I know," said Nora. She sighed and hung her head. "God, how could I get myself in this position? I don't even like her!"

David laughed. "Yeah, keep preaching that line to yourself and maybe you'll be okay."

Nora left the pub after that second drink, too down in the dumps to pretend to be sociable after David's astute observations had exposed her. How could she be falling for Maggie? It was just…impossible. She grew grumpier by the minute as she walked up the road towards the Tube station. Gradually, she became aware of the chill in the air as she stomped up the road and shoved her cold hands into her coat pockets to warm them.

The fingers of her right hand rustled against a folded piece of paper. Trembling, her heart suddenly pounding, she curled her fingers around it and pulled it from her pocket. It was another note—same paper, same font. She hurried over to a streetlight, which cast its yellow-orange glow across the paper as she read.

Watching you leave tonight was so desperately hard. Another two days without your face to gaze upon, your smile to warm me. Another two days of dreaming crazy dreams, of wondering what could be. I have retreated into one of my all-time favourites, Jane Eyre, this week. I imagine you would class that one in your top five somewhere, just like me.

Nora nodded to herself, smiling, then read on.

And I came across this verse, and it seemed to me it said all I wanted to say at the end of this week.

Her coming was my hope each day,
Her parting was my pain;
The chance that did her steps delay
Was ice in every vein.

Until Monday...

Nora read it again, struggling to breathe. Oh God, who *was* this woman? And how could she elicit such a reaction in Nora? She prided herself on always remaining calm, rising above the nonsense of the hearts-and-flowers treatment that a lot of women seemed to think constituted the perfect romance. But if *this* woman presented her with a dozen red roses and another note full of wondrous words, she would literally swoon. She folded the note, slipped it into her bag with its two partners, and took a deep breath before walking on. She was going to do everything she could to work out who this admirer of hers was—if nothing else, her mystery woman would be a welcome distraction for this stupid attraction to Maggie.

Come Monday, Nora was a woman on a mission. She was going to share the contents of the third note with David, and they were going to crack this mystery once and for all. And then she reached her desk and stopped in her tracks.

Laying across her keyboard was another note.

She quickly glanced around. Not a soul in sight. She snatched up the note and hungrily immersed herself in it.

> *Good morning, beautiful. I hope your weekend was good. I was happy that mine passed by so quickly, as it drew me nearer to you with each minute that fled. And I decided something over the weekend, once again inspired by our Jane: 'I would always rather be happy than dignified.' I may lose some dignity in revealing myself and risk your rejection. But the chance that I could be immeasurably happy if you do not reject me, and you yourself take a risk in knowing me, and learning me, is worth the potential cost.*
>
> *So, come find me, if you care to. I am waiting and will wait until ten this morning. Please, come find me—I am on the bridge, and I hope you will know me when you see me.*

Nora's breath stalled in her throat. Oh God, she was out there, waiting! She glanced at her watch. Nine fifteen, plenty of time. Was she ready? Definitely, yes. But nervous too—so many doubts about who the woman was. Still desperately hoping it was a woman, of course. But again, somehow, the way the notes were written, something just told her it had to be a woman. Oh God, what if it was all some awful prank, and she was about to make an utter fool of herself? What if the woman was in a relationship and just trying to charm her way into Nora's pants for a quick fling? What if—?

She stopped herself. She could do the *what ifs* all day, but where would that get her? Safe? Yes. But always wondering what might have been? Yes.

Time to be bold.

Nora stepped out of the building into a light drizzle, strong enough for an umbrella, which—of course—she had left upstairs in her mad rush to get out of the office once her decision was made. Whoever was waiting for her on the bridge would just have to take her looking a little damp and frizzy. She took a deep breath and turned left towards the bridge.

Someone was waiting, huddled under a plain black umbrella and wrapped in a long black coat. She had her back to Nora, but the figure was unmistakably that of a woman, and Nora breathed a huge sigh of relief at having passed that first hurdle. Pushing herself onwards, despite the shakiness in her legs, she tried to calm her breathing as she reached the end of the bridge and stepped onto it. She skirted a couple of men, and then, for a few moments at least, it was just her and the other woman. The heels of Nora's boots clicked on the bridge, and the sound was just loud enough to reach the woman because she turned her way. She lifted her umbrella, which revealed her face, and Nora froze.

Maggie.

It took a moment to register. It was Maggie. Maggie was standing in the centre of the bridge, waiting for her.

Maggie smiled, tentatively, and then walked slowly towards Nora.

It's Maggie, thought Nora numbly. *Maggie has been writing me those astonishingly wonderful notes? Maggie?*

Maggie stopped a pace or two away, her smile fading at the lack of reaction from Nora, but Nora was too stunned to get her face muscles working. They stood staring at each other for a few seconds, and then Maggie shrugged and made as if to walk past Nora.

"Wait!" blurted Nora, finally finding her voice.

Maggie stopped alongside her, her expression questioning, yet fearful.

"You?" whispered Nora. "The notes...they were from you?"

Maggie nodded and started to speak and then stopped, waiting.

"But...I mean...really?"

"Really what?" asked Maggie quietly. "Really they were from me, or really that's how I feel about you?"

"Both, I suppose." How could it be possible that the brash, arrogant woman who'd asked her out in her first week on the job was the same woman who had, well, *wooed* her with such heartfelt letters and poems in the weeks since?

"Yes, to both," whispered Maggie as she took a step closer. She gazed into Nora's eyes, her own filled with nothing but sincerity. Maggie took a deep breath, as if bracing herself. "I'm not the woman you met that first week." Her voice was quiet but determined. "I fell into my usual self-protecting act, allowed my own urban myth to cloud my judgement and make me as obnoxious as everyone has come to expect me to be. I went home one Friday night, unable to get thoughts of you out of my head, and I had a good, long talk with myself. I decided it was time to be the real me, the one they"—she gestured towards the office block behind Nora—"never see. The woman I really want to be. The woman I really am. The woman who is completely and utterly captivated by you."

Nora's heart did a great big thud. Maggie's spoken words, like her written ones, left her reeling.

"And I couldn't just walk into the office on a Monday morning, tell you all this, and expect you to believe me. I needed you to *hear* me before you could *see* me."

"But, how...? You knew so much about me, what I was doing. How?"

Maggie tilted her head. "I hope I didn't alarm you."

Nora smiled ruefully.

"Oh God, that wasn't my intention! I just got lucky, I guess, with circumstances. That Friday night, when you went out with Joanne the first time, by sheer fluke I was out with a friend, and we sat at the table behind yours. I eavesdropped all evening—very rude, especially to the friend I was eating with."

Nora giggled.

"In terms of getting into your locker—again, just luck. I was standing at the printer near the lockers when you entered your combination one morning. I...I was watching your hands." She blushed.

Nora found herself smiling at the implication hidden in Maggie's words.

"The others were easier. I only had to wait for you to be away from your desk. And this morning..." She paused, letting out a small sigh. "I knew I had to do this, to risk telling you who I was, so I got up extra early and made sure everything was in place before you arrived."

Nora took a moment to absorb all that Maggie had said and to work out how it fit with the events of the last few weeks.

"What about the woman you were seeing?"

Maggie's face scrunched into a frown.

"David overheard you telling Michelle you were off the market because you had found someone. How does she fit into this whole...scheme?" Nora tried to keep her voice neutral but wasn't sure she succeeded.

Maggie's eyes widened, and then a blush stole across her cheeks.

"That was you," she whispered. "I was talking about how I felt about you. I wasn't seeing anyone. I was just trying to put a stop to whatever gossip was doing the rounds."

Nora slowly shook her head. This was extraordinary. Her mind and body whirled from the emotional onslaught of coming to terms with the resolution of the mystery. Of discovering that the beautiful woman in front of her had written the words that had set Nora alight. Of realising that the dream the notes had dangled in front her had every chance of becoming a reality. A reality she could literally grasp with both hands, if she just took one step forward.

And so she did.

She took Maggie's free hand in hers and wrapped Maggie's cold fingers in her own much warmer ones.

Maggie's instant smile was brilliant enough to generate its own rainbow in the drizzle around them.

Nora smiled back and then giggled and then laughed out loud with the sheer joy of the moment. She didn't resist when Maggie bent her head and placed the gentlest, tenderest of kisses on Nora's lips. A kiss that stayed gentle for only moments before Nora clutched at Maggie's coat, pulled her in closer, and urged Maggie to kiss her with a hunger that seared its way deep into Nora's soul.

Maggie lowered the umbrella over their joined bodies, shielding them from the rain and any onlookers, and they lost themselves in each other, with no words needed.

ROMANCE ON A SIDE NOTE
BY CHRIS ZETT

LIZ CHECKED THE TITLES ON the table against several lists in her head as she went through the stacks of books. There were thousands, maybe tens of thousands of books to go through this weekend. She didn't expect to discover anything worth a decent commission, but she never knew. She would probably find some of the items on her *unpaid* list, though. She sighed. That list was ever growing, but how could she refuse her grandmother and her book club? *Ah, there's one.* She crouched down and reached into a box under the table.

"No, I need that!"

Something hard and narrow hit Liz from behind. Sharp pain shot from her lower back into her right foot, and she lost her balance and fell into the box of books. *What the fuck?* She struggled to free herself from the mess of books and squashed cardboard and turned to tell the rude person behind her exactly what she thought of people shoving and fighting at a library sale. This was not Black Friday after all. The scolding died on her tongue as she looked into the worried face of an elderly lady behind a walker.

"I'm so sorry, dear! Did I hurt you? Did you break something? Let me help you up!"

The woman's concern convinced Liz that it had been an accident, rather than intention, that had landed her on the floor. She waved away the outstretched hand, afraid the fragile woman would break if she had to lift her weight. Not that Liz was that heavy, but even a paperback edition of *The Complete Works of William Shakespeare* seemed too much for her attacker. The woman clutched her walker with one hand; the other trembled at her side, and she looked pale as if she might faint any minute.

"It's okay. I'm not hurt." Liz turned back to arrange the fallen books in a stack and to reclaim the book that had caused the incident. It was an illustrated edition of *Little Women* in good condition from 1947, if she remembered correctly. The same sketch of a woman was repeated in alternating red and white on the front and back. It was a beautiful book, but not rare and certainly nothing to fight over. She stood and turned to the woman.

"Are you really all right? I swear it was an accident. I'm so, so sorry. I'm not yet used to this contraption." The woman pointed at her walker and frowned.

"I'm fine, don't worry. I'm Elizabeth Fray, but you can call me Liz." Liz smiled and held out her hand.

"Oh, I'm Elizabeth too, Elizabeth London, but I go by Beth." She took Liz's hand, and her grip was surprisingly strong. Beth gazed at the book in Liz's other hand but didn't say anything.

Liz offered the book for inspection. "Do you want it?"

Beth hesitated. "May I have a look inside?"

"Sure." Liz shrugged and gave it to her.

Beth swiftly leafed through the book, not pausing to study the illustrations or the condition of the binding as

Liz would have done. Finally, she shook her head and gave it back; she sighed and grasped her walker with an unsteady hand. "You can keep it, dear. It's not what I'm looking for."

Liz took a quick look at the book and put it in the shopping basket she had brought. "I saw another edition somewhere over here. Maybe that's the one you're looking for."

Beth looked down and blushed. "No, no. The edition is right, I'm sure of it. But I need a different copy." She seemed to shrink behind her walker as she slowly turned toward the next table. "Maybe I'll get lucky over there. Thank you."

Liz watched her go and debated whether she should follow her. The blush and the forlorn expression intrigued her. There was a story behind Beth's search. *Stop helping old ladies and concentrate on customers that pay the bills!* Liz closed her eyes and mentally reviewed her long list of books she needed.

A few hours later, she found what Beth was looking for. Another copy of the same edition was stuck between travel descriptions, and she nearly overlooked it because she found a book that would pay some of her bills for this month—a first edition atlas with illustrations of southern France, the region her client's great-grandfather had immigrated from. This version of *Little Women* was even more worn than the first one and had obviously gone through many hands. It had been repaired several times, and the spine had been exchanged for a generic one, probably sometime in the late fifties. She carefully opened the book and checked if anything on the inside was different from the others. Several comments in two distinctive styles of handwriting filled the inner margins with lines in thin pencil. Sometimes the comments consisted of just one word or a short sentence. Sometimes there was a conversation between the two writers. One had signed with JS, the other with BL, and they not only discussed the book but life in general. It was not difficult to guess that BL stood for Beth London.

Liz searched for Beth but couldn't find her. Maybe she had given up.

Liz went to the checkout counter, where a librarian was handling the sale of the books. She patiently packed each purchase in totes with the logo of the library and chatted with the customers. Liz had enough time to admire her as she waited in line. She was probably around Liz's age, and the brown corduroy skirt, the green woolen sweater, and the neat knot of her dark hair would have looked old-fashioned on most women but it didn't on her. Liz couldn't pinpoint how she pulled it off. When it was Liz's turn, the librarian's smile made her forget what she wanted for a moment.

"Excuse me, have you seen an elderly lady with a walker, maybe that high," Liz motioned to somewhere beneath her shoulder, "with curly white hair?"

The woman, Jane her name tag said, gave her a look that was the perfect mixture of incredulous and amused. It lightened up her classic stern librarian look, which Liz found cute. Jane raised her eyebrows and pointed to several women that matched the description in the near vicinity.

Maybe she had been a little bit vague. Liz tried her best charming smile and explained the situation to Jane. She finished by handing over her card. "So, if you hear from Beth, could you please give her my number and let me know?" She searched for the right words to convey an interest in talking to Jane again. As usual, she failed to come up with a clever line and settled for something simple. "Or you could call if you have any questions."

Jane nodded and put the card in her pocket. "It's not very likely, but I'll keep it in mind."

Her expression had softened during the explanation, and Liz wanted to linger and chat with her, but a line had already formed, and the other customers grumbled behind her.

Liz decided to take the book with her and see if she could find Beth herself, which should be easy. Working as a professional book finder regularly included finding people. When she was on the trail of rare first editions, she sometimes needed to find the past owners to research the current one.

Locating Beth proved more difficult than finding a Gutenberg Bible. Not really, but it certainly felt like it. She wasn't listed in the phone book and seemed to lack ties to the region. Liz's usual sources and the Internet came up empty. After losing fifteen minutes reading about the new tube line in London that was named after Queen Elizabeth, she gave up and focused on paying customers. But the urge to find her remained for the rest of the week.

Sunday was her regular day to visit her grandmother. She lived in a retirement home, for the social aspects more than anything. She got to see her friends every day, and they had formed a book club. Currently, they were rereading their favorite classics and planned to start *Little Women* next. Should she show her grandma Beth's copy? She finally decided against it. The way Beth had blushed made it somehow seem too personal.

Liz greeted her grandmother with a hug and a kiss.

"What treasures have you brought me today?" Her grandmother reached for Liz's bag even before the hug ended. Her eager smile and enthusiasm always reminded Liz of herself as a little girl on Christmas.

Liz unpacked the stack of books she had found at the library sale and several used-book stores. "You won't believe what happened when I found the copy of *Little Women* Aunt Jo requested."

"Did you have to fight for it?" Grandma chuckled.

Liz wasn't surprised. Her grandmother had fantastic intuition. "Nearly." Liz told her about meeting Beth and finding the book she was seeking. She left out the written conversation and Jane, the cute, but sadly uninterested librarian. Liz sighed. Complaining to her grandma about the fruitless search for Beth felt good, but it didn't alleviate her regret of failing to find her.

"Maybe she's like me," Grandma said after listening patiently. "She could be living in a retirement home and wouldn't have an individual listing."

Why didn't I think of this? That's so simple and obvious. Liz stood and hugged her. "That's a great idea, thank you. I'll make some calls tomorrow."

After Liz had talked to her grandmother, it was embarrassingly easy to find Beth. All it took was a couple of phone calls, and the next thing Liz knew, Beth was inviting her over for coffee. Liz waited to surprise her with the book when they met the next day.

Beth fussed over the flowers Liz brought. "They are so lovely, thank you." She set them on the perfectly decked table with fragile porcelain cups, plates, and a silver coffee pot. She offered cookies to Liz and winked. "It's been a long time since a beautiful young woman gave me flowers."

Was that an innocent comment, or did Beth just out herself? Liz's gaydar was faulty at the best of times and certainly not tuned to elegant old ladies that resembled her grandma. She decided to ignore it for now and presented the wrapped book to Beth.

"Thank you, dear. That wasn't necessary." Beth carefully removed the paper.

Liz just smiled and studied her expression.

Surprise and hope warred on Beth's face as she looked from the book to Liz and back. She slowly opened the cover and hesitated before checking the pages. Liz could tell the exact moment when Beth found the first note in the margin. A wide smile stretched from one side of her face to the other, and she squeezed her eyes shut, making the wrinkles around her eyes more pronounced. Tears streamed from them, and she sobbed.

Liz hurried to Beth's side of the table and carefully laid her arm around her shoulders.

Beth returned her hug as she laughed, cried, and thanked her simultaneously.

After Beth had cried herself out, she told her story to Liz. "When I grew up, we didn't have much money for books. I went to the library each week and went home with as many books as I could carry. I'd read everything that was deemed appropriate for my age and was rereading my favorites when I discovered the comments in this book. At first, I was furious. How could anyone dare to write in a book? In a public library! It just wasn't done. I planned to report it to the librarians on my next visit. But then I found myself agreeing with the comments. They were witty and reflected exactly what I was thinking. I even thought of clever replies to one or two things and wanted to point out important passages the commenter had overlooked." Beth chuckled. "The night before my next visit to the library, I wrote my first remark next to the others. I was mortified. What if someone noticed when I returned the book? I would never be allowed to go back to the library." Beth paused to pour more coffee. She looked pensive as she stirred sugar and cream into it and took a sip.

"And were you found out?" Liz gently prompted.

Beth shook her head. "No, not for a long time. To make a long story short, we wrote to each other for over a year. She, or maybe he, was called JS. We started with our thoughts about the story and the writing, but we soon turned this into a conversation about everything that was important to us." She played with the tiny silver spoon that looked big in her petite hands. "I don't know if you've ever experienced this, but sometimes being anonymous frees you to admit things you barely allowed yourself to think, let alone say out loud."

Liz laughed. "Well, that's the joy of the Internet now. We can reinvent ourselves without looking anyone in the eyes."

"Exactly. I've never had such a close friend since. Well, that's not strictly true. I've had lovers, partners, and we shared intimate conversations, of course. Maybe the first time is just more memorable than the rest. I just wished I could have met her. Or him."

"What do you think? Was JS female? Didn't you get clues from the writing?"

Beth thought about that for a minute. "I always thought of JS as a girl my age. We were too similar for her to be someone else, but then JS started flirting with me." There was that blush from their first meeting again. "Or I with JS, I don't know who started it. But girls didn't flirt with girls in the fifties. Or so I thought." She grinned.

Liz couldn't help grinning back. "Yeah. It always takes some time to figure that out." She hesitated to turn the mood, but she wanted to know more. "Why did you stop writing? Because they found out?"

"No, not really. My father was in the army, and we had to move on short notice. I didn't have time to check out the book again to let JS know, so I risked writing something in the library. I wanted to leave her a message to explain and ask her to write to the post office of the town we moved to. I should have just put a piece of paper in it or something, but I wasn't thinking straight. The librarian saw me writing in the book and went mad. She screamed at me, and I ran away, leaving the book behind. I was always afraid to go back into that building." She shook her head. "With my teenage imagination, I thought they had *wanted dead or alive for desecrating books* signs with my face hung up everywhere."

It was tragic that their friendship had ended so suddenly. Liz wondered what JS had felt when BL had stopped writing. "Have you ever tried to find her?"

"No, how could I? I knew nothing but the initials." Beth looked down into her cup. "And to be honest, I nearly stopped thinking about her. At first, it was too painful, and then life took over. I lived on the other side of the country for most of my life." She tried to drink from her cup, not noticing that it was already empty. "Last year I broke my hip, so I sold my house and moved to a retirement home. Nearly all of my friends had either died or moved closer to their kids, so I decided to return here. When I read about the library sale, it seemed like a sign. I figured with all these wrinkles and white hair, they wouldn't recognize me now." She took Liz's hand. "It was a sign. I've met you, and now I have that book again to keep me company."

Liz hadn't wanted to promise anything to Beth, but the idea of finding JS lingered in the back of her mind for days. She knew her initials, probable age, and the town where she lived in the fifties. It shouldn't be impossible to find her. But it was. At least with the tools she had at her disposal at home. She needed to pay the library another visit.

She tried to avoid it because she was hesitant to explain the case of the "desecrated" book. It felt like a betrayal of Beth's trust. Finally, she made an appointment with the head librarian to see what she could find out. He wasn't overly enthusiastic and sent her to a colleague in charge of the archive.

Liz went to the main floor in search of Ms. Tome. She bit the inside of her cheek to avoid making jokes about the name that was only too fitting for a librarian. The first staff member she spotted was Jane. Liz jumped on the opportunity to talk to her again.

"Hi, uh, Jane?" Liz hoped she wasn't making too much of a fool of herself. She always got nervous around women she found attractive.

Jane turned. "Oh, hi. You're the book finder, Liz, right? I'm sorry, I haven't seen any elderly customer named Beth yet."

She remembers who I am! She forced herself to concentrate on the conversation and not to stare into Jane's dark brown eyes that shone like a well-polished leather cover. "I've actually found her. Thank you for keeping a lookout. Now I'm searching for someone else. The head librarian told me that Ms. Tome could help me. Do you know where she is?"

"You've just found her. What can I do for you?" Jane smiled.

Liz could imagine a dozen things. *Do not go there. You're here for Beth.* "It's a complicated story that might take a while."

Jane nodded. "Do you want to go to my office? It doubles as an archive of sorts, but I have enough space for two chairs and a desk."

Jane walked toward the back of the building, and Liz followed. They stopped to pick up two mugs of coffee from the break room. The office wasn't really small, but the walls were higher than wide and completely covered with filing cabinets and bookcases that were nearly twice as tall as Liz. It gave the room a crowded feeling, and Liz immediately loved it. The unique scent of old books, in combination with a little bit of dust, wood polish, and a trace of vanilla smelled like home to Liz. She sat in the comfortable visitor's chair and sipped her coffee as she told Jane the complete story.

They silently drank their coffees. It was difficult to gauge Jane's reaction. She smiled at times, and Liz took it as a positive sign, but then she wrinkled her brow in either concentration or displeasure. Sometimes it was much harder to read people than books.

"I fear it will be nearly impossible to find JS after all that time. We haven't computerized anything before the late eighties. If JS is still registered, we might be lucky. And I'm not sure about giving the contact information to anyone else, but I can contact her if we find her. Or him." Jane tilted her head and studied her. "What do you hope to gain from that? Do you want to write a book about it or something?"

Liz shook her head. "No, nothing like that. I just have a soft spot for elderly ladies that remind me of my grandma." She tried to ease the tension with a joke. "And I might be a hopeless romantic, always searching for a happy ending."

It seemed to work. Jane started to laugh. "Okay, let's start with the current records first. What year of birth are we guessing?"

Liz relaxed into the chair. "Beth was fifteen in 1952 when they wrote to each other. I suppose JS was around the same age. Let's have a look at anyone born before 1940. Beth mentioned that JS was born during the summer. She'd complained that no one came to her party because it was during summer vacation. She must have lived relatively close because she came every week."

Jane opened a program on her computer and clicked and typed for several minutes. She frowned and hummed with increasing frequency. At last, she looked up and shook her head. "It's depressing to see how few elderly customers we still have. None of them have matching initials. I even looked at the birth names in case it was a woman who married later. I'm afraid we have to look manually at the files." She pointed towards the cabinets looming over them. "Going through all the files will take a while, and we have no guarantee that it's even the right name. If J married and changed her name, the file will be in a new category."

The task seemed nearly too much. It would take weeks, maybe months to find anything. If they did it, it also meant she would spend weeks or hopefully months in Jane's company. Liz's mood brightened. "I'm up for it. I can't come here every day, because I need my day job to pay my bills, but my schedule is flexible. If you don't mind, I could come whenever it's best for you and work my way through the files."

Jane smiled, and Liz's heart missed a beat.

"I'd like that. I'll help when I can. Can we start now?"

Liz had been right. It took them several months working on and off to plow through the "S-files" as they called them. She took time off to visit an auction for a client, but the commission had enabled her to work full-time in the library for a few weeks afterward.

Most days, she worked on her current projects from home for a few hours and then went to the library to work with Jane until her lunch break. In the afternoon, Jane spent her time mainly out of her office but came back to bring her coffee, snacks, and funny anecdotes about the customers. They started to bring each other lunch, and Liz enjoyed their conversations, which ranged from books to movies to politics and always returned to books. She had finally found her match in obscure literary knowledge. She used to bore her girlfriends whenever they discussed literature. Jane, on the other hand, actually seemed to enjoy their talks, rather than just tolerating Liz's ramblings.

Sometimes, the names in the files reminded one of them of people they used to know or places they used to visit. Over time, they learned each other's history. Jane told her about the year she worked and studied at the British Library in London, and Liz told her how her love of books had been supported by her grandma since she'd been little. They even found the file of Aunt Jo, who wasn't really Liz's aunt, but her grandma's best friend. Liz couldn't stop giggling when she found out Jo's real name was Marjorie.

They talked for hours and flirted subtly. Some days, Liz was sure she imagined it, so she held back because she was afraid it was all wishful thinking. On other days, she was sure she'd interpreted the signals right and basked in the warm glow that Jane's smile cast over her.

"That's it. The last one." Liz put the file carefully on the tall stack on Jane's desk. She wanted to fling it in the corner of the room instead. Only two files were possible matches in their last batch.

Jane sighed. "Let me put them away, and then we can discuss how to proceed." She took the files and climbed a few steps up the ladder to gain access to the correct filing cabinet.

Liz allowed herself to eye the legs and perfect figure emphasized by the long narrow skirt. Jane completed the look with a purple-and-green-plaid pantyhose that Liz found incredibly sexy. She always brightened her conservative attire with little details that showed her mischievous side. Liz suppressed a sigh. It might be the last time they saw each other. She shook her head. *Don't be so negative.* They were friends now, bordering on more. Even if they didn't have an excuse to meet several times a week, they would stay in contact. Liz was sure of it. She had only to work up the courage to ask Jane out on a date.

"I have some useful tools to find people on the Internet. Let me try those first." Liz opened her laptop and started searching. It didn't take long to come up with some information. "The woman died. That leaves the man, Jim Sedge."

Jane rested her hands on the back of Liz's chair and leaned over her shoulder.

The smell of vanilla distracted Liz. She bit her lower lip to keep herself from sighing out loud.

"Oh. I had hoped to talk to all of them. Now we'll never know for sure. What did you find about him?" Jane spoke much too close to Liz's ear.

How could she concentrate with that warm breath playing through her hair? "I have... Uh, that tickles... I found someone, I think." Liz was disappointed when Jane pulled back.

"You think?" Jane walked back to her side of the table and slumped into her chair. Usually, she sat very straight. Now she slouched against the back of her chair.

Liz wrote down the telephone number and slid the paper over the table. "We can't be sure this information is up to date, but we can at least try."

As Jane made the call, Liz felt as if she were reading a really bad novel. It didn't feel real. She was missing something vital. She massaged both temples with her hands. Maybe she was just too tired.

Jane hung up, shook her head, and grimaced. "Humorless old guy. He made a speech about wasting tax dollars with my call. He denies ever writing in a book. Even if it were him, I wouldn't want Beth to meet him."

That certainly was anticlimactic. After all the work they had done, they were back where they had begun. "So, that's it. Maybe it was the woman."

"Maybe."

They both stared at the files for a moment. Then Jane looked at Liz with a completely different expression. A smile began in the corner of her mouth.

"Would you like to meet for lunch on the weekend? What are you doing on Sunday?"

Liz gasped. She hadn't expected Jane to ask the question she was afraid to ask herself. It took her three tries to clear her throat before she could answer. "I'd love to." Her mind was already making plans for a date when her speeding thoughts came to a crashing halt. "Wait, no, I can't."

"Oh, okay. Maybe another time." Jane's voice was carefully neutral.

Now she's thinking you don't want to go out with her. "It's just that I promised to go to my grandma's book club." Liz hesitated. "I know it's probably not how you planned to spend your only day off, but would you like to join us?"

"Talking about books in my free time? Why would I want to do that?" Jane winked at her and laughed. "If it's okay with your grandmother, I'd love to go and meet her. You've talked so much about her and your aunt Jo that I feel as if I know them already."

Sunday presented itself with sunshine and perfect spring weather. The members of the book club were happy that most of the other residents went outside and they had the comfortable community area for themselves. Coffee and cake were served, and they were ready for a lengthy interrogation. Liz had underestimated the attraction of a newcomer. The usually placid ladies fired question after question at Jane, which she fielded without missing a beat. Liz tried to intervene but was shushed and told to sit and wait. Jane smiled at her as if to say she shouldn't worry. So, Liz took a piece of cake and watched the show. Jane didn't show any signs of uneasiness and even seemed to enjoy the interaction.

"Liz," Grandma said suddenly. Her voice still held that school-teacher quality, and Liz sat just a little bit straighter. "Tell us what came of your research project you've been working on. Did you finally find the person you were looking for?"

Liz looked at Jane, who nodded slightly. Nobody here had met Beth before, but she decided not to mention any names. She explained to the others about the chance meeting, the friendship documented in the book, and their futile search. Everyone was quiet for a change and listened. Without warning, Jo jumped out of her seat and bolted from the room. When she didn't come back, her grandmother followed Jo. What was that about? Was she sick? Liz wondered if she should follow them. The ladies' questions drew her back to the conversation, and she finished her tale.

After a while, Grandma returned and approached Liz. "Step outside with me for a moment."

Liz stood up. "Is Aunt Jo okay?"

Grandma looked at the others. "Shh. Just come." She hurried to the door.

Liz followed to where Aunt Jo was waiting. Her face was flushed, and her eyelids were swollen. What was going on? What made her cry? Jo was generally relaxed and hard to ruffle, no matter what happened.

"Do you still have contact with...with the woman who wrote in the book? What's her name?" Jo clutched Liz's arm, her hand trembling.

"Aunt Jo, are you okay? Do you need to sit down?" Jo looked as if she might faint. Even though no one would call her fragile, she definitely looked her age today.

"No. Don't fuss. Just answer my question. Do you?"

Why was this so important to her? The answer hit her like a book tumbling from the highest shelf. Why hadn't she seen it before? She'd even found her file a while back. "You are JS!"

Jo just nodded and smiled shyly.

Liz grinned like a fool. She was nearly jumping up and down with excitement. "I can't believe it. All this time, the answer was that close. I'll call Beth right away." She reached for her phone, but Jo stopped her.

"Beth... Do you think she might want to talk to me after all that time?" The trepidation in her voice slowed Liz down.

Liz hugged her. "She came to the library to find the book, maybe even to find you. Everything will be fine."

The next hour was chaotic. Liz decided to break the news to Beth in person and drove to her retirement home, which was surprisingly close. After a short talk and a longer cry, Beth insisted on meeting Jo right away. Because Beth's hip was acting up, Liz drove back to get Jo and Jane. Now she was sitting with Jane on one of the benches in the garden. At the other end of the park, Beth and Jo talked animatedly about something.

Jane had the same mixture of delight and excitement reflected in her expression that Liz felt. "I'm happy for them."

"Me too." Jane slowly turned until she was facing Liz. Her gaze moved over Liz as if she was searching for something. Her smile softened and became marginally more sensual. "This is the best date I've ever been on."

"Me too." Liz moved closer until their arms and thighs were touching. Warmth spread from the points of contact through her body and finally settled behind her breastbone. She desperately wanted to kiss Jane, but she managed to restrain herself. They had enough time later. "What do you think they're talking about?"

"Books." Jane leaned against her and took her hand. Her fingers were warm, soft, and strong. They felt just right. "And what do you think we'll be talking about when we reach their age?"

They both laughed and answered together. "Books."

WROTE TRIP
BY CORI KANE

PATRICE HURRIED INSIDE THE HOUSE and did a quick scan to see if she'd forgotten something essential. Her backpack was sitting on a kitchen chair, with her phone, sunglasses, and suntan lotion on the table next to it. She was set for her vacation.

She would have liked to start it in peace, but her phone obviously had other ideas as it started ringing. "You just *had* to do that, didn't you?"

A look at the display confirmed Pat's suspicion: Kasey.

Better now than when I'm on the road. Pat answered the call. "Isn't it a little early for you?"

"Good morning to you too. I wanted to get you before you left. You haven't yet, right?"

"You caught me just in time. I'm on my way out the door." Pat slid her sunglasses into place. Granted, the sun hadn't entirely come up yet, but for Pat their shielding effect worked against the entire outside world sometimes. She needed them now to fend off whatever Kasey wanted from her.

"And you're not about to reconsider, sit down your ass, and write that novel? Like, right now?"

Pat took a deep breath. She'd explained before that she needed a break, that she needed to recharge her metaphorical batteries, but either Kase didn't listen, or she didn't care. Both options stung. "No," was all Pat said.

"RJ, please, I…"

"Don't call me that. You know RJ Patrick is just a pseudonym. I'm Pat, and I'm not a machine, Kase. I haven't had a vacation in almost five years. I've written the *Dusty Shades* series, then two books for the *Blue Troop* series, and I'm finally out of imagination. I got an idea but can't put a single sentence to paper, virtual or otherwise. It's just not coming. If you think someone else will do a better job writing that last book in the series, please let them. I'll even give you my notes. At this point, I'd be thankful to be rid of it." Pat was almost yelling, so she hastily clenched her teeth together. They'd been over this. All she wanted now was to be left alone for two weeks.

"I know you don't mean that." Kasey sounded contrite. "I'm sorry, Pat. It's just that this series is so goddamn successful. Everybody's got their knickers in a twist over the delay."

"I'm aware, but I'm just not feeling it at the moment. I need a break."

"Yeah." Kasey sighed. "Well, I hope it helps. I hope you find your muse, drag her back home, and write the best in the series. And…I also hope you get some rest. Maybe a tan and a good lay?"

Pat laughed. "I'm not aiming that high, but a tan would be nice."

"All right. Come back in one piece, and you know how to reach me should something…develop."

"You want me to call if I get laid?" Pat joked.

"Well, given that you'd be the only one of us getting any, please do. You know what I mean, though?"

"Yeah, I know." Pat shouldered her backpack, grabbed her keys, and the bottle of lotion. She looked around the house one last time. "Time to go," she told Kasey.

"All right, have a good trip."

"Thanks, Kase. Don't work too hard."

"Haha," was the only answer she got before Kasey disconnected.

Pat slipped her phone into her pocket and left the house. She locked the front door, walked to her car, and dropped her backpack on the passenger seat. After a few minutes of puttering with her iPhone and stereo, she started the engine and music flooded the interior of the car.

Pat smiled. Before she pulled out of the driveway, she pushed her shades up on her head because it really was still too dark for them. Then she started the trip that she hoped would bring her some rest and relaxation and return her muse to her side.

The traffic thinned out rather quickly after Pat had left the city. No commuters drove out this way; it was the kind of one-way highway out of the city to a new part of your future, another city, another life. Naturally, it wasn't really a one-way highway, because people also entered the city with the same kind of hopes. The point was Pat felt as if she was leaving everything behind.

She would come back, but first she got to drive away from all her responsibilities, her deadline, her computer. And it felt good. At least, it felt good for the first hour when she was singing along with her music, carefree and relieved of her burdens.

After that first hour, however, things got decidedly boring. There were hardly any cars around, and she didn't need all her concentration on the road. But what to do with the rest of it? She didn't really want to sing to her music all day and arguing with religious programs or sports commentators on talk radio was only fun for half an hour.

She couldn't read, of course. Pity. Maybe she should have just rolled herself into a ball on the couch with all the books she'd always wanted to read and done just that. Maybe this road trip was a bad idea.

Ah, her brain, the relentless force behind her personal achievements. It couldn't go long without entertainment. But she wouldn't just find the next exit and return home. No way. She'd promised herself some time away from home, some time away from her work. Too bad she wasn't able to leave her brain behind too.

She started a mental list of sights she wanted to see, towns and cities to stop at, foods she wanted to have for dinner. After a few minutes, her thoughts wandered, and she started tapping restlessly on her steering wheel.

"Road trips are boring," she said, then sighed. She should have asked someone to come along, just to talk. But whom would she have asked? Her neighbor Lee? He was nice and friendly and sometimes hit on her because she was a woman and he was a man and he thought that was how the world worked. Her ex Lena? She'd left because Pat wasn't paying her enough attention. Well, now she could have all the attention she wanted. Of course, Lena was involved with another woman and in a "serious relationship." The way she'd worded it made Pat wonder what their relationship had been. Fun and games?

Then there was Kasey. Her editor didn't go on road trips and probably couldn't even remember when she'd been on vacation the last time. Kasey was happiest when she was working, which also included harassing Pat about when her next sentence, chapter, novel would be finished.

Pat sighed again. There really wasn't anyone who would have just dropped everything to accompany her on this road trip. Anyway, it was supposed to be *her* time. Alone time. Thinking time. Something new age, something spiritual...

Oh, a hitchhiker. A girl. What was she doing out here in the middle of nowhere?

Pat slowed down, set her blinker, and stopped at the side of the road.

The girl hesitated for a moment and then ran toward her car.

She was young, possibly twenty if not younger. Pat leaned over the passenger seat and unlocked the door. Then she took her backpack from the seat and put it in back.

The young woman opened the door and looked inside the car. "Hi, I'm Jen. Are you going in the direction of Belington?"

"Sure, hop in. I'm Pat." She smiled.

Jen slipped into the passenger seat. She looked at Pat a moment, a frown forming between her eyebrows. "I didn't really expect anyone to stop for me. It's not the liveliest part of the world."

"How did you end up here anyway?" Pat asked, as she steered the car onto the road.

"A fellow student said he was going my way and would drop me at home. Well, that's at least how I interpreted what he'd said. He really meant he was going my way and would drop me at an intersection where he would leave me to find my way home, six hours later, presumably." Jen made a face.

"If you're walking fast. Belington is just behind that town with the brewery, isn't it? I forgot what it's called."

"Elkins? Well, it's actually a little farther than that. But if you don't go that far, just drop me off at another intersection. I can find my way."

Pat wanted to shake her head at the recklessness of youth but resisted. "I'm sure you can, but I would feel better if I dropped you off at…where you're going."

"My mom's house," Jen supplied helpfully.

"Your mom's house, then."

"You sure you wanna go all that way? I mean, don't you need to be somewhere?"

Pat laughed. "Not today. Not for two weeks, in fact. I'm taking a vacation."

"That sounds nice."

"Yeah," Pat said with a lot less enthusiasm than when she'd started the trip. "I hope so."

"Why wouldn't it be?" Jen sounded genuinely interested.

"I'm taking a vacation from work. I'm just… I work in a creative field, and I kind of lost my inspiration. But there's this huge project I'm working on. Everybody's… Anyway, what if I can't get back to that project? What if I can't reconnect?" Pat shook her head. Why was she talking about this with somebody she didn't know?

"Do you think that maybe you're putting too much pressure on yourself?"

Pat looked over at Jen for a moment, then back at the road.

"It's an important project."

"But is it a project that's important to you?"

Pat didn't know how to answer this question, so she didn't. Instead she filed it away as something to think about on her trip.

"So, where are you going for your vacation?" Jen asked as she searched through her backpack. After a moment, she gave up and put the bag on the floor. She leaned comfortably against the door where she could look at Pat rather than outside.

"West."

"Speaking of vague, but if you don't wanna talk…"

"No, no, that's not it, sorry. I just really haven't made a plan. I thought I'd drive west for a week and then turn around and drive back."

Jen chuckled.

Pat looked over at her and couldn't help smiling. "Do you think that's stupid?"

"No, I think it's kinda cool. And a lot unprepared. I thought the thirties would all be about planning your life, but that's obviously not how you roll."

That made Pat laugh. "I'm usually making lists about everything. The trip was kind of spontaneous, I guess. I just needed time away."

"Good for you."

For a few moments, only the low music from the stereo could be heard between them. Surprisingly, Pat didn't rush to say anything. She was comfortable with Jen setting the pace of their conversation or silence, whatever Jen preferred.

"But you are, though, aren't you?" Jen finally asked.

"Am what?"

"In your thirties?"

Pat glanced sideways, and Jen grinned cheekily.

"Are you trying to find out how old I am? Don't be shy, just ask."

"Okay, how old are you?"

"Thirty-six. You?"

Jen chuckled. "Should've known. I'm twenty-two. Currently an English major at NYU. Single..."

Pat turned her head. Their eyes met.

A slight tingle went up Pat's spine as she gazed into Jen's dark eyes. She quickly looked away. It would be too easy to get lost in the depths of her stare.

Get yourself together, Pat. Just because Kasey thinks you should get laid, doesn't mean you're gonna get some from a far-too-young hitchhiker. This is not a porno. It's life, remember?

Heat crawled up her neck, and she cleared her throat.

"How about you?" Jen asked.

"Oh, it's been a while since I graduated from Chapel Hill. English too."

"Married?"

Pat looked over at Jen, who was once again smiling.

"No, I'm not married."

"Engaged? In a serious relation—?"

"Serious, what does that even mean? Are there relationships which aren't serious?" Pat interrupted more forcefully than she'd wanted to. Her face heated once again, faster this time. She shook her head. "Sorry."

"Not at all. I mean, yeah, there are relationships that aren't all that serious. Sometimes you like someone, but you don't wanna make a commitment. But, of course, you have to talk about these things, about whatever you want to have with someone. Did you just break up with someone?"

Pat shook her head. "No, it's been almost half a year since *she* broke up with *me*. We were together over three years, and the other day she told me she was now in a serious relationship. I guess I got kind of testy over that word."

"Well, three years *is* a serious relationship. Sounds to me like your ex has a chip on her shoulder."

Pat nodded, amazed with herself for talking so casually about her ex. Generally, she didn't tell strangers she was gay. Maybe it was because Jen was a woman or because she was younger. Or maybe it was because Pat got a vibe from her—a gay vibe.

"Yeah, maybe she does," she answered.

Fifteen minutes later, they passed the exit leading to Elkins.

"Since you're over twenty-one, is the Elkins beer any good?" Pat asked.

"No idea. I'm not a beer fan."

Pat chuckled. "And you claim to be a student?"

"Ha, yeah, but I prefer tequila."

Pat threw her a look to see if she was serious. Jen wore the same easy smile. She seemed bemused, but never entirely serious.

"Tequila? Not for me. I like wine."

"Bad experiences with tequila?"

"Tequila, vodka, rum, you name it. But my college days are thankfully far behind me. I'm not drinking much these days."

"I was kidding about the tequila, by the way. I do enjoy some alcohol sometimes, but it's usually just something girly colorful."

Pat nodded. "Nothing wrong with that. I mean, nothing wrong with drinking alcohol on occasion, even if it's tequila. I've had my share, and maybe we were overdoing it back then. But even that..." She shrugged, refraining from saying it was okay. There were moments, memories which weren't really okay. Things had gotten out of hand, and not just once.

"Some of my friends are overdoing it sometimes. I try to stay out of that."

Pat looked over again.

Jen looked back at her earnestly.

"I'm the designated driver a lot," Jen added.

"Then you do own a car?"

"No, but most of my friends do. We're usually a whole bunch of people going out together."

"Safety in numbers," Pat remarked.

"That too. It's always good to have some guys with you just in case some asshole doesn't understand what 'no' means. That's my exit." Jen pointed ahead.

Pat slowed the car as they neared the exit to Belington.

"Does that happen a lot?" she asked, getting back to their earlier conversation.

Jen sighed. "Sometimes. It's usually drunk frat boys. I don't like frat parties. I prefer a club or a party at some venue. Even sororities are okay. Though sometimes girls can be assholes too."

Pat snorted. "Tell me about it."

"I sure could," Jen said, the grin back on her face.

Pat once again cleared her throat and scratched her head. She wasn't entirely sure, but she had an inkling that Jen was flirting with her. Just a little.

"Sooo," Pat drew out. "You're into girls?" She bit her lip, not sure if the question was appropriate. Would Jen be insulted? She hadn't reacted much to Pat telling her about her ex, but she never knew, especially with strangers.

"And how."

Pat turned to look at her, but Jen had turned toward the window. She was pointing out something. "This is where I went to elementary school."

Pat looked at the red brick structure.

"Turn here," Jen said, and they rounded the building, a playground coming into view behind it.

"That's where I first kissed a boy," Jen supplied. "And a girl."

Pat had to laugh. "Early bloomer?"

"Not really. I mean, I did go out with boys until senior year. That was when I stopped lying to myself that anything sexual could ever happen between me and a guy. You a lesbian? Or bi?"

"Lesbian, but it took me a while longer to come out. I was already twenty-seven."

"Ever married? To a guy, I mean?" Jen asked.

"Fortunately not, though I was with a guy for six...seven years before I came out. That was not easy."

"I bet."

Silence once again filled the small space of Pat's car. She turned another corner at Jen's behest. It was her destination. A cul-de-sac.

Jen pointed at a house on the left. "That's where I live. Drive all the way to the end. You can turn there."

Pat nodded, and a minute later, she stopped the car in front of a purple house. "It looks cozy."

"It's home," Jen said. "I really appreciate you going out of your way like this, you know?"

"Actually, I enjoyed the company. Road trips are only half as fun as they look in movies."

Jen smiled.

Pat lost herself in her eyes for a moment. Jen was a pretty girl…a beautiful young woman, really.

"Well, I hope it won't get too boring for you on your trip."

"When it does, I'll just stop for the next lost young woman on the way," Pat joked.

"You say I'm so easily replaced?"

"No, I didn't—"

"Relax, Pat. It was a joke." Jen touched her arm, smiling.

A spark ran through Pat, and it made the little hairs on her arms stand up. "Well," she said, but it was hardly audible. She cleared her throat.

"You want to get back on the road. In the name of my mom and my own, thank you for bringing me home safely. My mom hates when I hitchhike."

"I can believe that, but I guess there was no other choice this time. Except for walking."

Jen nodded. "I wouldn't have gotten into the car with a guy. I'm not an idiot."

"That's what I thought."

"Would you give me your number?" Jen asked quietly, looking at her hands folded in her lap.

At first, Pat thought she'd heard wrong, but then Jen looked up again. Their eyes met, and there was that spark again. Pat nodded before she even knew what she was doing.

Jen pulled her phone from her pocket.

Pat took hers from the dash, and they synched their phones quickly.

Jen took a picture of Pat.

"Beautiful," she murmured as she clicked a few buttons. She lifted the flap from her backpack and put it inside.

Pat happened to look down at that moment and caught sight of a book inside the backpack. Her eyes widened, and Jen chuckled.

"Ah, yes. I should've said…" Jen pulled the book from the bag and turned it so that Pat could see her own face smiling back at her. "Love your book." She leaned over, kissed Pat, and then opened the door and got out. "Thanks again for the ride," she said, leaning into the car.

"You're welcome," Pat said, still slightly stumped. Then she smiled.

Jen closed the door and walked toward the house. She turned and waved.

Waving back, Pat put her car in drive and left Jen behind. She looked back in the rearview mirror to watch Jen walk up the stairs to the front door. Another sigh escaped her.

Pat sat in a truck stop diner, smiling up at the waitress as she refilled her cup. "Thank you." A familiar ringtone disrupted the customary noises of chatter and cutlery on plates. "Sorry," she said to no one in particular. The waitress had already left her table for the next customer. She pulled her phone from her pocket and looked at the display.

It was Jen.

Pat smiled.

"Hi," she answered the call.

"Hey, how's it going?"

"Well, I'm at a truck stop about two hours from your home."

Jen laughed, and Pat decided she liked the sound.

"Well, yeah, you might think I was already missing you, but I'm actually calling with a message from my mom."

"Really?"

"Yes, indeed. She wanted to say thanks and ask if you'd like to stop by on your way home. She'd like to cook you a thank-you meal."

"Please tell your mom that it was my pleasure. No thank-you meal required."

"Does that mean you're not coming by on your way back?" Jen sounded disappointed.

"That wasn't what I meant. I'd love to…come by, to see you again."

"Phew, you almost got me worried there for a second. I was wondering if I should be apologizing for kissing you. I mean, we had this elaborate discussion in our sexuality class about consent, and I feel kinda guilty for not asking permission."

Pat cleared her throat. "Well, I don't want you to think it's okay to just kiss people, but I think there are moments when the permission is given…non-verbally, like…"

"You could just say that you liked it," Jen said.

Pat could hear the smile in Jen's voice and had to laugh at how flustered she was. She usually wasn't this complicated. "I did like it, Jen. I liked it a lot. I'm just a little worried because you're so much younger than I am."

"I didn't ask you to marry me, Pat. I just like you and thought that you liked me too. And maybe we can get to know each other a little better. So what if I'm younger? I know when I like someone."

"Yeah, you sure do. And you're right about me liking you back."

They were quiet for a while. Pat took a sip of her coffee, savoring the taste.

"How is your soul searching coming along?" Jen finally asked.

"Soul searching? I thought of it more as a recharging of empty batteries."

"So, how is that coming along?"

Pat rubbed her cheek. "Not sure. I had a thought earlier. You said I'm putting too much pressure on myself. I think maybe you're right. When I started this series, I wanted it to be fun. I guess I kind of lost the fun between deadlines and interviews and what-nots."

"Is this about the *Blue Troop* series?"

Pat hesitated. She'd tried so hard not to let herself get influenced by the opinions of others. Since Jen was obviously familiar with her work, it didn't seem fair to let her have a say when so many didn't. She didn't even listen to her sister. Then again, her sister always just said her books needed more sex. What she meant was hetero sex, of course.

"It is, but I'm not really comfortable discussing my works in progress."

"Oh." Again, Jen sounded disappointed. "Well, that's okay—"

"You know, screw that. I'm actually at a point where it can't get any worse, even if you tell me to put more sex in it."

"Why would I say that?"

"That's what my sister always says."

"I see. Well, I was actually thinking of introducing a new character. Your characters are such a tight, well-oiled group of people. Why not disrupt the chemistry a little by bringing in someone new? And queer. I need a queer character in that series. It's the only thing missing from making it perfect. It would also be nice if that character had sex at some point, but no pressure."

Pat had to laugh, but only for a moment. "A new character," she mused.

"You like the idea?" Jen asked.

"Hmmm." Pat took a notebook from her pocket. She went over some notes for the book, notes she'd made when the series was still a distant dream.

"Pat?" Jen pulled her from her thoughts.

"Oh, sorry, I was just looking at some notes. I guess I could introduce someone new. It wouldn't interfere with the plot points, but would definitely add some tension."

"Well, it sounds like you have something to think about on your trip, then. And if that doesn't work, I have about half a gazillion other ideas, so just call me when you're stuck?"

"I may actually do that," Pat said, thoughtfully.

"Even though you don't want to." Jen guessed at her hesitation.

"Well, writing is my job. I should be able to figure out my own stories without help, shouldn't I?"

"Maybe you're just too close at the moment. Or too stressed. It's not like I want a piece of your cake. I would be satisfied to be mentioned in the acknowledgments."

This made Pat smile again. "You definitely earned that already. Thank you."

"Will you call me? I mean, even if you don't want or need my input?"

Pat wondered at this for a long moment. Her rational mind told her that Jen was too young, that it would never work between them. But the tingling sensation in her lips reminded her of the almost chaste kiss Jen had pressed to her lips. The tingling spread, and Pat took a deep breath. "I'll call."

"That's a promise, right?"

"It is."

"Good. I'll let you get back to your trip or notes or food. Whatever you're doing."

"Thanks for calling. And tell your mom I'd be happy to come by on my way back and have dinner with you both and... Is there anyone else?"

"Just my cat, Dumbledore. My brother is camping with friends during the break."

"Then I'm looking forward to meeting your mom and Dumbledore."

"Okay."

Another moment of silence followed. It bound Pat to her promise and made her realize that she wanted to drive back to Belington right now. But she wouldn't. She needed time to figure out her work problem. She needed time to herself before she could invest the time to get to know someone else.

"I'll talk to you soon," she finally said.

"Drive carefully."

"Will do. Bye, Jen."

"Bye, Pat."

ORPHANS' CHRISTMAS
BY KATHY BRODLAND

I SAT IN MY CAR for a good five minutes, trying to summon the courage to get out and go up the stairs to the brightly decorated house a few yards away. Did I really want to be the oldest "orphan" at Clare's annual Christmas party just because she was my favorite beta reader? She'd made it quite clear that if I didn't show up, she'd send her wife to get me. I'd never met Barb, but I'd seen pictures of her. A retired firefighter, she wasn't somebody I wanted to argue with.

Even my sister had gotten involved. "Oh for heaven's sake, Edie! Go have some fun for a change. Who knows, you might even meet someone!"

That was all very well for her to say. She lived on the other side of the country with a husband and two kids. She wasn't a sixty-something who'd been on her own for three years.

I huffed and finally decided to get my act together. I fished my folding cane from the passenger seat and gathered up the bag holding the veggie platter and the unwrapped gift I had been instructed to bring.

Someone—probably Barb—had shoveled the steps leading up to the house, and I made it to the sidewalk without falling on my ass. As I walked, my cane poked little round holes in the snow. From the sound of it, the party was well underway. Warm light blazed from the downstairs windows. Laughter and Christmas carols wafted out on the crisp cold air.

The unmistakable crunch of feet against fresh snow sounded to my left. A woman in a black hoodie was heading my way at a brisk trot. Given that she carried a bag similar to mine, she was probably on her way to the party as well.

I waited at the foot of the steps for her to catch up with me. At least I wouldn't have to brave the crowd on my own.

"Hi there," she said, her voice a pleasant alto. She glanced at my cane. "Do you need a hand there?"

"Thanks, I'm fine. Just catching my breath after making it this far." I waved my cane in the general direction of my red Mazda parked two cars down.

"Well, fear not, fair maiden, I shall endeavor to deliver you unharmed to the castle gates." She whisked my bag away and linked a sturdy arm through mine. "Shall we?"

I tried not to grin as I cast her a sidelong glance.

She smiled back, keen blue eyes sparkling. "Almost made you laugh, didn't I? You were looking a bit lost standing there about to turn into a snowman."

By now, we'd reached the front door. A huge wreath decorated with red berries, pine cones, and a big silver bow obscured most of the frosted window. The other woman pushed the doorbell. Seconds later, the door swung open.

"Hey, Clare! Edie and Frankie are here." The large individual looming in the doorway had to be Barb. She waved us into the foyer. My coat was whisked away to a closet; my boots ended up on a large rubber tray along with an assortment of other footgear.

Frankie handed over our parcels, and Barb rumbled, "Thanks. Clare is in the kitchen, making like a domestic goddess. Venture in there at your peril."

"I heard that!"

I peered around Barb's girth to see the goddess in question in a wheelchair heading in our direction.

"Edie!" Clare squealed. "You made it."

When I bent down to hug my friend, she pecked my cheek. I stood back and peered down at the bright, cheery face looking back up at me. Her black curly hair bounced in all directions. I had seen photos of Clare on Facebook, of course, but meeting the woman I had come to think of as strong and confident was a treat. The accident that had left her confined to a wheelchair did nothing to diminish her vibrant spirit.

She waved in the general direction of the living room. "Go make yourselves comfortable. If there aren't enough chairs, let Barb know. She can rustle up a couple more for you. I'll swing by and chat later. Right now I have a turkey that needs to be dealt with." She took my hand. "I'm so glad you came. I've been looking forward to meeting you."

She gave Frankie a poke in the ribs. "You take good care of this lady. She's very special."

"Oh, I don't think that will be a hardship." Frankie came around to my left side, away from my cane, and took my arm again. "Shall we?"

I was still trying to decide if she was always this protective when I found myself facing a room full of women, all looking at me. It wasn't until most of them glanced away that I finally remembered to breathe. Apparently, they weren't overly interested in the elderly gray-haired woman who had just appeared in their midst. Only the redhead in the far corner of the room seemed to take more than a passing interest. By the time I found a chair, she'd shifted her focus to Frankie. What caught my eye, though, was an enormous tree decorated from top to bottom with shimmering red and gold ornaments.

Frankie touched my shoulder. "Can I get you something to drink?"

I hesitated. All this attention was a bit unnerving.

Frankie's smile was a bit lopsided. "I'm under orders from her highness to take good care of you."

"Thanks. A Diet Coke would be great."

"Consider it done."

While she was off on that errand, I got myself settled and took a surreptitious glance around. There were about a dozen women, and much to my delight, at least half of them were well into their fifties, maybe even a little older. One or two smiled my way.

Frankie returned and handed me an ice-cold can of Diet Coke and a paper napkin. She sat next to me, popped open a can of her own, and took a sip. "I have been informed that dinner will be ready in about fifteen minutes. I don't wish to assume anything, but will you need help getting around in the dining room?"

I pictured myself juggling my cane and plates of food. "Yes, I think I will."

"Okay, well, there's a little bit of everything there." She rattled off a list of the foods.

"The baked salmon sounds good. And a salad would be nice as well."

"Okay. As soon as Clare announces dinner, I'll get something for you."

"Thanks. Oh, I was wondering about something. Clare's in a wheelchair, but there is no ramp at the front. How on earth does she manage?"

"Oh, Barb put in a ramp between the kitchen and the garage not long after Clare's accident. I think there was some talk about selling the place and moving to somewhere that was all on one level. But they love this house, so they finally decided to stay here and renovate."

There was a flurry of activity, and then a small brown and white dog came dashing in. It made the rounds, stopping to greet each of the guests in turn.

Frankie chuckled. "Brandy's the welcoming committee. She just loves company. I suspect she is the other reason why Barb and Clare don't want to move. They have a big yard with lots of room for Brandy to run and play. Clare has a veggie garden out there as well."

Brandy made it to me and put her paws on my knees.

"Hello, there, little one." I scratched behind her ears. She wagged her tail enthusiastically in response. I leaned back in my chair and patted my lap. "Wanna come up?"

Apparently, she did, because I soon had a lapful of wriggling puppy planting doggy kisses all over my face. The paper napkin came in very useful.

Clare poked her head around the corner. "Brandy! You get down right this minute!"

Brandy cast a sheepish glance in her mistress's direction and slunk off my lap.

Clare shook her head. "Sorry, Edie. I guess she really liked you, but we don't usually let her get up on guests' laps."

"Oh, that's okay. I didn't really mind. I love dogs."

Frankie laughed. "Apparently, the feeling is mutual."

A writer's life could be a solitary one. Especially if said writer was single. Having a pet would be good for me—I mentally patted my expanding waistline—in more ways than one.

Dinner was announced, and Frankie did her vanishing act again. She returned a few minutes later with a plateful of food for me.

Barb was close behind her with a TV table, which she set in front of me. She grinned in Frankie's direction. "Is she behaving herself?"

Frankie growled at her. "Don't I always?"

Barb scratched her chin. "Well, let me see now..." She winked at me, then headed back to the kitchen.

"I take it you two are good friends," I said as I tucked into the salad.

"Oh, yeah, we've known each other for years. Even though we worked for two different departments, we managed to get together at shared functions."

"So what kind of work do you do?"

"I was a cop. Retired now. Have been for the last year. Decided it was time to hang up my shield."

"And you are one of Clare's orphans too?"

"Yeah. Unfortunately." She concentrated on the turkey on her plate for a few minutes. "So, what's your story? How do you know Clare and Barb?"

I started on the baked salmon. "I don't really know Barb. Chatted with her once in a while on Facebook, but that's the extent of it. She's quite a character, though."

"She certainly is."

"I met Clare when I asked online for beta readers to go through the book I was working on at the time. We became friends and have kept in touch ever since. I was delighted to discover that we live in the same town."

"Oh, so you're a writer?"

"Yes."

"What do you write?"

"Fiction. Mostly paranormal, with a bit of romance thrown in for good measure."

"A bit of romance is always nice."

"I suppose so. Haven't had much experience with it lately."

She arched her eyebrows but didn't pursue the matter.

The wounds left behind when my partner of twenty-five years dumped me were still a bit raw. By the same token, I didn't ask how she became one of Clare's orphans. That felt too much like forced intimacy.

It became too noisy for us to carry on a conversation at that point. Clare wheeled into the living room, with Barb close behind her. She parked in front of the Christmas tree and waited until she had our attention.

"Ladies, those of you who've never been here before aren't familiar with this part of the evening. You each brought an unwrapped gift to the party. We put them in a box, and Barb is going to pass it around so you can each take one. I'm going to read a story to you, and you will pass your gift to the left or to the right when I say the words 'left' or 'right.' When the story is over, whatever gift you're holding is the prize that you take home."

Frankie murmured, "This should be fun."

I had to smile. I hadn't played this game in years. It would indeed be fun. When the box came my way, I closed my eyes and reached inside. I almost burst out laughing when

I retrieved a ceramic plaque showing a large coffee cup. The words *Shhh* and *Almost* were written at different levels on the cup. At the very bottom it said, *You may speak now.*

I needed a cup like that. I glanced sideways to see what Frankie's prize might be.

She had a large black apron with the words *The* Real *Boss* written across the bib portion. She grinned back at me. "I'm not giving this up."

I showed her the plaque I had. "I'm not giving this up either."

Clare clapped her hands. "Okay, folks, here we go." She cleared her throat and started reading. "I'm a person who always likes things done *right*. I *write* notes to my wife to make sure things get done *right*. One day, I wrote a note to my wife, asking her to deliver some cookies to Ellen *Wright's* home. My wife *left* the house *right* before nine Friday morning, with Ellen *Wright's* cookies. *Right* before she *left*, I made her take the cellular phone in case she got lost. She did, *right* about nine-thirty. She called me and said she was lost and she was sure I did not *write* the directions down *right*..."

By the time Clare finished reading the story, my sides ached from laughing so hard. I wiped tears from my eyes with the back of my hand. Frankie wasn't in much better shape. Of course, I wasn't holding the plaque I wanted, and she didn't have her apron either. Fortunately, Clare wasn't finished yet.

"I can see some of you were hoping for the prize you started out with. If you like, you can offer to trade with whoever has it."

It was time to stretch my legs and wander around a bit. I stopped to admire or chuckle over other people's prizes. My search paid off when I spotted the plaque set to one side on a table. I pounced and offered the bronze candlesticks I'd ended up with in exchange. The woman eyed the candlesticks with obvious longing and eventually handed over the plaque. She admitted, she never drank coffee herself.

Frankie stooped to kiss an elfin blonde woman on the cheek. As she straightened, clutching the apron, she caught sight of me. She smiled and shook her head. When she came close enough to be heard, she said, "What a butch won't do to get a prize."

"Hmm. Yes, you did seem to be suffering a great hardship there."

"Oh, it was dreadful." She looked around at the doorway leading into the dining room. "Damn, no mistletoe in sight, or I would see who else I could kiss." She winked at me. "In the spirit of the season, of course."

"Oh, of course."

She linked her arm through mine and steered me in the direction of our chairs.

We were halfway there when the redhead who'd stared at Frankie earlier cut in front of us. She ignored me as she ran a manicured finger along the unbuttoned front of Frankie's shirt. "So," she said with a purr, "Handsome, I'm bored. Why don't we make our own fun somewhere else? You live just around the corner."

Frankie blew out a long breath. "Marilyn, we've had this conversation before. You already know my answer. Let's not go through it again."

Marilyn glanced my way. Her lip curled. "You could do so much better than this old hag. I could show you a real good time, Frankie, darling."

I tightened my grip on my cane, wanting to slap her smirking face. Instead, I moved away before I lost it in front of these strangers. Marilyn's words rang in my ears. She sounded so much like my ex when she'd hurled similar words at me before she took off with a woman twenty years younger than I. I headed for the front door, eager to put as much distance between me and her as possible. I almost made it when Frankie appeared in front of me.

"Don't let her spoil your evening, Edie. For what it's worth, I'd rather be here with you."

Behind me, Clare tore a strip off Marilyn. "You just wore out your welcome here. Get your coat and leave right now."

Frankie and I moved out of the way as Marilyn yanked her coat off a hanger in the closet and slammed out the front door.

Clare wheeled into the foyer. "Please don't leave, Edie. I'd be heartbroken if you let that woman spoil your evening. She's just jealous."

I couldn't imagine why anyone would be jealous of me. All I really wanted to do right then was find someplace to hide the tears that threatened to fall.

Frankie took my hand. "Edie. Please stay."

I blinked to clear my vision.

"Besides," Clare added, "you can't leave until you have some of my famous fruitcake. I will be hurt if you don't try at least one piece."

I plastered a smile on my face and swallowed my injured pride. "Well, what are we standing around out here for? Lead on, McDuff."

Shortly, I found myself ensconced in a comfy chair, a plate of dark fruitcake on a folding table in front of me.

Thankfully, Clare didn't use marzipan on her cakes. My mother used it all the time, and I would carefully pry it off and bury the evidence in the garbage can. I took up my fork and sampled a piece of the fruitcake. "Oh Clare, this is awesome. I don't suppose you'd share your recipe? I haven't tasted anything this good in years."

"Sorry, sweetie." She laughed. "That recipe has been in my family for generations. If you want more of it, you'll just have to come visit us again." The smile vanished. "I can promise you one thing: Marilyn will never darken our door again. She didn't just insult you. She insulted almost everyone here tonight. I'm probably the youngest woman here, and I'm fifty-three."

That bit of news startled me, and I almost dropped my fork. I would have guessed Clare to be in her forties perhaps, but no more than that.

"Now, enjoy the rest of your dessert." She patted my hand. "There's more where that came from. I might even be persuaded to send some home with you."

She wheeled back into the kitchen, leaving Frankie and me pretty much on our own. Just about everyone else had left. Not because of Marilyn, I hoped.

I waited until Frankie finished her queen-size portion of cake and then asked, "Just out of curiosity, is there history between you and Marilyn?"

"Oh, hell no. She's definitely not my type. Told her so on more than one occasion. She thinks she's the Goddess's gift to butches and can't imagine why I would turn her down."

I let that sink in for a moment. "So what is your type?"

She sat back in her chair and looked off into the distance. Finally, she turned to me. "Someone like you."

Oh. Now what did I say to that? Several flip remarks came to mind. I dismissed them and simply said, "Now, why would you want someone like me?"

She held up her hand, her eyes filled with warmth.

I fell silent.

She shook her head and smiled. "I know where you were going with that, Edie. You walk with a cane. I have a hip that gives me trouble at times. So you're losing the battle with gravity. So am I."

I glanced at the red tank top underneath her open shirt. "I doubt you have gone from 44 D to 44 long."

She choked on the piece of cake she just put in her mouth.

I thumped her on the back and handed her my glass of milk.

When Frankie could speak, she mopped her face with her napkin and gasped. "You might warn a person before you come out with remarks like that."

"Sorry about that. I put mouth into action before putting brain in gear."

"You certainly did. Bad girl."

I started to smile, then changed my mind. I still couldn't shake the memory of Marilyn's words and the pain they had caused. After a glance at my cake, I pushed it aside, my appetite gone.

"Clare will be hurt if you don't finish that fruitcake," Frankie said.

"I can always take it home. Speaking of which, I should be heading home soon before the bar scene lets out."

Barb stuck her head around the doorway. Her face was flushed, and snow clung to the shoulders of her jacket. "You might want to rethink that notion. I was just out shoveling the sidewalk again. It's snowing like it means business, and the weather forecast is saying we are in for a major storm. I don't know which car is yours, but there are five of them out there parked bumper to bumper. I could dig you out, but you still won't be going anywhere until they move."

Oh great. I followed her to the front door and looked out into the night. Visibility was almost zero. I couldn't see past the row of cars lined up. I wasn't even sure which white blob was mine.

"Sorry," Barb said. "Wish I could do more."

I wandered back to the kitchen and just stood there, weighing my options. They were few and far between. Calling a cab was out of the question. They would be so busy I could walk the five miles between here and my place before a cab would make it here in this weather.

"I'd offer you our spare bedroom, but we use it for storage," Clare said. "We do have a fold-down couch if that helps." She smiled. "You might have to put up with Brandy trying to keep you warm, though. In the meantime, why don't you have a cup of coffee and sit and visit with Frankie?"

I could think of worse ways to pass the time. After shooing Brandy down, I reclaimed my chair. She promptly lay down at my feet, her head on my shoe. I bent and patted her head. She wagged her tail as she tried to lick my hand. I gave her another pat and sat back up.

Frankie wandered in and sat next to me. "I've just been informed that I am not allowed to walk home in that mess. So, it looks as though we are both staying here tonight. Do you think you could handle sharing that hide-a-bed? I'd take one of the chairs, but my hip would be killing me by morning." She chuckled. "I'm sure Brandy will make an excellent chaperone."

I had to smile at that idea.

She was silent for a moment. "I was wondering…would you be interested in spending some time with me later on? You know…the usual. Coffee, the occasional dinner. Things like that."

As much as part of me wanted to say yes, I shook my head. "Thanks, but the way I reacted to the hurtful things Marilyn said makes me think I'm not ready to be with someone else just yet."

Frankie laid her hand over mine. "That's all right. I'm not asking for more than friendship right now. But it's a good place to start. Will you at least consider my offer?"

I'm sure I must have given a good impression of a deer caught in the headlights of an oncoming car as I struggled with conflicting emotions. Fear was at the top of the list. After my ex left me high and dry, I swore I would never let anyone hurt me again. Opening myself up to someone new in my life was too scary. Time for an exit, stage left. "I'm going to give Clare and Barb a hand with the cleaning-up. It's the least I can do."

As I rose to leave, Frankie caught my hand. "Wait up. I'm coming with you."

Thankfully, Clare didn't turn down my offer to help.

I put my cane to one side, leaned against the sink, and tackled the dishes.

Frankie was put to work tidying the dining room. Barb packed up leftovers and put them in the freezer or in the fridge. Several boxes were put to one side for Frankie and me to take home. That would be a treat. All I had for a

Christmas dinner was a turkey roast that would probably still be in my freezer next year. I hadn't decorated. There wasn't much point just for myself.

Through the pass-through between the kitchen and the dining room I watched Frankie as she helped Barb take the leaves out of the big table and stack them in the corner. I could see why Marilyn was attracted to her. With a smile that could melt the coldest heart, those blue eyes, and that close-cropped salt-and-pepper hair, Frankie was handsome.

Frankie chose that moment to glance my way, and I found myself wondering what it would be like to be with a woman as kind and as attentive as she was.

With the kitchen cleaned up and nothing much left to do, it was time to get ready to turn in for the night. I wasn't looking forward to sharing the hide-a-bed, but there weren't too many alternatives.

Barb showed up with sweatpants and a couple of T-shirts draped over her arm. "Here you go, you two. There's extra toothbrushes in the bathroom if you need them. See you in the morning."

Once Barb headed off, we divided the clothing between us. Frankie smiled. "After you."

When I finished my usual bedtime routine and pulled on the sleepwear Barb had provided, I looked in the full-length mirror on the back of the bathroom door. Neither of my hosts were tiny women. The T-shirt was two sizes too big, and even after I rolled up the cuffs on the sweatpants, I still looked like a kid playing dress-up. I smothered a giggle, gathered up my clothes, and headed for the makeshift sleeping quarters.

Fortunately, Frankie was too preoccupied cuddling Brandy to notice my night attire. Or maybe she was just too polite to laugh at my comical appearance.

I was snuggled under the blankets, with Brandy curled up at the foot of the bed when Frankie joined me a short while later. Even though the bed was made for two people, I noticed a sizeable gap between us. I muttered a sleepy "good night" and got an equally sleepy reply.

Of course, in spite of my fatigue I lay there wide-awake, unable to relax. It had been a long time since I had shared a bed with anyone, even under these innocent circumstances.

A soft voice in the darkness said, "You still awake?"

"Yeah, I always have a hard time sleeping in a strange bed."

"Me too."

Brandy squirmed her way up between us and planted doggy kisses on my face.

Frankie's chuckle said she was getting the same treatment. She shifted in the bed, and I sensed her lying on her side, facing me.

"Edie, I hope you will reconsider my earlier offer. We both have wounds. I lost my wife to cancer just a year and a half ago. I'm guessing you have a similar story. Perhaps we could help each other heal."

"I'm sorry to hear about your wife. While I appreciate that you want to move on, I'm not sure I can. To be perfectly honest, I didn't even want to come here tonight. After my wife left me three years ago, I turned into a recluse. My writing sustains me for the most part. This is the first social event I've been to in months. Clare threatened to send Barb after me if I didn't show up."

"Oh, I can just picture that."

So could I.

I lay there, motionless, for several minutes, thinking about the woman lying next to me. We had only just met, but so far she had been everything I wanted in a friend, never mind a lover. She was kind, attentive, smart, and funny. And best of all she seemed to like me. It was a bonus that we were both about the same age. Perhaps it was time I started living again and let my heart take over from my head.

I drew in a deep breath and let it out slowly. "What were you saying about coffee or a dinner sometime soon?" I whispered.

"Mmmm. Let's see now. How about all of the above?" The blankets shifted as Frankie moved closer.

"I'd like that."

"Good. I really would like us to be friends. I mean, how could you resist someone so incredibly handsome?"

I muffled my laughter with the edge of the coverlet. "Don't forget modest."

There was laughter in her voice when she replied, "No, mustn't forget that."

When Frankie took my hand in hers, I held my breath and then relaxed. Her hand was warm, and its gentle pressure on my fingers was oddly comforting. I lay motionless for a few minutes, suddenly wishing Brandy would move to the bottom of the bed. She really did make an excellent chaperone. Not that anyone determined enough would be put off by the presence of a small dog.

I sighed and wished I had that kind of courage.

Brandy chose that moment to move to the bottom of the bed. The space between us suddenly seemed far too wide. I turned on my side so I was facing Frankie, careful not to dislodge her grip on my hand. The darkness that enclosed us felt warm and intimate. I sighed and settled in closer to her body. Something told me I was not going to be an orphan much longer.

VEGAN DELIGHTS
BY HAZEL YEATS

In the pre-dawn gloom, Kate struggled to wake up, disoriented and groggy. She opened her eyes one at a time. Oh goodie, a new day. A cold one at that. She pulled the comforter up to her chin. To her right, a thin sliver of light peeped through a gap in the curtains. She thought of spring mornings—of walking barefoot on damp grass while watching the magnificent sunrise; of fragrant flowers and birds chirping. She closed her eyes and drifted off to sleep again.

A sudden loud rap on the door made her sit bolt upright, her heart thudding in her chest.

"Kate!" Lara, her neighbor, shouted. "Are you up?"

Oh shit, she forgot she asked Lara to make sure she was up this morning.

"I am!" she hollered. "Almost!"

"Can I come in?" Lara said, her voice softer now. "I'd like to run something by you. Are you decent?"

Kate lifted the edge of the covers and glanced down. Was she? She was decent enough, for someone who was alone in her own bed. Were her thoughts decent, though? She moaned softly. Last night's dream began just like this, with her in bed and Lara pounding on the door, asking to be let in. But then her dream had taken a wonderful turn—a turn that this scenario, in the cold light of day, definitely wasn't going to take. Not by a long shot. She shook her head to chase away the images. She didn't do crushes on straight women—not since eleventh grade, when Hayley Thompson had turned her world upside down.

"Kate! Did you go back to sleep?"

She hurried out of bed and opened the door to her apartment. The hope that Lara, too, would look disheveled and cold was crushed instantly. Because there—O Lord—she was. Kate blinked. What was it that worked so well about Lara? The skinny cargo pants, leather jacket, and skimpy tank top? The jet-black hair? Whatever it was, Kate's breath got stuck in her throat. She coughed to dislodge it.

"Are you okay?" Lara came nearer. Her hair was still damp.

Even from where she was standing, Kate could smell the faint scent of soap and shampoo. She nodded and managed to bring out a hoarse, "Sure, I'm fine."

Lara looked at her for a prolonged moment.

Kate froze. Here she was, in her faded pajama bottoms and her Property of Litchfield Federal Women's Correctional Facility T-shirt, with tousled hair and morning breath, being scrutinized by this enigmatic super girl who lived across the hall and made her life hell. Or was it heaven? She closed her eyes for a second as she imagined herself falling into Lara's arms.

"So I'll see you around." Lara made a half turn.

Kate nodded. "You bet. And thanks for the wake-up call." She struggled for something else to say, something suave, but nothing came to mind.

"Sure," Lara said. "No problem."

After she left, Kate tried to pinpoint the exact moment her sanity had flown out the window. Young Lara was involved with an athletic, twenty-four-year-old dream of a man, who, to further his appeal, was the proud owner of a master's degree in computer science. There was no doubt in Kate's mind that he was a hacker. Maybe even an alien one.

"So how's the new neighbor?" Carol nodded at the waitress as she filled her cup and then walked away. She took a careful sip of the coffee and made a face. "Ugh. Why, Kate? Why do I have to drink this battery acid? I live in a city where making coffee is a higher art form, for God's sake." She pouted. "I'm not asking for much, am I? A simple half-caf, no-foam, non-fat, vanilla soy latte will do."

Kate looked around. The coffee house *was* unpretentious— to the point where some people might call it grubby. There was only one reason she liked to hang out here. "Nostalgia. I've been coming here since college."

"Exactly." Carol pointed to her cup. "And this coffee has been on a hot plate ever since."

"You're right," Kate said. "From now on, we'll meet at your uptown crappuccino place with the hunky barista, okay?"

Carol nodded. "Deal." She pushed her glasses more firmly onto her nose. "Now, about young neighbor…"

"Her name is Lara, and she's okay." Kate sighed. "But I keep out of her way. I want to concentrate on work."

"Speaking of which, I got us a gig," Carol said. "We're catering a sweet sixteen party next Saturday."

"That's great!" Kate beamed. "Where?"

"Greenwich Street," Carol said, a proud smile on her face.

Kate patted her friend on the shoulder. "Well done, partner. Let's give it our best shot, and then who knows, The Tartlets may well be asked to cater every celebration in Tribeca."

Carol's face dropped. "About that. The name, I mean. I thought it was cute when we first came up with it, but now I'm just afraid people are going to think we're hookers. And even if they don't, won't they assume we're running just another boring cupcake business? I think of us more as queens of the savory treat, actually."

"Good point," Kate said. "So how about The Crab Cake Wizards?"

Carol made a face. "How about something a little more grown-up, like—"

"The Merry Caterers?"

"You can't expect us to be merry all the time," Carol said. "And even so, I really want the focus to be on our product rather than on us. Who cares if we're cranky when our food is heavenly?"

"So let's just go with The Tartlets," Kate said. "For now. Or at least until we've used up the thousand business cards I ordered."

Carol nodded. "So what does young neighbor girl do anyway?"

"She writes for some obscure women's magazine." Kate made a shushing sound. "It's very hush-hush. They're all about this new millennium approach to feminism, which basically comes down to the notion, if I understand correctly, that whatever you are, it's okay."

"Sounds like a healthy principal," Carol said. "Although I doubt whether *that's* the new millennium approach to feminism."

"If it is, it's a cop-out," Kate said. "Whatever happened to taking a stand?"

Carol shrugged. "But why is it hush-hush?"

"O, I don't know—they're young; they love a little mystery. Unveiling conspiracies, that sort of thing." Kate leaned over. "Apparently, they're on to some multinational corporation that turns a blind eye to sexual harassment and age discrimination. Or maybe it's all a smoke screen. I've asked her to get me an issue, but she never has. Maybe they're really Mulder and Scully. I think they're involved in something way more dangerous than they let on."

"Who's *they*?"

"Lara and her streamlined fiancé."

Carol shook her head. "Your imagination is running wild again. *The X-Files* can really mess a person up, you know?"

"I assure you," Kate said, "that I have both feet firmly on the ground. But I do think that there are forces in this world beyond our control." She folded her hands on the table. "We're on the threshold, as a species, of incredible things. Technologically, I mean. A hundred years from now, we may well have evolved into some kind of super androids."

Carol nodded. "Probably. And that whole process is actually beginning right across the hall from your apartment. How very convenient."

"Mock me all you want," Kate said, her tone surly.

"You know what I think? I think women should stop whining." Carol shoved her coffee cup across the table. "I refuse to drink this."

"I know, we went over that."

"The thing is," Carol said, "you can't pay feminism a better service than by outsmarting men." She smiled at a young girl walking toward their table with a tray in her hands. She sat up straighter. "Climb that corporate ladder, I say!" She banged her fist on the table. "Cheat on your wife with your secretary!" The coffee cup splashed over.

The girl looked at her with an alarmed expression and scurried past.

Kate nudged Carol's foot under the table. "Calm down, okay? You're scaring people. And isn't your view of men just a little clichéd?"

"I'm right, though, right?" Carol said. "What feminists have wanted through the years is to stop men from being nasty to them because they deserve pity and sympathy. But I'm telling you, the only road to equality is beating them at their own game."

"There's a balance that needs to be restored," Kate said. "Men still call the shots."

"So anyway, what's Lara's deal?" Carol said. "I mean, relationship-wise? Is she really getting married?"

Kate shrugged. "I don't know, but I have a feeling they're pretty serious. I sure see them together a lot. There's this incredible vibe between them. It's almost like they're one person." She stared at a spot on the wall. "I can just picture them flying through Gotham City side by side, doing their saintly work and then afterwards having wild, intergalactic sex—*while* flying."

Carol shook her head. "The guy in Gotham City doesn't actually fly. And there's nothing intergalactic about him."

"Really?" Kate said. "So he's just a regular dude in a cape?"

"Pretty much." Carol's head snapped up, and she eyed Kate suspiciously. "Isn't an X-Files adept supposed to have at least a working knowledge of this stuff?"

"I was just trying to make a point."

"It *would* require an out-of-this-world limberness," Carol said dreamily. "Having sex while flying, I mean." Her gaze strayed. "To think that there are people who live like that, huh? And then to think that Ray tried to worm his hand under my top last night when we were brushing our teeth together." She sighed. "That's foreplay for you after ten years of married bliss."

Kate made a face. "*Way* too much information."

"Sorry." Carol grinned. "Love him, though."

"She's really okay, you know?" Kate wasn't ready to drop the subject of Lara just yet. "I was afraid I was going to be late for our appointment this morning, so I asked her to knock on my door at seven, and she did."

"Aw." Carol cocked her head. "That's *so* delightfully transparent. As if you don't have an alarm clock and an iPhone all perfectly capable of raising anyone from the dead."

"Shut up, okay?"

"So is she decent to look at?"

"Well—"

"Oh God, never mind." Carol shook her head. "The way your eyes light up is all the answer I need!"

"She wears a lot of black," Kate said. "And leather. She told me she was a vegan for a while, but then she started missing her leather, and now she's just a vegetarian. When people give her a hard time about it, she says, 'I'm not *eating* the damn jacket, am I?'"

Carol grinned. "It *does* seem like a bit of a double standard."

"Why?" Kate shook her head. "Why is it that people who take a moral stand are always criticized for not taking a more profound moral stand? Yet people who don't give a damn about anything are never criticized at all?"

"There are saints in this world, and then there are mere mortals," Carol said. "And the bar is raised higher for the saints, obviously." She tapped her index finger on Kate's hand. "But, honey, if I can give you a piece of advice? Stop lusting after her. She's out of your league."

Kate flinched. "Ouch?"

"I don't mean that you're not hot enough," she cast Kate a seductive glance over the rim of her glasses, "obviously."

"That's something, at least," Kate said.

"But you tend to fall for the wrong women. All they do is wear you out and then dump you. Because what *you* want is to sit on the couch at night with your sleepy time tea and your little candles, and what *they* want is to paint the town red. Nobody's fault. The women you're attracted to are simply not the women who are right for you. You can't hold on to them."

"Are you saying I'm boring?"

Carol shook her head. "I wouldn't say boring. More like...stable." She looked at her watch. "But anyway, I have to go pick up Janey from school." She got up, pulled a ten-dollar bill out of her back pocket, and then immediately put it back. She pointed to the battered Formica table. "This whole bash is on you. For obvious reasons." She picked up her bag and slung it over her shoulder. "Let's get together at your place tomorrow night to plan for the sweet sixteen party, okay?"

"Sounds like a plan," Kate said. "Chips and dip?"

"More like smoked salmon and quesadillas."

Kate smiled. "Ka-ching!"

It wasn't until Kate was back in her building, staring at Lara's door as she groped in her bag for her keys, that she remembered something Lara had said that morning. Her heart began to flutter. Lara said she wanted to run something by her. But in the confusion of the early morning encounter, she had forgotten to ask what that something was. A thrill of excitement ran through her. What an excellent reason to see her now. She knocked discreetly on Lara's door.

No answer. Which, in retrospect, was a blessing. Because now, Kate could plan the visit for a later time, and when that time came, she'd pull out all the stops—look strikingly great, be scantily dressed, and smell beyond heavenly. If only Lara hadn't seen her in her dowdy nightwear that morning, with the pattern of the creased sheets imprinted on her cheek. It would be quite a challenge to erase *that* image from her mind.

She and Carol spent the next evening trying out new recipes, most of them based on what Kate considered to be God's gift to vegans—the chickpea.

"Why vegan?" Carol ran her finger through the hummus and slipped it in her mouth. She moaned. "Jesus, that's really good."

"Because we're versatile," Kate answered. "We can cater any shindig, whether it's vegan, vegetarian, kosher, halal, or what have you." She threw a bunch of coriander and a handful of cashews in a blender. As she was whizzing it up, Carol rested a hand on her arm. She switched off the machine. "What?"

"Are you sure we're not concentrating on the vegan delights because you want to impress the vegan delight across the hall?"

Kate shook her head. "I told you, I don't mix business with pleasure. I'm totally dedicated to us, you know, to The Tartlets, or whatever we call ourselves."

"All right, then." Carol opened the fridge and scanned the contents. "Where do you keep the sour cream?"

"Hello!" Kate said, fiddling with the blender. "No dairy, remember?"

"Right." Carol sighed. "What a hard life that must be. Like missing an arm."

A knock on the door.

Kate wiped her hands on her apron and blew a strand of hair off her forehead. She opened the door, and there was Lara, looking like some deliciously androgynous anime character. Once again, she was fresh out of the shower.

"Hi," Carol said from behind the kitchen counter. "Come in and sample our homemade falafel." She smiled in Lara's direction. "It's to die for. Even if I do say so myself."

"Oh..." Lara's eyebrows went up. "I didn't know..." She waved hello to Carol. "I'm intruding," she said, looking at Kate. "You're busy."

"We need a head taster," said Carol.

"I brought wine." Lara's voice was almost apologetic, as if bringing wine was considered bad manners.

"I hope it's vegan wine," Carol said, "because we're having an exclusively plant-based party here."

Lara smiled. "Actually, it *is*."

"Wine is just grapes, right?" Kate said. "How is a grape un-vegan?"

"Oh dear, you still have so much to learn." Carol walked up to Lara, introduced herself while she shook her hand, and took the bottle from her. She studied the label, clicking her tongue admiringly. "An organic, vegan Merlot. Happens to be my favorite. And Kate's too. Because in spite of what you might think, she actually *can* talk." She walked back to the kitchen, sat the bottle on the counter, threw a cucumber on her cutting board, and began slicing it up.

"She knows I can talk," Kate snapped. "We talked only yesterday."

Lara nodded. "Which is why I'm here." She stared at Kate intently for a second, then brought a hand to Kate's face and ran a thumb down her cheek. "You have a little—"

"Flour!" Carol chimed in.

Lara stared at her thumb and wiped it on her jeans. "Anyway, I was going to ask you if you'd be up for me interviewing you."

Kate gave Lara a blank stare, still feeling the spot where she'd touched her. She leaned her hand on the headrest of her easy chair for stability.

Lara tilted her head. "You know, for the magazine."

"For *your* magazine?" Kate said. "Why?"

"For our series on powerful women."

"But…" Kate laughed. "I'm anything but a powerful woman. I'm actually more of a house plant."

"You're setting up your own business, right?"

"We are, yes," Carol hollered. "And pending our big break, Kate pays the bills by working her ass off at some dead-end secretarial job. She's every inch the alpha female."

"That's great," Lara said, never taking her gaze off Kate. "So when are you…available? To talk about this, I mean. I'll give you the ins and outs, and then you can decide whether you're up for it."

"Why not give her the ins and outs now?" Carol pointed to the couch with the tip of her knife. "Make yourself comfortable. Have some wine and food."

Lara shook her head. "Thanks, but I have things to do. Maybe some other time."

"If you really think I qualify," Kate said, "then I guess I'm in. Can't think of a reason why not. It might even be good for business and win us some new customers."

"I guess," Lara said. "Not sure the readers of *Glopax* are the sort of people who have their parties catered, but I guess it won't hurt."

"That's okay." Kate wondered what sort of people the readers of *Glopax* might be and how many there were. "I have nothing planned tomorrow night. So I suppose we could set it up. How about we meet at your place?" She smiled. "I know where it is."

"Good. That's great." Lara lingered and then suddenly turned on her heel. "I'll see you tomorrow, then." She looked over her shoulder, waved at Carol, and left.

"Now *that*," Carol said, grinning from ear to ear, "was a booty call if ever I saw one."

Kate walked back to the kitchen and leaned against the counter. She felt flushed and a little confused. "Stop it, okay!" She frowned at Carol. "You're weirding me out. It wasn't even a call to start with. It was a visit, to discuss a business transaction."

Carol grinned mischievously. "She brought wine. She smelled like a goddess."

"Still." Kate pouted. She wanted it to be true, but she was afraid that saying it out loud might jinx it.

"You were right," Carol said. "She really is... What's the word? Luscious."

"Don't think I ever called her luscious."

"In a Katniss Everdeen meets Lisbeth Salander kind of way."

Kate shook her head. "Shut up, okay?"

"And the way she wiped the flour off your cheek. I thought I was going to faint."

"Didn't you say only yesterday that I wasn't supposed to lust after her?"

"I changed my mind," Carol said. "Go ahead. Lust! You have my blessing."

For some reason, Kate hadn't expected Lara to have a couch. But she did, a ratty one, but still. It was thin and faded, just like the carpet. Looking around, she didn't know *what* she'd expected. Maybe bean bags. As she was waiting for Lara to get her stuff, Kate realized that the whole apartment was actually disappointingly boring. There was no telling what kind of person lived here. Apart from the couch, there were a couple of mismatched chairs, a fruit box that served as a coffee table, a withered potted palm, a small television on a console table, and a floor lamp. A wicker basket, half hidden under the couch, aroused her curiosity, and while keeping an eye on the door through which Lara had disappeared, Kate looked through the stack of magazines in it. There were no surprises there either—no seditious periodicals of any kind, just some issues of *Cosmopolitan* and a few fitness magazines.

On the walls, a fairly tacky picture of the New York skyline by night hung next to two nondescript abstract paintings that looked as if they were done by a five-year-old. Lara's apartment reminded her of a set for a low-budget movie, a room filled with borrowed stuff.

The door opened and Lara walked in, not with some kind of state-of-the-art recording device in her hand, but with a notepad tucked under her arm and a pencil in her mouth.

"It's very different from your apartment, right?" she said with some difficulty. She grabbed the pencil from between her teeth. "I was actually wondering if you'd give me some pointers. The place could do with a woman's touch." She laughed.

Okay. Kate's mind went into overdrive. What did she mean, a woman's touch? Was she playfully mocking her own butchness? And was the butchness a gay thing after all? She looked her over. It might be. It might *so* be. But what about her symbiotic attachment to Boy Wonder? If she was gay—which was definitely too good to be true—than where was *he* in the equation?

"I'd be happy to," she said, trying to process it all.

The interview wasn't a ploy or a smoke screen or any kind of excuse to do anything other than to actually conduct an interview on the subject of women executives and the alleged glass ceiling, the question of whether the world would be a better place if women called the shots, and the pitfalls of starting one's own business.

Lara scribbled on her notepad like a maniac, and even when she asked questions, she hardly made eye contact. She seemed distant. A little timid, even.

Kate searched her face for a clue as to what she was thinking, but she couldn't manage to establish a connection. Her heart sank. Where was Lara's spirit? And where was all that wonderful sexual tension she'd felt between them? Where was the thumb wiping the flour off her face?

It was barely nine when they said good-bye. Lara promised to let her read the interview before running it, and it wasn't until Kate was halfway out the door that the spark seemed to return to Lara's eyes, and she said, "Oh, before I forget. I actually have another huge favor to ask you."

Thank God. Ask me something, anything, no matter how inappropriate or weird. Or even illegal. Let's salvage this night.

"You probably know," Lara said, "that most journalists dream of writing a book, right?"

Kate had no idea. "I guess."

"Well, I do anyway," said Lara. "Because, as fulfilling as it is to make the world a better place or to at least contribute to doing so, I've come to realize that it doesn't match up to the joy of creating a fictional world."

"You write fiction? What are you working on?"

"I have something... Hang on." Lara disappeared again, only for a minute, leaving Kate in the doorway, and when she came back, she handed Kate a pile of paper.

The pages were printed, to Kate's relief—she had half feared, as she stood waiting, that the masterpiece might be written by hand. On hemp paper.

Lara looked at her, her eyes dark and large and moist. "This, I hope, will one day be a novel. I would love for you to read it. I really trust your opinion."

"Okay." Kate tried to think of abandoned puppies and gory stuff to stop herself from planting her lips on Lara's.

"I'll be glad to take a look. A novel in the making, wow, that's so great. Good for you."

Lara put both hands on her chest. "This piece is very close to my heart, Kate, but I want you to be brutally honest. Tell me exactly how it makes you feel." She smiled. "Is that all right?"

The smile made Kate melt. "I'll get on it right away."

And she did. Once back in her own apartment, she took a shower, made tea and a sandwich, and then crawled into bed, with just her bedside lamp on and the manuscript in her hands like a Christmas present she'd stolen from under the tree before anybody was up. If Lara's writing turned out to be really bad, she would have to find a way to break that to her gently, but if her stuff was Pulitzer Prize material, then it was incredibly exciting that she was the first to see it. Some of Lara's future fame might even rub off on her, and then her and Carol's business would skyrocket if they played their cards right.

The top page was blank, followed by a page with just the title, in italics.

The Force.

Lara's name was at the bottom of the page in admirably modest lettering.

She wasn't sure what to think of the title. *The Force?* May the force be with you? She was almost sure it would be a sci-fi or fantasy story. Maybe Lara was dreaming, like so many, of being the next J.K. Rowling.

She started reading.

The first chapters weren't badly written, and they meandered pleasantly enough, if not very excitingly—no sorcerers or vampires; no intergalactic warfare; definitely no having sex while flying. It was a coming-of-age story. An idealistic, small-town girl and her equally righteous twin brother, born to a family of tobacco-chewing, dim-witted hillbillies (who sat on a porch all day, trying to shoot birds out of the sky—the family was so stereotypically portrayed that Kate found herself cringing at the description), move to some big city more than a thousand miles away, where they embark upon the task of writing manifestos about the deplorable state of the world and what world leaders (and indeed citizens) should do to avert the decline.

Kate was relieved to find that the manifesto writing and the following struggle to publish some sort of underground periodical were no more than a backstory—the focus was on the way the twins tried to make a life for themselves in the dazzling complexity of the unnamed metropolis.

All in all, it wasn't bad, although it might not be the sort of thing she was willing to lose any sleep over.

But then, there was chapter four.

And like any good writer must, Lara presented her main character with a problem that deterred her from her chosen life path. While her life path was to end famine, male supremacy, dictatorship, and a great many other unsolvable wrongs, something happened—she fell in love. And being in love completely filled her heart and mind and senses, to the point where all she could manage to think about was getting her hot crush into bed and fucking until the sun came up.

By this point, Kate had sort of understood that the story, while written in the third person and featuring a protagonist named Hermione, was strongly autobiographical. And she knew that in chapter four, she was in for a cringe-worthy description of Hermione's (read Lara's) hot nights with Boy Wonder. And even if she was willing to read it (she *had* promised, after all), it would probably be easier to do if she had a little something to cushion the blow. So she went to the kitchen and poured herself a big glass of the wine that the object of her affection had brought her—using it, ironically enough, to console her while reading a detailed account of said object's straight sex adventures.

Once more snuggled under the covers with her glass in her hand, she drew a deep breath, and started to read.

Chapter 4

The first time Hermione met Sam, it was as if her soul recognized Sam's, as if they were twins, separated somewhere in a cruel space and time, but reunited, now, in this most unlikely of places—a dimly lit hallway in a less than impressive apartment building.

The coincidence of there being another person pining for someone in the darkened hallway of an apartment building didn't escape Kate. It made her heart race—here was someone sharing her plight!

There were moments in Hermione's life when she felt not just out of place, but out of time—not in the way one longs back for a period of more happiness or stability, but like a time traveler,

misplaced in the wrong era. But when she met
Sam, her life made sense for the very first time.
She was finally where, and when, she belonged—
Samantha was her home, her destiny.

Whoa! *What?*

Sam was...(something inside her seemed to explode)
...Samantha?

Hermione had been with women before.

Kate sprayed a mouthful of Merlot all over the bed. The wine sloshed over the rim of her glass.

"Shit!" She put the glass on the nightstand. The sheets were wet, but who cared? She got up, rounded the bed, and got in on the other side, her head spinning. She took off her drenched T-shirt, threw it on the floor, and got back under the covers, half naked, because that felt okay.

Hermione had been with women before!

She flipped the pages impatiently.

She had fallen in love with women, slept
with them, drinking their nectar (Kate rolled
her eyes—oh Jesus, their nectar? Ugh!), *waking*
numerous times in the arms of attractive but
nondescript bedpartners. They were one-night
stands, and at best, they relieved her loneliness
for a couple of hours. They were interchangeable.
They satisfied her physical needs as she did theirs,
but none had touched her heart.

It was obvious, from a literary point of view, that Lara was trying just a tad too hard. Kate struggled to overlook the flowery style as she waded through the pages, stopping herself, with some difficulty, from skipping ahead to the good bits.

But the endless exposé on the merging of the souls and Hermione's nocturnal ponderings on the nature of time and space really got on her nerves after a while, and so she cheated a little, skipping about twenty pages and picking it up again at the beginning of chapter six.

Chapter 6

Hermione had bought a bottle of her favorite wine at the organic market—the wonderful Merlot that was her own favorite. A wine for a very special occasion. She loved to give Sam presents. Loved helping her. Even if it was simply by knocking on her door when she was afraid of oversleeping.

Kate stared at the page wide-eyed, gasping for air. Her heart began to pound at the thought... But she shook her head—*surely* this was a coincidence.

She was worth it. Hermione wanted to give her so much more. Everything, down to her very soul.

Kate made a face. Enough with the souls already!

It seemed that tonight the universe was calling the shots, for while she had decided to wait for the right opportunity to tell Sam how she felt, this night seemed to present itself in a way that wouldn't take no for an answer. Hermione knew that Sam was home; she could hear her on the other side of the door when she was standing out in the hall. She imagined her, in all her long-legged glory—her wonderfully creamy skin, her eyes blue as the ocean, the wavy, strawberry blonde hair cascading down her shoulders. She was a picture of femininity, in her short skirts and her tight, satin tops. But she was also a go-getter like no one else Hermione knew—determined, energetic, ambitious; a master chef whose talent would one day be recognized by all.

O, God, Kate thought, as the dizzying truth began to dawn on her. Did she really just read what she thought she read? Was the resemblance between her and Sam not a coincidence at all? She brought the page so close to her face it touched her nose. She squinted. Was this about...her? Or at least about some perfect version of her? She took a second to consider if there was any other explanation, and when she failed to find one, she raised her hands in the air, causing the manuscript to slide to the floor.

"She's me!" she shouted. "*I'm* Sam! This whole thing is about us!"

And as she realized this, she understood, in a flash, that Hermione's twin brother was, in fact, *Lara's* twin brother. Boy Wonder was her brother! No wonder she'd felt as if they were the same person. They *were.* Well, kind of. A surge of heat went through her, and she threw back the covers, remembering only when she saw her naked breasts that she wasn't wearing a shirt. How fitting!

She exhaled loudly as she picked up the pages off the floor.

> *The disappointment, on calling, that Sam had company over, made her want to lie down and weep.*

"No!" Kate said out loud. "Don't be a wuss! Kiss her! I mean me. Kiss me!"

> *But the company (Sam's less than subtle business partner and friend) was just about to leave, and it wasn't long before Hermine and Sam found themselves alone in the apartment. It was a gentle spring night, and through the open window, a blossoming tree sent a sweet scent of lilac their way, filling their nostrils with hope and purity.*

O, please. Filling their nostrils with hope and purity? Blech.

On a happier note, Lara seemed to be upping the ante here. Kate could just sense it. Apparently, Lara had taken last night's scene and moved both Carol and the winter out of the way. Good call.

Hermione couldn't help but picture Sam naked.

"Come on, sweetheart," Kate said to the empty room. "Do me proud."

Again.

But by now, even Hermione's creative mind had stretched her imagination to its outer limits, and where she had been able, before, to arouse and excite herself to the point where she screamed for release (Kate exhaled loudly as a delightful shiver went through her) *by simply imagining herself and Sam in the throes of passion, it wasn't enough anymore. She needed the real thing. She needed to touch Sam, the real Sam, not some image of her. Needed to feel her skin, to touch her in that most intimate of ways* (tell me how, exactly!).

As they sat side by side, sipping wine, Hermione moved closer, brushing her thigh firmly against Sam's.

Sam's breath hitched.

Kate snorted derisively. Lara imagined her breath hitching at the brushing of a thigh? She'd have to do a little better than that.

Neither of them spoke. It was too late for that. Tonight was all about a wordless acting-out of their fantasies. Hermione put her hand on

Sam's thigh, feeling the strong muscles beneath the smooth spandex of her pencil skirt.

Sam leaned into her (not that easy in a spandex pencil skirt!), her full lips like a sweet promise, moving closer. Hermione closed her eyes. It was better than anything she could have ever imagined. The tender gentleness of her lover's lips on her own, the soft touch of her hands on her face—she was afraid of fainting.

"Go easy on the vanilla, sweetheart," Kate said, flipping through the pages excitedly. "This is *so* not going to lead to having sex while flying."

Things went into a tailspin from that moment on. Hermione could control herself no longer. She took Sam by the hand and led them to Sam's bedroom. Once there, Sam lay down on the bed while Hermione began to perform a slow striptease. Sam watched Hermione's every move, her eyes large and blue as the ocean, her breathing ragged. Hermione took off her shoes and socks, her jacket. She pulled the tight, black top out of her jeans, removed it, and threw it on the floor. She unhooked her bra and slid it down her shoulders. Sam stared at her small breasts, mesmerized, watching the nipples grow dark and erect.

This time, Kate's breath *did* hitch.

She unbuttoned her tight (tight was definitely Lara's thing) *black pants and took them off. She was naked but for her panties. Sam's breathing became heavier still as she sat up, pulled Hermione toward her, hooked her fingers under Hermione's panties, and slowly slid them down her legs. Hermione stepped out of them. She was finally whole. There was something incredibly arousing about standing completely naked in front of a Sam who was fully dressed.*

Sam looked at her with eyes full of lust. Hermione sat down on the bed. Sam brought her face close and began to kiss her, more eagerly this time, pushing her tongue far into Hermione's mouth—a sweet merging that made Hermione want more, much more than this. Sam's hands were all over her. Her mouth trailed down, her tongue drawing lazy circles around her nipples. She took one nipple in her mouth, sucking on it, and then went over to the other one, making them harder still. Hermione felt herself getting wet, getting flooded, and as Sam kept her eyes locked with Hermione's, she began to move her hand, trailing it maddeningly slowly over Hermione's breasts, over the taut stomach, and down to her core. Sam's hand found the wet folds waiting for her. Allowing her fingers to play and explore endlessly, she finally entered Hermione, and Hermione, pushing against her, climaxed almost instantly, in a way she'd never climaxed before—in glorious waves of pleasure.

Kate swallowed hard.

Sam caught Hermione in her arms, kissing her as the convulsions subsided. Hermione closed her eyes, and when she opened them again, Sam was naked beside her. She gasped for breath—this was what she'd been dreaming of for so long. Sam's perfect, alabaster skin, the bountiful breasts (Kate looked down her naked torso—not sure she'd call them bountiful, exactly), *the perfect legs, meeting in that most mystical of places* (well…), *a place where she wanted to dwell, and drink,* (??) *a place she could call home.*

As if there was no time to waste, Hermione ran her warm hands along the length of Sam's glorious body, shivering. She drew a trail of hot kisses along Sam's perfect skin, her mouth teasing, sucking, caressing. A moan escaped Sam that wouldn't be stifled.

A familiar throb started somewhere deep inside of Kate.

Hermione moved along Sam's body, slipping between her thighs, spreading them. She groaned as she took in the beauty of the perfect rose (Oh God—no corny flower euphemisms!) *with the delicate dewdrops* (ew!) *that was the center of Sam's body and now the center of Hermione's universe—the place where everything came together.*

She brought her mouth there, and it felt almost like a sacred act. Hermione teased Sam with her tongue, drawing circles, tormenting her. When Sam could take no more, Hermione brought her hand close to her face, and while she continued to suck on Sam's clit, she inserted two fingers into her wetness, withdrew them with a stroke, and then entered her again, slipping in and out of her, and again, and again. Sam's hips bucked against Hermione's fingers, and as she cried out Hermione's name, her body stiffened and convulsed, as a mind-blowing orgasm ripped through her.

This time, it was her own moan Kate couldn't stifle. For in spite of the distractingly baroque style, the prose was alluringly sexy and yet, in a way, dark and mysterious—much like Lara herself. Kate had to admit that reading the scenes, while imagining herself and Lara as the leads, had gotten her into a definite...state. A state that required...taking care of. She put the manuscript down and closed her eyes, her hand trailing down her body.

But then, she stiffened, and her eyes flew wide open.

Surely, there was a better way to deal with this!

She got out of bed, smelled herself for traces of the wine (it would just have to do), put on a clean shirt (no bra) and some jeans, picked up the manuscript, walked out of the apartment and, once in the hallway, knocked on Lara's door. Loudly, because it was... What time was it anyway?

She went back to her apartment, checked the clock on the wall, and then once more positioned herself in front of

Lara's door. One in the morning. It was one in the morning. But all bets were off now. Lara may be asleep, but she only had herself to blame for this.

The door was opened wide. Lara wasn't asleep, and by the looks of her, she hadn't been (did she *ever* sleep?), because she looked the same way she always did—sprightly and beautiful.

"Kate!" she sang. "I was just thinking about you." She moved forward and arched her back. "Have you—?"

"I read it." Kate held up the manuscript. "Well, parts of it."

Lara smiled seductively. "Good parts?"

Kate nodded, feeling weak in the knees. "*Very* good parts."

"Oh, Kate." Lara swooned. "Did you get who—?"

"Yes! I totally got that."

Lara sighed deeply and stepped closer still, ending up practically in Kate's arms. "What'd you like about it?" she whispered, her lips almost brushing Kate's.

"Everything." Kate looked deep into Lara's eyes. "It's brilliant." She wrapped her arm around Lara's waist. "My place. Now."

Lara kicked against her front door with her boot to close it, and Kate led her into her apartment. Once inside, Kate took Lara's hands in hers. "Listen. I want to do this *exactly* the way Hermione and Sam did."

Lara brought her lips to Kate's ear. "Me too," she whispered. "That's why I wrote it the way I did."

Kate shivered as she kissed Lara's fingers. And while they were headed for the bedroom, leaning into each other, Kate's head all but exploded when she realized that any minute now, Lara (Lara!) would be naked in her bed, licking the delicate dewdrops off her perfect rose.

She could only hope she'd survive it.

CRUISE
BY JACELLE SCOTT

"I can handle it, really," said Cathy. She'd been followed down the narrow gangway of the *North Star* by a young porter anxious to earn a generous tip merely for showing her the way. "Seriously." She swiped the key card through its slot at B-298 and motioned for him to *shoo*.

The porter slunk away. Cathy dumped her backpack—full enough for an expedition to Everest—onto the bed with a thump.

Her respite was short-lived.

The stateroom door swung open. A smiling, slender woman entered, slipping a polyester scarf from her neck. "I promise you, Ramon, my bags aren't filled with cement," she said to yet another porter. The young man struggled with her three pieces of matching green Samsonite, including the makeup case, and a buckled leather satchel. "Oh, hello! You must be my 'shared accommodation'!"

"That would appear to be the case." Cathy turned from her task and offered her hand. "I'm Cathy Mackenzie."

"Louise—actually, Lou," she said. "Lewandowski."

Cathy could see that the strain of holding Lou's bags was testing the porter's stamina. Tiny beads of sweat glistened in his unevenly plucked eyebrows.

"Miss?"

"I'm sorry, Ramon! Here, just set them down." Lou immediately crossed to the vacant bed.

"Not to worry, Miss," said the young man. "I am very strong." Despite his dismissal of her concern, he grunted as he wrestled the bag onto the luggage stand at the foot of the bed.

Lou gestured for him to hold on as she dug into her handbag. In a small change purse with an old-fashioned pinch-clasp, she discovered two dollars and pressed it into the luggage carrier's hand.

"Oh thank you, Miss," he said, backed out of the room, and pulled the door closed behind him.

Lou sighed as she returned the change purse to her handbag. "I hope that was enough." She ran a hand through her slightly mussed hair. "I really don't know the rules for tipping." She looked at Cathy as she spoke, as if waiting for some advice.

"That won't be the only tip you'll be giving," said Cathy, knowing full well the confidence of the room service people, stewards, and excursion guides. Since no ports of call were scheduled for the *Cruise to Nowhere*, she could only imagine how much more indulgent the staff and crew might be. "You're fine."

Lou pivoted and squinted at her reflection in the mirror opposite her bed. "I look a fright. My taxi from JFK got snarled in awful traffic. I didn't think I'd make it for our departure time!"

Even as she spoke, a low, long bellow of the ship's horn sounded, and a subtle rumble indicated that the engines were firing.

"Well, you're here now." Cathy glanced at her watch. "We'll be underway before you know it."

Louise rubbed a finger over her teeth. Apparently satisfied, she lifted her eyes and set her hands on her hips. "The space is pretty small for the price, I think."

"I guess that's how they get you into the shuffleboard matches," said Cathy. She pulled four hardcovers out of her backpack and tossed them on the bed and then continued rummaging. "I can't believe I forgot my toothbrush," she mumbled.

Lou perked up at the mention of shuffleboard. "Do you like it?"

"Like what?" Cathy was determined to paw down to the bowels of her bag.

"Shuffleboard."

Cathy snorted. "Pa-lease. I detest games of *any* kind." In spite of her athletic build—well muscled, trim—she eschewed virtually all kinds of sports, with the exception of pistol shooting. Deirdre had hated that Cathy owned the compact, powerful Glock. But there was something comforting about the solitary mastery that target practice required. After Deirdre decamped from their house and relationship, Cathy'd relished some afternoon solace as she took aim at Deirdre's left-behind collection of Schlitz and Billy beer cans. But, of course, her new roommate didn't know any of that. "I'm sorry," she said with mild chagrin. "I shouldn't assume. Do *you* like games?"

"Scrabble, mostly. Trivia, sometimes. Bingo, occasionally. I like the casino, but only for the penny slots." Lou opened her suitcase and extracted a tissue-wrapped statuette.

"Right," Cathy said. "I see you've brought your good luck charm."

"You mean the Infant of Prague," Lou said with a curious pride and fussed with the statue's garments. The gold imperial regalia was pristine, and a tiny bird was firmly affixed on the Infant's right hand. "Is He good luck?" she murmured softly. She kissed the Infant's face briefly, and positioned Him on the edge of her dresser. "Something like that."

Warily, Cathy regarded her cabin mate. *Two thousand passengers and I get stuck with the superstitious bingo-playing keeper of St. Christopher or whoever the fuck he is. They all look alike in those weird getups. She's probably got the homemaker's grotto in her backyard—a bathtub turned upright and painted a robin's egg blue on the inside. She definitely had to get her hubby's permission to go on vacation.*

Lou gestured toward Cathy's books. "Looks like you plan to do some reading. What are you into?"

"Non-fiction, mostly. Right now, I'm on the latest biography of Anna Freud. And that top one," she said, as she pointed, "is new. Critical essays on Virginia Woolf."

Lou began to forage in the narrow closet next to the mirror.

"Some extras in here," Lou said, her voice muffled. A small mountain of pillows began to accumulate on the bed. She leaned back. "You want a couple?"

"No, thanks." Cathy's backpack, finally empty, would fit in the cupboard beside the sink.

Lou must have realized how foolish she looked. Still hugging the last of the pillows to her chest, she settled herself on the foot of her bed. "It's my back...for support when I'm reading. I don't mean to take all of them, but if you're not—"

"How about you?" Cathy asked. "What do you like?"

"Literary fiction." Louise began, quite unceremoniously, to arrange the pillows in a throne-like structure. She then opened the makeup case and stacked a wobbly tower of glossy romances on her bedside table.

"Really? *Literary* fiction?" The collection of paperbacks didn't seem to support Lou's assertion. Cathy swallowed to mask her amusement. "Very nice. Tell me what you're reading. I might know it."

"I'm afraid you wouldn't," Louise said kindly, palms outward and wavering like two Chinese fans. "Right now I'm working on Daphne Heartwell's *Love's Eternal Passion.* I've got manuscript pages in my satchel. It's quite good. I'm a beta reader for Tryst House. I plan to finish it tonight and start on the sequel tomorrow."

"A beta reader?" asked Cathy. "I'm not sure I'm familiar with the term…"

"My contribution to the literary world, you know. The publishing house enlists beta readers to generally comment on the state of a manuscript before they're invested with the costs of publishing. I'm intrigued with plots and characters, but if I find something I don't like, I let the press know. It's volunteer work—they pay me in copies—but I love to do it!"

Cathy frowned. "Sounds like love stories, right? What's the title of the sequel?"

"*Love's Passion Rekindled,* I think. Same characters, though."

"Well, *that* saves time," Cathy said wryly. "With their complex lives and all."

Louise's face lit up in a broad smile. "Exactly! So, you're familiar with Heartwell! Isn't she wonderful? A genius, I think. You know, a lot of people don't realize she's written seven books in the last three years."

"Yes," Cathy mumbled sarcastically under her breath. "Remarkable."

Louise finished patting her pillows into place. Another blast from the ship's horn was followed by an announcement. The ship was ready to weigh anchor.

"I think I'll go out to the rail," Lou said. "I want to watch New York fade into the distance. Do you want to come?"

"No, thanks. Go ahead, though, and enjoy the show."

Lou gracefully re-wound the polyester scarf around her neck. "Do you know anyone on board?"

"Just you, now," said Cathy.

"Shall we have dinner together?" Lou's hand was on the cabin door.

How could she say no? Why not get all of the required courtesies out of the way on day one? Then, hopefully, the cheery Catholic might leave her to read in peace.

"All right. See you back here in a while," said Cathy. "Six?"

"Perfect."

After Lou left, Cathy glanced at the statue once more, as if it had been rigged with a nanny-cam. After a split second's hesitation, she strode to the table and the shaky pillar of paperbacks. She flipped over the topmost book. On the cover, a brunette with long, wild hair (and whose semi-buttoned blouse fell dramatically off her left shoulder down to a hint of cleavage) lay in the passionate embrace of a muscular man with wavy black hair and a tight shirt. He appeared desperate for a kiss. Cathy shook her head and chuckled. *So. Louise Lewandowski, Ambassador of the Holy See, likes Harlequins.* She turned the book face down on the tottering pile, suddenly regretting that she hadn't gone on that South Dakota backpacking trip instead.

Considering the weightlessness of their banter—
something Cathy normally had little taste for—dinner had
been unexpectedly pleasant. Lou was a chatty woman who
readily exposed everything from her experiences in Catholic
school to her opinion of Yorkshire terriers. She hailed from
Port Dickens, an unremarkable town in upstate New York
whose claim to fame, long gone, relied exclusively on its
proximity to the Erie Canal. After raising three kids and
paying off the mortgage on a four-bedroom cape—all
products of a twenty-eight-year marriage—her husband,
Walter, had died eight years ago and left her reasonably
comfortable. Lou's concise discussion of Walter reflected
an indifference that surprised Cathy, but then, men were
generally legitimate objects of indifference, in her opinion.

However pleasant dinner had been, Cathy was talked
out for the night, and especially with her cabinmate's cheery
chatter. She looked forward to her pajamas, some quiet, and
some bourbon. When they reached the cabin door just after
sunset, Cathy had her keycard at the ready. With a flourish,
she bowed demurely at the waist, pushed open the door, and
waited. "After you, please," she said with a bit of drama,
cocking her arm and ushering Lou inside. "Join me for a
drink?"

"It's been years—"

Cathy retrieved the small bottle she'd set on the mini-
fridge upon arrival. "Where's the porter when you need him?"
she mumbled, skimming every flat surface in the space. "I
don't see any glasses."

Slowly, Lou let her scarf—bedecked with tiny birds that
floated among tiny twigs and succulent purple berries on a

cream-colored background—drift to the floor. Bright and fluid silver bracelets, one on each wrist, tinkled lightly as she tousled her short, reddish hair with both hands for the umpteenth time. Perhaps a nervous tic, thought Cathy.

"In there, I suppose." Lou gestured toward the bathroom. An oval, pewter medallion on a silver chain lay motionless— or trapped—in Lou's upper cleavage as she bent to retrieve the scarf. Shrill voice or not, there was something becoming about her, something enticing.

About to grab the glasses from the bathroom vanity, Cathy caught sight of Lou's profile in the mirror. Perched on the edge of her bed, Lou unbuttoned her shirt and lazily fell onto her back. "I'm absolutely *stuffed*!" she called. "More than I normally eat in a week." She slid her arms upward over the gray-blue comforter and arched contentedly, hands behind her head. The edges of Lou's blouse draped downward, highlighting the elegant, deep curve created by the slope of her bottom rib to her waist.

A flash of Deidre demanded that Cathy avert her gaze, but she wasn't eager to obey.

Lou's waist tapered out to sumptuous hips and then sharply inward for the long, unbroken line of her thigh. Her skin was smooth for a woman who must be in her fifties. Cathy pulled her eyes away from the mirror abruptly. Deidre was right. She shouldn't watch.

Cathy scooped up the small glasses with one hand. "Got 'em," she announced cheerfully.

She poured an inch for Lou, who gingerly sniffed at the lip of the bar glass.

Cathy laughed. "Not your poison? I picked it up last week in Kentucky." She tipped her glass toward the statue on the dresser. "Or would your boy there disapprove?"

Louise's frown made it clear that the Infant of Prague was off-limits for any sort of levity. "I thought you were from Vermont."

"Visiting a friend," Cathy said. She upended her glass and stared into its emptiness for a minute. "So, tell me more about the life of a beta reader. How did you get into it?"

Lou didn't seem anxious to respond. "My friend Maureen—she was a beta reader before I was—brought me some books. One of them was Heartwell's first novel, and I've been hooked ever since."

"On the Heartwell's? Or do you and Maureen read other titles?"

"I read anything the press sends me," Lou said crisply. "But Maureen?" Her voice assumed a wistful tone. "Well, she died recently. She was my best friend..."

Clearly, the pain was still fresh, evident in the sad anguish that subtly etched itself into the corners of Louise's eyes, even though she continued to hold her good-natured smile in place.

"I'm sorry," Cathy muttered. She placed her glass on the floor and unlaced her boots, ambivalent about the silence after all. She cleared her throat. "Looks like you've got quite a handful of pages there."

"Yes, about 275." Louise smiled, and listlessly riffled the stack beside her with her finger. "I'm nearly finished with it. The next one will probably keep me busy until we get back to New York."

"You'll forgive me for saying so," began Cathy, "but isn't that sort of romance narrative a bit on the lightweight side? I mean, it's not very intellectually challenging..."

"No, I suppose it isn't," Lou agreed. "But Maureen liked the work, and so do I. We were on the same bowling team."

She distractedly caressed the medallion around her neck. "She was a smart woman—a brilliant, wonderful woman."

The loving stroke made Cathy wonder whether the medal had been a gift from Maureen. Maybe a birthday gift or a token pressed into Lou's hand at Walter's funeral. Cathy chided herself for her curiosity; she was not usually one to trespass. "They're all the same, though, no? Pampered rich girl falls for bad boy even though she's committed to another man? In the end, the woman inevitably ditches her intended, reforms the scalawag, and falls into his arms." Cathy screwed the top onto the bourbon bottle. "Or some variation of that. I mean, seven books in three years? C'mon. That's not literature; that's pulp."

"There *is* a formula," Lou conceded. "And it's not like reading Proulx or Sontag. But some of the authors capture something powerful about romance. You know what they say—it's an escape."

Although Lou indulged the discussion, Cathy sensed that her thoughts were still with Maureen. "Right." She rubbed her knees and stood. "Maybe you'd like some privacy. I could go out to the Promenade Deck," she offered. "They've got some sort of telescope set up for the meteor shower…"

"She got sick quite suddenly and passed within a few months." A meager sparkle of tear increased Cathy's uneasiness. A meteor shower sounded like a lot more fun than Heartbreak Alley.

When Cathy returned to the cabin two hours later, Lou was in her pillow nest. As if she had anticipated drifting off, she was cozily buttoned into a white flannel nightshirt. Her mouth was agape, head fallen to the side. A manila envelope lay on her lap, undisturbed.

Cathy brushed her teeth and climbed into her own PJs, a light gown. The clear night and the telescope had combined to produce a spectacular show in the dark sky. It was a magnificent thing to see and feel and comprehend the depth of the world.

The tiny, razor-focused travel light she had clipped to her headboard was just what she needed. She reached for the volume of Woolf criticism and ran her fingertips over the cover. The first time she taught Woolf—twenty years earlier—her classroom of college seniors had insisted that gender issues were passé. For most of them, *A Room of One's Own* was a dreary, forced march, but for her, it had always read like fire.

Until last June, she had been used to reading two or three books a week; now, two or three pages a day sufficed, wearing her out with rereading each time she returned to her text. Still, she carried the books. How could she not? They had reflected her sensibilities, provided her a platform, and filled each crevice of her mind's life. She wouldn't abandon them now, and they wouldn't abandon her. It had been a long and affectionate marriage.

Her relationship with Falconer College, by contrast, was much more complicated. After twenty-five years and every possible award of distinction, her dismissal the previous summer had been discreet but resolute after she berated— and then failed—an entire senior seminar. She'd been given a chance to reverse her decision, naturally, since in all but one case, students required the course for graduation. But the students could not read. It wasn't that they couldn't read something especially challenging or something that *she* liked—she had a sterling reputation for being generous with her students and for not desiring admirers or clones. No, it was that they couldn't read *at all*. They had nonetheless managed to get through four years of college and now expected to be barcoded as "educated."

One by one, students were interviewed and asked to read from the assigned book; one by one, they confirmed the professor's claim. Highly embarrassed administrators, cajoled by angry parents, begged Cathy to reconsider, but when seven of Falconer's best did not graduate that May, there were headlines. So much for academic freedom.

And then in June came her diagnosis, the timing of which could not have been more fortuitous for administrators, who immediately exploited her illness. Letters of apology were mailed to the parents of the failed students. The professor was ill, the letter explained, and the mistake had been rectified. And then, in a repulsive act of hypocrisy, the administration flipped for a lavish party and retired her, emeritus.

Fuck them.

Whether she knew it or not, Lou snored. Not obnoxiously, but with a persistence that demanded respect—and, perhaps, ear plugs. But then, it was the first time Cathy had shared a bedroom with a woman in nearly five years. Deirdre had her flaws, to be sure, but snoring wasn't one of them. Cathy regarded Lou's low, semi-raspy voice as somewhat charming and actually kind of sexy. And her smile was, well, kind. But Harlequins—and the boy statue—annoyed her. Who was Maureen, anyway? Surely not a lover; at least, Louise didn't look the "type."

Cathy wondered if she should turn off the cabin light, which still glowed on the table between them. Oh, what the heck, the old girl was clearly out for the night. She got to her feet and deftly removed the manila envelope from Lou's lap and casually laid it on the edge of her own bed. As if she had done it a thousand times, Cathy pulled the comforter up from the foot of the bed and covered her roommate. Still asleep, Lou reacted to the blanket's sudden warmth; she shifted into a crouch, drew up her knees and turned toward the blank wall, away from Cathy.

She stared at Lou's folder, pretty sure that it didn't contain the manuscript of a Pulitzer winner. Yet, Cathy was curious. Whoever this Maureen was, she had a big enough impact, even after she was dead, to keep a seemingly intelligent woman fascinated by this schlock. When Lou's light snore confirmed her slumber, Cathy opened the folder and read.

The rare, half-hearted rainstorm that hung over the Atlantic on the fourth morning thwarted Cathy's plan to wrench Lou out of the cabin. The balcony door was open a crack, and a cool, damp breeze ruffled through the room.

Except for dinner that first evening, Lou spent the lion's share of three days so focused on her work that Cathy began to wonder why she had bothered to leave Port Dickens in the first place. But then it occurred to her that the reading might be all tied up with Maureen's recent demise, as though Lou needed to be in new space to accomplish an old task.

Lou emerged from the shower, wrapped in a bulky towel.

"I'm thinking of watching a movie," Cathy said. "I don't want to disturb your work. I can keep the volume low."

Louise scrabbled among the cosmetics on the dresser-top for her half-glasses. "What?"

"A movie." Cathy waved at the flickering TV screen. "Will the noise bother you?"

With a quick catch of herself, as if she might lose her balance, Louise leaned to her left as she brought her glasses to the bridge of her nose. "What are you watching?"

Cathy wiggled the remote in a sort of *tick tock* in her left hand. "I'm not exactly sure. It's in French." The flutter of black and white images over Cathy's shoulder barely made any noise at all. "I haven't quite mastered this contraption…"

"Toss it here," said Lou. "They charge for the in-room movies, too, you know. They're $11.95!"

"I guess I didn't read that in the brochure…" *Or did I?* Cathy couldn't remember just exactly what her payment covered on the trip. Before she'd left Vermont, her friend Violet (the only one who really understood, who had gone to the doctors' appointments with her, and who—even now—was watching over her rescue mutt, Petunia) had encouraged Cathy to deposit money in an onboard account. "That way," Violet had said, "You won't have to worry about the bar tab or the theater tickets. It'll be a breeze! Just say, 'Put it on my tab.' Easy-peasy."

Cathy was grateful for—and simultaneous annoyed with—her friend's helpfulness; she wasn't an invalid *yet* and didn't need Violet to treat her like one. The doctors had consistently reassured her that, with medication, Alzheimer's could be slowed to a snail's pace. She had plenty of time.

Cathy bent her arms and pressed them backward, uncoiling a mild tension. The TV's menu materialized.

"Except this classics channel," Lou continued. "These movies are free." She began to scroll. "Do you like old movies? Look, they've even got *It Happened One Night!* Have you ever seen it? Maureen and I must have watched it a hundred times!" Lou seemed fixated on the sleek black remote, her thumb purposeful and focused as she cued up the movie. The opening credits began to bleed across the plasma. "Is this all right?"

Cathy planted herself in the easy chair. "Sure. Why wouldn't it be all right?"

"Well, you don't seem to care much for romantic fiction, so I'm guessing you might also not care much for romantic comedies, that's all." Lou pitched the remote onto the table. "Let me get dressed."

She had already laid out her clothing—a pinstriped camp shirt, pink panties, pink bra, and dark capris. In a fairly immodest—and thoroughly unanticipated—act, Lou allowed her towel to fall to the floor, turned her backside to Cathy, and wiggled into her drawers and brassiere. Cathy could hardly help but notice how large her breasts were, pendulous and supple, tipped with small, delicate, rosy nipples. Lou seemed to study her blouse before pulling it on.

"Close the door?" Cathy asked, gesturing to the sliding glass.

As Lou tugged the stubborn door, the vertical blinds rattled, and she wrapped the blinds' draw-cord loosely across her palm and gave it a yank. "It's better in the dark, don't you think?"

Cathy chuckled at the double entendre. "I usually think so, yes," she said as Lou settled into the patterned love seat and propped her feet up on the coffee table before them.

"Okay," Lou announced. "Ready when you are."

Cathy delicately nudged the remote away from its spot next to Lou's ankle and hit the *play* button.

They watched the first half hour of the movie until the television cut out. Patiently, they waited for their connection to be restored.

"Why did you come alone?" Lou had cocked her elbow on the arm of her chair and rested her cheek in her hand.

The question seemed to come out of nowhere. "Why *wouldn't* I? I'm not afraid to travel by myself."

Lou wiggled her toes back and forth in thought. "I just mean, I don't know many details about you other than that you taught history at Falconer College." She yawned. "Are you on break?"

"Retired," Cathy said flatly. "But you didn't ask why I'm here *now*. You asked why I'm here *alone*."

Lou grinned. "Caught me," she said. "I'm just curious. Is there a partner somewhere back in Vermont?"

Partner. Peculiar word choice for a straight woman. "Nope. I answer to no one."

"But you *did*."

"I did."

"What was her name?"

Cathy fiddled with the remote in an attempt to bring back the movie. *So, the Harlequin beta reader is perceptive.* "Deidre," she finally said.

Cathy's response didn't seem to disconcert Lou. "How long?"

Cathy shrugged, as though she didn't quite know the answer. "Five years, give or take." The ensuing silence was large and cumbersome. "And Maureen?" she asked. "Were you and Maureen…"

"Involved?" Lou finished, as though she considered the question mechanical, part of an interminably boring scene. She inhaled and cast her eyes upward. "Well, yes and no."

Cathy cocked her head and looked at Lou. "More 'yes' or more 'no'?"

Lou let out a light, genial laugh. "Caught me again. Pretty dumb thing to say, huh? I know that's supposed to be a simple question."

Lou's comment, however blithe, poked at Cathy. She was well aware that the *social* question was not always the same as the *sexual* one; it was not, for everyone, a "yes/no" proposition. But still, she generally identified women who couldn't answer that question (neatly) as equivocal and expedient. At the very least, she deemed them confused. Inexplicably, though, she resisted that handy conclusion about Lou.

"It's not always simple," Cathy grudgingly acknowledged. It was worth some teeth-gritting to get Lou to expound. This elegant, bereaved, trashy fiction reader—who *was* she? And what, for Lou, clouded the answer to a question that deserved absolute clarity?

"No." Lou looked sad. "Not at all."

Cathy considered jumping in to fill in the silence but thought better of it.

"Maureen and I were 'just friends,'" Lou continued, as she marked the space with her fingers, "for a very long time. Maybe fifteen years. Figuring out that it was more than a friendship took most of that time." She grinned. "But I'm pretty sure I figured it out when I preferred

Maureen's company to Walter's—by far—and when I started daydreaming about her. Hell, I searched the paper for groups we could join, just because I couldn't stand to be away from her." Lou laughed. "Once, I even forced her to take a dog grooming class so I could spend Wednesday evenings with her. And we didn't have any dogs!"

Cathy shifted in her seat. "Is it time for bourbon?" she joked.

"It's only eleven o'clock!" Lou exclaimed. "Anyway, I forced Maureen to join my trivia team. That covered Thursday evenings." Lou's eyes teared up. "I just couldn't live without her. But then, one evening—about a year ago—she was at my house, and we were reading one of the manuscripts. And we decided, for a laugh, to act out one of the scenes that seemed particularly hilarious."

"And?"

"And I kissed her. She kissed me back, and we clumsily made love—it was the first time for both of us—and we had a fabulous six months after that. We had just started talking about living together when she was diagnosed with melanoma. She died about four months later. Not much pain, physically, but in the end, she didn't know me. That was the worst part, watching her fade into the distance, just like New York when we left the harbor. It was excruciating to be forgotten." Lou stretched her toes to touch Cathy's.

Lou was right. Cathy found it terrifying to think about the decline of her cognitive function. And it had already started—misplacing things, unable to read for long periods, and more recently, unable to recall her dog's name. Of course, it eventually came to her, standing in her kitchen with the smelly can of Alpo as she searched her brain for the word that would bring the wiry terrier mix to his bowl. But when I go, thought Cathy, no one will be standing at the rail.

"Sounds like you loved her very much," said Cathy.

"People always say 'move on'—so easy to say—but they never seem to have any suggestions about how to do that."

"Well, it's cliché, of course, but what about another relationship?"

Lou pursed her lips. "I'm not sure. Maureen's death is so recent. But I admit, I hate to think of that part of my life as over. What about you?"

Cathy shook her head. "No intention of pursuing anyone."

"You sound sure about that."

"I have health problems myself," she said quickly. "Early onset Alzheimer's. Medication slows it down, so they say. I have two or three more years of clear thinking, but eventually I'll lose my mental faculties." She briefly gave her skull a lackluster tap with a finger. "So it hardly seems fair to put somebody in that position, although I agree—I hate to think that part of my life is over."

"Oh, Cathy! I'm so sorry. What an awful burden," Lou mused. "You know, it's strange. You just said you have two or three years of *clear* thinking, and you connected that to fairness. And I was considering the same thing—only in reverse—just yesterday. I figure I have two or three years of *muddled* thinking—to get over Maureen, I mean. But we came to same conclusion. It wouldn't be a decent thing to do, and yet, where does that leave us?"

The rain continued unabated throughout the early afternoon, and the movie could not be resurrected. Lou took advantage of a minor lull in their back-and-forth to begin her packing. They agreed that a room service pizza was preferable to standing in line at yet another buffet.

"You've got all tomorrow morning to pack," Cathy reminded her.

"Ah, but you see, I have a plan!" Lou continued, untangling a couple of wire hangers. "If I pack now, then tomorrow morning I'll be able to squeeze in a couple of hours in the casino. Did I tell you I won sixty-three dollars yesterday?" Lou paused, and scrutinized the lacy camisole in her hands, as if she were unsure if it were clean or not.

Cathy dialed the kitchen but was immediately placed on hold. She waited and restlessly dug her hand into her pocket. From the corner of her eye, she saw Lou quickly snatch the Infant of Prague from the dresser. Again, she kissed His porcelain face briefly, then wrapped Him in the camisole, and tucked Him safely into her suitcase.

Several times throughout the afternoon, the women reminded themselves that it was their last full day at sea and that they really should go above deck, yet neither of them moved toward the door. The persistent drizzle, they agreed, made the prospect unattractive. But when the sun peeked through the blinds and Lou reported, with some shock, that it was four o'clock, they each marveled at how the day had nearly disappeared.

Somewhere during the afternoon, the toes that touched had expanded to include ankles, and the room had become a lazy tangle of convivial laughter and eye-catching. The talk was smooth and even, resistant to the gutter of past pain or future plans.

Twice—maybe three times—Cathy felt that a kiss was in the making. Their cozy gabfest had been too close—too intimate—to simply leave behind without gesture. She wondered whether Lou would invite her to move to the love seat or contrive some equally awkward act. But she underestimated Lou's capacity for forthright disclosure.

Lou dabbed at her mouth with a napkin, leaned forward, elbows on knees, and bit her lip. She seemed to be falter for the next thing to say. Cathy noticed that the pewter medallion was still safely at rest between Lou's breasts.

"I'd like to make love with you," Lou said. Straightforward and unapologetic, her statement momentarily stunned Cathy.

"We hardly know each other." Cathy stumbled over her thoughts. "One conversation—even a *great* one—isn't enough..." She searched for the right word.

"Context?" Lou suggested.

Cathy nodded.

"Maybe this *is* the context. I'm obviously not over Maureen, and I can't 'go on' and create context with someone else out of thin air. For your own reasons, you don't feel able to develop context with anyone, either." Lou seemed pensive. "But we *could* remind each other that we're alive right now. Just right now."

Lou's gaze was searching and charmingly, seductively authentic.

Their lovemaking was fierce and unceremonious.

Without prelude, they pushed aside the pizza box and cracked the balcony door. Lou swiveled the cord of the vertical blinds to allow splinters of sun to em-dash the wall, and Cathy double-locked the cabin door. In silence, they stripped to their underthings and dragged back the comforter from Cathy's bed before slipping between the sheets. Each propped on an elbow, they stared at one another.

For the first time, perhaps, Cathy thought, she was able to take in her cabinmate's features close up. Lou's bright, round countenance consisted of an effervescent smile, made all the more fetching by an inconsequential crowding of her lower teeth and supple mouth framed by lips that pulled out at the corners. Her blue-gray eyes were unremarkable except for their large irises, flecked with miniscule black cinders, as if a tiny explosion had taken place behind her corneas.

Lou was not beautiful. But there was something strong and vulnerable in her hopeful face, something eager and still serene, something troubled yet tranquil.

They didn't talk.

Lou, who had been so chatty all day, had placed a finger to her lips to insist on quiet, and then reached for Cathy's jaw to draw their mouths together. The softness of her kiss was startling, and Cathy immediately opened her mouth and pulled Lou's tongue inside. Lou placed her hand on Cathy's sternum, her fingertips imprinting over her heart.

Cathy jostled herself closer, looped her arm across Lou's ribs, and busied her hand at the task of unsnapping Lou's bra. The garment flew away, swung aside to the floor, and Lou's breasts spilled into the space between them. Cupped in her hand, Cathy fondled the swell and curve and sweep of flesh, and circled her over a hardening nipple; it wrinkled with arousal at her pinch. Then Cathy discarded her own bra, and pressed herself against Lou; her mouth and tongue focused on Lou's eyelids and cheeks. Between the mash of their breasts, Cathy felt a fusion of heat and friction.

Lou pushed Cathy to her back and quickly straddled her, her hands on Cathy's wrists, her breasts swaying above Cathy's mouth. Cathy obliged her, drawing in first one breast, then the other, and Lou groaned and threw her head back, then dropped it forward, stuffing Cathy's mouth. She released the wrists, and raked her fingers through Cathy's hair, its tangles suffused with sweat.

They wrestled for nearly an hour, first one on top, then the other, their hands and legs a skein neither wanted to unravel, their mouths searching for yet another inch of unwet skin, their fingers reaching deep into the dark clefts of excitement, hips grinding, hearts pounding, thighs tested and wrapped and crushing.

"I can't wait anymore," whispered Lou as a trickle of perspiration escaped her temple.

Cathy grasped her shoulders and pushed her up and away. "Then don't," she said, as she shifted her ass downward and spread her legs.

Lou tasted like the cool sweetness of a river.

Cathy awoke to the sound of the cabin door closing. She rubbed the sleep from her eyes, unwilling to rise. Lou was gone. *Oh shit, what had she done? Exploited the grief and loneliness of an almost complete stranger to soothe her own self-pity?* The encounter had been spontaneous and sober, and neither of them had offered the other any promises of undying love and commitment. It was just sex—raw and hot and affirming.

Still, Lou had exited the room without a word. Was she upset?

A shower, Cathy thought. I need a shower. She sat up and cast her eyes about the room. Her jeans and shirt remained in a compressed silo on the floor; somewhere—she extended her legs and poked around under the jumble of sheets—she knew, her panties had been nudged deep underneath the sheets.

The clatter of room service plates and silver came from the hallway; she glanced to the door and noticed two sheets of paper. Undoubtedly, the invoices for their outstanding charges, as well as a reminder to gather their belongings. The ship was due to return to New York by one in the afternoon.

A shower, a quick breakfast, Cathy resolved again, as she hauled her limbs across the mattress. Then she'd pack, stuff her trusty backpack with her dirty duds, and make her grateful good-byes to Lou. All in all, Lou had been a decent roommate, and the sex had been a bonus. No, more than a bonus, she admitted; it had been a precious, albeit unforeseen, gift.

She picked up her books—mostly untouched during the voyage—and selected a slim volume near the bottom of the stack, allowing the others to tumble to the bed. It was *A Room of One's Own*—the very copy she had used for over twenty years—dog-eared and margin-noted and definitely the worse for wear. "Women and fiction," the book's ostensible theme, suddenly struck Cathy as entirely fitting for Lou—the lively, honest reader of fiction.

The theme worked as well, if more subtly, for their encounter, she thought; what was their lovemaking but an example of women and their many fictions? She glanced at Lou's Samsonite next to the door. *Why not? Being forgotten really must be a horrible thing.* On her way out, she tucked the book into the bottom of Lou's bag.

The breakfast of waffles and bacon, grapefruit juice and coffee was not spectacular, but it hit the spot. The dining room was filled with robust, delightful laughter, and one table of guests spontaneously broke into an Irish folksong. Although she had eaten alone, Cathy felt welcome and warm, especially after being asked to join a table of four fat ladies in pink-collared sweatshirts emblazoned with the ace of hearts and *The Bettin' Bitches* scrawled across their ample chests. Declining the invitation had been pro forma, but the ladies' chatter breezed across the space between their tables. Cathy nodded at them as she pushed her chair away from her table and headed for the exit.

On her way back to her stateroom, she ducked inside the large, windowless gift shop to peruse the mostly made-in-China offerings—seashell necklaces, nautical caps, Hawaiian shirts, flip-flops, towels, and tote bags. Somewhere, she hoped to snag a portfolio of postcards, which Violet, who collected the gaudy pictures, would appreciate. She spied Lou at a carousel of keychains.

"Hey," Cathy said.

Lou fingered a row of tiny surfers encased in a slosh of suspicious, oily liquid in Lucite. "Maureen would like this one." She prodded the chains into a cheerful jingle. "She loves kitschy crap like this."

Present tense. She's talking about Maureen as if she doesn't even remember that Maureen is dead. "You were gone when I woke up." Cathy sighed. "Are you all right?"

"I'm just trying to find something to take home," said Lou. She moved her hand to another row of bobbing palm trees. "I'm good."

"Should we talk?" Cathy asked, her voice low and hurried.

Lou's smile was bemused. "I don't think so. I've asked Ramon to get my bags, and I'm going to hit the slots until we land." She tilted her head slyly. "It's my last chance to gamble."

Cathy swayed for a moment on her feet. So, Lou had been serious after all. There wasn't to be a tearful goodbye, any wrenching regret, or declarations of love. Briefly, she fixated on the word *intimacy* and all of the private, energetic, captivating excitement and magnetism it implied. Impulsively, she reached for Lou's upper arm and turned her toward her. "I feel like we should say more," she whispered.

Lou raised an eyebrow. "We talked about this last night, remember? It's okay, really. What happened was wonderful and spontaneous and comforting." Lou lowered her voice and grinned. "And terribly sexy." She patted Cathy's hand. "When I got on this ship, I wondered if my life was over. But now? I'm not so sure, after all. I'm grateful I got to spend the week with you. But you're going back to Vermont, and I'm going back to Port Dickens." She leaned into Cathy's ear. "Thank you."

"It's just, it seems like—" Cathy sputtered.

"Don't," Lou insisted. "You'll make your own cloth of it, no? What it meant to you, I mean. Even if you forget, it still happened, Cathy. It *happened*."

Cathy released Lou's arm and looked down at her boots. "I enjoyed feeling my mind," she acknowledged and then glanced at Lou with a wink. "And other things."

"See? It was important for both of us. A real moment. But solitary."

"Right," Cathy nodded. "It was real. Not fiction."

"Not fiction." Lou's laugh was full of gentle light. "Let's leave the romance to Heartwell." Lou gave the carousel another languid spin; it stopped at the row of dangling surfers again. She plucked one off the rack. "This one," she said again. "I think Maureen would like this one…"

Cathy stuffed her hands into her pockets and stared. The surfer bobbed in its little plastic world, alone on its slippery wave. "Yeah," she said. "She probably would."

SEX SELLS

BY JAE

KILLING SOMEONE NEVER GOT ANY easier. In fact, it got harder every time. Mara had thought about how to off Sue for days, but nothing she'd come up with sounded right.

Shoot her?

No, that was lame—and a bit too messy. Slitting her throat or stabbing her were out for the same reasons.

What about pushing her off a cliff? Mara gnawed on the end of her pen and considered it for a moment.

Tempting, but it had been done to death already—no pun intended.

Hire a hit man?

Not personal enough. Plus a professional killer would do it quickly and with a minimal amount of suffering, and that wasn't what Mara wanted. Not for this particular victim. After cheating on her just when Mara had thought the relationship might be going somewhere, Sue deserved a more gruesome death.

Mara leaned back in her seat and swirled her spoon through the foam left over at the bottom of her mug. Normally, the soothing background noise of clinking ceramic cups, the hiss of an espresso machine, and the murmur of conversations inspired her, but today even the familiar sounds did nothing for her.

She wanted to kill the noisy group of tourists who apparently presumed the other customers wanted to hear every word of their conversation. But then again, she'd have to find an effective murder method first. The loud hip-hop music blaring from the earbuds of the teenager slouched at the table next to hers didn't exactly help either.

She sent him a glare. Maybe electrocution would work. Could you get zapped into the great beyond by your cell phone or MP3 player?

Probably not. Besides, she'd already killed someone off with electricity. No. She needed something else. Something unique.

Sighing, she dropped the spoon into her empty mug. She needed another caramel macchiato. Hey, could that be the perfect method she was looking for? Was there such a thing as caffeine poisoning?

Her cell phone rang before she could get herself another coffee. She fished her cell phone out of her backpack and flipped open the protective cover. Her mood instantly improved when she saw the name on the display—Hayley Wheeler.

"Can you die of a caffeine overdose?" Mara asked instead of a greeting.

A moment of silence filtered through the connection.

"Good morning to you too. I'm doing just fine, thanks for asking." Despite the mild rebuke, Hayley's sexy voice was laced with humor.

"Good morning," Mara repeated dutifully. "How's my favorite editor today?"

"I'd be flattered if I didn't know for a fact that there's not exactly a lot of competition in that category."

"Details, details. Okay, you're my only editor, but you'd still be my favorite even if I had a dozen."

"I'd better be, since I single-handedly saved the main character in your last book from wearing a T-shit instead of a T-shirt."

"Hardy-har-har," Mara said. "I will hear that until I fall face-first onto my keyboard and croak, won't I?"

"Oh yeah. You bet you will."

Mara groaned, but the familiar banter still made her smile. God, she loved a woman with a sense of humor and a way with words. Add to that a killer smile and a good command of grammar and syntax, and Mara was a goner. Too bad that this particular woman was her editor—and Mara wasn't even sure she was gay. Chances were she was either a lesbian or bi, considering she edited lesbian fiction for a living and had even put together a pretty hot lesbian erotica anthology last year. But it wasn't a sure thing, and Mara had never managed to come up with an inconspicuous way of finding out. How did you ask the person whose gently wielded red pen had helped garner you a half dozen literary awards if she might possibly be interested in women?

Mara's overactive imagination immediately presented a scenario where she sent Hayley an e-mail saying, *Do you think I should cut the prologue and start with the detective's point of view? Should that sentence at the beginning of chapter eighteen have a comma or a semicolon? Oh, and while I'm asking you questions... Are you gay?*

Nope. Out of the question. Mara switched her cell phone to the other ear. "So, what about that caffeine overdose? Do you think a grown woman could die of it?"

"No," Hayley said without hesitation. "Trust me. If that were possible, I'd have shuffled off this mortal coil at least an hour ago."

Christ, now she's quoting Shakespeare. Mara tried not to swoon and instead focused on what else Hayley had said. Her tone had been lighthearted enough, but after two years, four novels, two dozen video calls via Skype, and more e-mails than Mara could count, she knew Hayley well enough to detect the undercurrent of frustration in her voice. "Rough day?"

"Just a tight deadline for a new manuscript from a first-time author."

Some of the writers in Mara's critique group were newbies, so she knew how time-consuming and exhausting editing a debut novel could be. "Ugh. I don't know how you do it. All those dragging openings, heaps of adjectives, info dumps, and point-of-view violations..." Mara shuddered. "I think I'd be ready to commit hari-kari with my red pen after the first chapter."

"It's hara-kiri," Hayley said, making Mara smile.

God, she's so predictable. Predictable, but cute. Even the occasional text messages Hayley sent her used perfect grammar and proper punctuation. None of them ended with a string of acronyms such as *C U l8r*—unfortunately.

"Fine," Mara said. "I'd commit hara-kiri, then."

"Most manuscripts aren't that bad. I actually find it pretty rewarding to mentor our newbies and help them grow as writers."

That was typically Hayley. She never complained or gossiped about any of Mara's fellow writers, even the ones who deserved it. The woman was the epitome of professionalism.

Mara admired that about her, but it probably also meant that Hayley would never start a relationship with one of the authors in her charge, even if she was a lesbian.

"And every now and then, I get to work on a truly excellent manuscript," Hayley added. "Like yours."

Even knowing she probably looked like a Cheshire cat on an ecstasy high, Mara couldn't help grinning as if she'd just won the Pulitzer Prize for Fiction. "Flattery will get you everywhere." She paused. *Are we flirting? Or just joking around?* She wasn't quite sure.

Hayley cleared her throat. A creaking sound drifted through the cell phone, and Mara imagined Hayley leaning back in her office chair, the blouse stretching over her generous breasts. Good thing Hayley didn't suspect that she had inspired not just the description of Mara's latest heroine but also several late-night fantasies.

"So," Hayley said, "why are you asking about lethal caffeine doses? Are you overindulging in that five-hundred-calorie milkshake you call coffee again?"

Mara peeked at her empty mug. It had been her third. *Busted.* When had Hayley gotten to know her so well?

"Don't worry about the caffeine," Hayley said. "All the sugar in those things will kill you long before the caffeine does."

Mara sighed. "That's not why I'm asking. It's for the new book. I'm trying to come up with a halfway creative plot."

"And?"

"Zero, zip, zilch, nada, niente, rien, niets, nichts—"

Hayley laughed. "Okay, okay. I get it. Stop showing off your language skills."

Well, how else was she supposed to impress a woman who made her living with words? "Everything I thought of so far seems either lame or I've already used it in one of my previous novels. I need something fresh. I don't want to be one of those writers who basically write the same book over and over again."

"Agreed. Actually, I've been thinking about that too."

"You have?" God, Hayley would be the perfect woman for her. She lived in an imaginary world populated by fictional people for most of the day too and would understand when Mara started to scribble on napkins during dinner dates. She would probably even chime right in when Mara complained about the plot holes in the movies they watched. The same couldn't be said for Sue, the ex-girlfriend from hell.

"Of course," Hayley said. "As your editor, I have a vested interest in your continued success."

Was it really just that? Mara wanted to believe that they had become friends and Hayley wanted her to succeed for personal reasons too. "So, what do you suggest?"

"I love your mysteries. I really do. But I think you should consider...branching out a little. Make your stories a little... sexier."

The combination of Hayley's voice—smooth, silky, and confident—and her saying the word *sexier* distracted Mara for a moment. She nearly missed the meaning of her words.

"You want me to write a...a...*romance* novel?"

Hayley huffed out a breath. "Don't make it sound as if I asked you to write a trashy dime-store novel that involves a lot of damsels in distress, heaving bosoms, and moist love caves."

Mara burst out laughing. *Love caves?* Had any of Hayley's writers ever used that term in a manuscript? She was almost afraid to ask. "I don't know. Even without the heaving bosoms and the love caves…"

"Come on. Putting a little romance in your books wouldn't be that bad, would it?"

"Not that bad?" Mara's voice ended on a squeak. "Hayley, I kill people for a living!"

"On paper. Jesus, Mara, if you keep saying it like that, I'll have to bail you out of jail. Do I really have to remind you of what happened when you called the poison control hotline and asked how many belladonna berries were needed to kill a two-hundred-pound man?"

Heat flooded Mara's face. Just like the little T-shit mishap, she'd never live that down. She peeked up from her notebook. Several patrons of the coffee shop were now staring at her as if she were Ted Bundy, Jeffrey Dahmer, and Jack the Ripper all rolled into one. *Great.*

Loud enough for everyone to hear, Mara said, "I'm a mystery writer. I write police procedurals and murder mysteries. I don't do," she lowered her voice, now speaking just to Hayley, "sex. I mean, sex scenes."

"They're called love scenes, not sex scenes."

"Same thing," Mara grumbled.

"No, it's not the same thing at all. Love scenes are an expression of the characters' feelings for each other. It's all about emotional intimacy, even if, on occasion, it might be hard and fast and up against a wall."

Mara tugged on the neck of her T-shirt as heat pulsed through her body. *Jesus, Hayley!*

"Whereas a sex scene—"

"I know, I know." If she didn't stop Hayley, she would overheat and her attentive audience would call an ambulance because they thought she was having a stroke or something.

"Besides," Hayley said, "not all romance novels need to have a love scene, despite what some people might think, if that's why you're so reluctant to try writing one."

Wonderful. Now Hayley thought she was a prude. "That's not it. Really. I have nothing against sex. I mean sex scenes. Love scenes. Jesus." No other woman had ever managed to fluster her like this without even being in the same room—without *ever* having been in the same room.

A soft chuckle drifted through the line.

The erotic sound made Mara flush even more. She fanned herself with her notepad. By now, half of the coffee shop's patrons were probably listening in on their conversation. If any of the laptop-equipped people at the nearby tables were fellow novelists or, worse, comedians, she was providing them with some first-class dialogue. "I'm fine with love scenes," she said as calmly as she could. "It's just... I don't know. Romances are just not my thing."

Hayley was quiet for a moment. "On the page...or in real life?"

Mara's mouth went dry. In the two years they'd been working together, Hayley had never asked her such a personal question. Was she just trying to deepen her understanding of the woman behind M.C. McKinney, award-winning author of lesbian mystery novels, or did she have a personal interest in the answer?

"Sorry," Hayley said, interrupting the rare silence between them. "I shouldn't have asked that."

"No, no, it's fine." The last thing Mara wanted was for Hayley to think her private life was off-limits. If it were up to her, Hayley would *be* her private life. "When it comes to real life, I'm a big fan of romance. Admittedly, I haven't had

much success in that department lately. My last girlfriend...
Well, let's just say I had my reasons for naming my next
murder victim after her."

That should let Hayley know she was single and a lesbian,
right? Just in case Hayley hadn't read her author's bio.

Hayley chuckled. "Ouch. Let me guess... She dies a
horrible, excruciatingly slow, very painful death?"

"That's for sure. I just haven't figured out the details of
her demise yet."

"Nail gun?" Hayley suggested.

"Oooh! That has definite possibilities." Mara scribbled it
down on her notepad, underlined it twice, and drew a large
exclamation mark next to it. "Sounds like you've got an ex
or two you wouldn't mind killing off too."

Hayley gave a noncommittal hum. "Don't we all?"

Mara waited, but Hayley left it at that. *Damn.* No
mention of the ex's gender or whether Hayley was single too.

"Listen, Mara..."

God, she loved the way her name sounded coming from
Hayley's lips. She made the dot of the exclamation mark into
a little heart, then scrunched up her face and crossed it out.
Maybe she should try her hand at a romance novel after all.
She had the cheesy stuff down pat.

"I don't want to change your style or talk you into
writing something you're not comfortable with. If writing a
romance isn't for you, that's just fine. That wasn't what I was
suggesting anyway."

"Then what were you suggesting?"

"Have you ever considered romantic suspense novels?"
Hayley asked.

"Romantic suspense?" Mara drew out each syllable.

Another hum from Hayley. Somehow, she managed to make even that sound sexy. "Yeah. Or, in your case, romantic mystery. You could still have a mystery with dangerous criminals, nail-biting tension, and clever police work; you'd just add a romantic subplot."

"If it's not that different from what I've been writing, why try a new genre?"

"Easy. Sex sells."

"I thought they're called love scenes, not sex scenes."

"Touché." Hayley's tone revealed that she was smiling. "But you know what I mean. Lesbian readers prefer contemporary romance novels. Even established authors of mysteries like you will never sell as many copies as someone who writes romances or romantic suspense."

Mara knew that all too well. Her bank account knew it too. Some months, she had to take on copywriting jobs for local companies so she wouldn't have to go back to her day job. So far, she had never considered changing what she wrote just to make more money, and she didn't want to do it now, but maybe Hayley was right. There were only so many ways to kill a person. If she wanted to keep her writing fresh, she had to think of something else.

Giving Detective Walker a girlfriend might be an option. It would humanize her, make it easier for readers to identify with the workaholic detective, and provide a nice source of internal conflict. And if she included a little romance in her manuscripts, at least she would be able to live vicariously through her characters since her own love life was nonexistent. She could even model the love interest of the Hayley-inspired detective after herself. She shook her head at herself. Okay, maybe she wouldn't go that far.

"I know it's not fair," Hayley said. "But it's just the reality of lesbian fiction publishing, and I hate to see you struggle. You deserve a much wider audience."

Mara smiled. Hayley never failed to let her know how much she liked her writing, handing out praise along with constructive criticism, but it was still nice to hear it again. "Could I still kill off Sue?" Mara finally asked.

Hayley laughed that special laugh of hers, the one that had gotten Mara the first time they'd talked on the phone and that always made her smile in reflex. "We could put it in the publishing contract if you want."

"No, thanks. I trust you."

The laughter stopped. "Thank you," Hayley said, her tone now serious. "Thank you for hearing me out. Even if you end up not following my suggestion, that means a lot."

Mara didn't know what to say to that. *What? The great author is speechless?*

"You don't have to decide right now," Hayley said when Mara remained silent. "Think about it for a while. We can talk about it some more when we see each other next month."

Next month. The mere mention sent a tingle through Mara's body. They would both attend a lesbian fiction conference in Washington, D.C., and meet in person for the very first time. After having a crush on Hayley for nearly two years, the thought of coming face to face with her was equally exciting and terrifying. What if Hayley didn't live up to her expectations?

Mara suppressed a snort. As if. It was more likely that she would embarrass herself in front of three hundred and fifty lesbians—including her colleagues, beta readers, and critique partners—by confessing her undying love for her editor up on stage should she receive another award.

"All right," Mara said. "See you at the GCLS con, then."

"Right. And if you need anything before then, call me."

Anything? Did that include a date for the dance on the last night of the conference? Mara didn't dare ask. *Chicken. And you write bone-chilling mysteries for a living? Bah! Pathetic.* "Does that include...?" She took a deep breath. *Come on. Be a woman. Ask her out! What have you got to lose?*

"Yes?" Hayley prompted.

Mara clutched the edge of the table. "Does your offer include...? Well, I was wondering..."

"Yes?"

"Could we maybe...? I mean, would you have time to get together during the con to brainstorm ideas for unique murder methods with me? I'll even buy the coffee. Don't worry—black, no sugar. None of that five-hundred-calorie milkshake or those other horrendous additions that destroy a perfectly good cup of coffee for you."

Not hesitating for a second, Hayley said, "It's a date."

"Great. I will—" Mara snapped her mouth shut. Had Hayley just said...date? *Don't read anything into it, dummy. It's just a figure of speech.*

But Hayley made a living by choosing the right words in the right place. She wouldn't have said it if she didn't mean it, would she?

Mara's cell phone chose that exact moment to start beeping, indicating that the battery was about to die. No, no, no. Not now! "Oh, crap."

Beep, beep, beep.

"If you'd rather keep things strictly professional, I understand." Hayley sighed. "I just thought..."

"No!" Mara's heart beat so loudly that it drowned out the annoying beeping of her cell phone. "I mean, yes! I'd love to have coffee with you...as a date, not just a business meeting."

Only silence answered.

"Hayley? Are you still there?"

No answer.

Mara moved the cell phone away from her ear and stared at the dark display. "Shit! You stupid piece of technology!" She slapped the phone's leather cover closed with more force than necessary and stuffed it into her backpack along with her notepad.

If she ever included a romantic subplot in one of her novels and kept the two potential lovers apart by having the goddamn phone die, her readers would accuse her of relying on contrived coincidences.

The woman next to her got up, scraping the chair legs across the floor.

Yeah. Great. Show's over, so now you can leave. No happy ending today. Mara got up too. No reason to stay. She wouldn't get any work done now anyway. Not after this. She would go home and call Hayley back...if she didn't chicken out. Hayley might not even pick up if she thought Mara had hung up on her.

Instead of walking toward the exit, the woman from the neighboring table stepped up to Mara and held out her phone. "Here. Use mine."

"What?" Mara stared at her.

A flush crept up the woman's neck. She shuffled her feet. "Sorry. I couldn't help overhearing part of your conversation. You should call him back before he thinks you're not interested."

"Her," Mara said automatically.

The stranger shrugged. "Then call *her* back." She nodded down at the phone on her outstretched hand.

Mara stared back and forth between the woman's face and the phone for a moment longer before hastily reaching for the device. "Thank you."

Usually, she relied on speed dial, but there were two phone numbers she knew by heart—the pizza delivery service in her neighborhood and Hayley's cell.

Quickly, she typed in the number and lifted the phone to her ear.

It rang for quite a while.

Just when Mara thought Hayley's voice mail would pick up, that familiar sexy voice came through the line.

"Yes?" Hayley sounded cautious.

"It's me…Mara. Sorry, my battery died. Did you…um… hear what I said before the damn thing gave up the ghost?"

"No. The last thing I heard you say was *no*." For a few moments, no sound at all filtered through the phone, as if Hayley had even stopped breathing. "What else did you say?"

Mara smiled. "Well, since you want me to write a romantic suspense, I'll need a little more help with the book than I usually do."

"Of course. What kind of help do you need?" Still that cautious tone. "Brainstorming murder methods, as you said?"

"No. I can handle those. But I might need a little help researching the romantic part of the novel." Mara clutched the cell phone so tightly that her knuckles blanched and the woman next to her gave her an alarmed look.

"Oh," Hayley said after a while. "Sure. I mean, that's what we editors are there for, right? To help with whatever you need."

Mara was about to agree. It was easier to keep joking and hide behind a lighthearted tone and their familiar roles. But then she paused. Unlike her manuscripts, life couldn't be revised afterward if you didn't get it right the first time. And she wanted to get this right more than she'd wanted anything in a very long time. "Hayley?"

"Yes?"

"I'm not talking to the editor."

"I know. It wasn't the editor who agreed to help you with the romantic part of your novel."

Mara stood still for a moment, then hopped up and down like a preschooler who'd just been promised a visit to the zoo. "So you'll have coffee with me?"

"Like I said: it's a date."

A wave of giddiness swept over Mara, and now she could no longer resist teasing Hayley just the tiniest bit. "Shouldn't it be 'as I said'?"

"Smartass."

Yes, but I'm your smartass, Mara wanted to answer, but it was a little too soon for that. If she was patient, she might be able to say it one day.

After all, they were an award-winning writer and an experienced editor. Between them, they should be able to create the perfect happy ending.

FAUX PAS
BY ANASTASIA VITSKY

"I can't get the hook unfastened," Ally called from the bedroom. She rolled her right arm backward and squeezed her shoulder blades together in an effort to reach the tiny metal fasteners in the back of her undergarment. "Ow!" She'd put so much effort into this surprise, but the stupid clothing threatened to defeat her. Who knew sexy could be this difficult?

In the living room, a rat-tat-tat on their battered desktop computer signaled her wife hard at work. "Three thousand words!" Gia crowed. "I'm going to finish this chapter tonight!"

"I got a new panty and bra at Victoria's Secret this afternoon." Ally tried to make her voice seductive as she stroked the satin cups, pulled her hair to one side, and propped a bare heel on the edge of their mattress. She'd bathed and dabbed her favorite green-tea perfume behind each ear. Having a wife work from home had sounded great until Ally realized her wife never *left* work. Not even for a fifty-percent-off lingerie set Gia had admired for weeks. She'd complained about Ally's worn-out bras but couldn't be bothered to see the replacements.

"Shh…" Random profanities echoed through the still, unfriendly house. "No! You can't do this to me! The wheel of death! I didn't save my last chapter! Let me smash you against the wall and whack your brains out."

"Rather inelegantly expressed." Ally sashayed to the doorway, wondering whether she should abandon her plans for the night. Nothing attracted Gia's attention during NaNoWriMo. "I wanted impact play, but if you prefer to take me…"

"What?" Dark shadows under Gia's eyes made her look like a confused panda. "If I don't get this chapter back to my editor by tomorrow morning…oh. Oh, my." She leaned back in her chair, eyes widening at Ally with her red-satin glory.

"That's what we've come to? Oh, my?" Ally straddled the chair and bent over to wiggle her bottom in Gia's face.

"What, are you going to twerk?" Gia laughed and patted the tiny bit of fabric.

"Read, Ms. Writer," Ally ordered, trying to ignore the churning in her stomach. She was biting off more than she could chew, but she couldn't back down now. She'd spent too long poring over Gia's scenes of perfectly choreographed, mutually satisfying sex. Gia's characters always began with a long, sizzling spanking that led to torn clothes and record numbers of successive orgasms.

Ally had considered her strategy before deciding on the direct approach. Emblazoned across the back of her panties were the words, *Spank me.*

"What? I'm not going to…" Gia dropped her voice. "*Spank* you. That's crazy."

"You write it," Ally pointed out.

"Because it sells! No one reads plain erotica anymore. It's all toys and…"

Bored with marketing talk, Ally braced her hands on the dark gray carpet and gyrated in what she hoped was a suggestive manner. Instead, she bumped into the armrest and pushed the wheeled chair toward the desk. Coffee rained across her brand-new finery, and she screeched. "Ow! What the—"

"Are you okay?" Gia jumped to her feet.

Ally ran to the bathroom and stripped the soaked thong away from her abused flesh. *That's one way to get a sore bottom.* She walked into their enormous surround shower and turned the spigot to cold. "Yikes!" Gooseflesh rippled her skin as she adjusted the temperature to a more tolerable level. "I'm not okay!"

Gia stood in the doorway, a smile playing over her lips. She dabbed a bath towel at the coffee stains on her jeans.

"Don't get the towels dirty!" Ally shook the water from her eyes and held out her hand to Gia. The big surprise hadn't worked, but she might as well try to salvage the evening. "C'mon."

"I have to write..."

"Your computer's frozen, anyway. How long has it been since we showered together?" She squirted a dollop of foaming coconut body wash onto her left hand and held it out.

"I—"

"You know you want to." She smiled as Gia shucked off her jeans and sweatshirt in one fluid motion.

Or tried to. The hem of her pants caught on the corner of their wicker hamper, and Gia teetered like a one-legged stork trying to extricate herself. Poor Gia, graceful in her stitchery of words and yet awkward in real life. Gia's heroines kissed with perfect timing and never tripped on their own clothes.

Ally stepped out of the shower to give Gia assistance. She bent ever so slightly and lifted Gia's chin. What were the most inappropriate places and ways to kiss? She brushed Gia's hair back with her other hand, drawing the edge of her thumb along the edge of her jaw. Lifting Gia's hand to her lips, she interlaced their fingers and dropped a sweet, chaste kiss on the tips of the knuckles. Her gaze never left Gia's face. Ally poked out the tip of her tongue between her lips and drew Gia's hand to nuzzle next to her cheek.

"You should put that tongue to work," Gia breathed.

"You've told me not to promise what I won't deliver," Ally said primly. Shock clouded Gia's eyes for a second time, and Ally wriggled her naked buttocks in invitation. "First you say no tongue. Now you want more tongue. What's a girl to do?" She kissed the tips of her own fingers and touched them to the softness of Gia's lips.

"I'm...you're..." Gia raised her own hand as if to recreate the sensation of fingers on mouth.

"Spank me," Ally begged, turning around. She spread her legs and placed her palms against the bathroom wall, allowing the warm water to rush over her body. When Gia didn't comply, Ally raised her voice. "Hurry up." Gia was supposed to clap a solid but feminine hand against Ally's nether regions, spanking to a crisp pink and igniting unbelievable levels of passion. Ally longed for sheer animal instinct to overtake her placid, soft-spoken wife.

Instead, Gia took the pale pink shower puff, squirted it with body wash, and rubbed the luxurious foam over every crevice of Ally's body.

She squirmed, willing Gia's fingers to explore between her legs, but Gia washed efficiently before turning around and handing her own puff to Ally. Ally bit back irritation as she returned the favor. *How much more direct can a person get? The panties said it, I said it…what else can I do?*

Gia handed Ally a sea-green towel and wrapped a yellow one around herself. "Here you go."

Ally snapped the towel with a grunt and stalked into the hallway. Puzzled, Gia squeezed excess water from her hair. It couldn't be PMS, but why else would Ally be so touchy? Sure, they had quarreled in all of the usual ways during their courtship, engagement, and early marriage. Gia's inability to keep to a schedule and Ally's need for romantic displays had derailed many would-be dates, but seven years of married life had softened their rough edges. They'd gone through all of the major arguments often enough to skip to the shorthand version. *You know I hate that. We've been through this already!* What they lost in passion, they gained in comfort. Had they become too comfortable? Complacent?

Gia finished toweling off and ran a comb through her short, stiff boy cut. What would Lara, her current protagonist, do in this situation? Dashing fashion model by day and sex kitten by night, Lara Alexander seduced any number of women with her kinky prowess and bottomless toy bag. Gia couldn't horrify her sweet wife with the tricks Lara used to disarm angry lovers. Ally tolerated Gia's naughty writing, but they both agreed not to talk about it. Who wanted to live up to a twenty-something heroine with perfect buttocks and an acrobatic tongue? Lara was everything Gia was not, bold and rippling with sexiness. Brave Lara would take control of the scene without a second thought. Timid Gia would have to do her best without any super powers.

Stepping into the bedroom, where Ally was pulling on a denim skort, Gia cleared her throat. "Uh. Do you want to... you know? Have sex?" *Smooth, Gia. Real smooth. That's sure to get you lucky.*

Her fully clothed wife whipped around, hope and anger fighting for dominance on her face. "Really? Now? Not when we were..."

Ah, yes. Showering together. Gia could have smacked her forehead. No wonder Ally had gotten irritated. She should have remembered Gia needed neon signs to pick up on the romantic cues. Wasn't the point of marriage not needing to read unspoken requests? "It's hard to do it there." *Lame excuse, idiot. Are you a smut writer or not?* "It's too slippery. Wet." She cringed. *Lusty Lara wouldn't be that obvious. She'd have a snappy, witty comeback to regain control of the situation.* But how could Gia follow her protagonist's example without sounding crass? "I mean the floor."

Ally's cheeks turned pink. "There's something we could try here." She rummaged in a bureau drawer and took out a manila envelope. It was the same envelope she'd smuggled away when Gia asked about it.

So that's why Ally had been so secretive about the mail! What had she ordered? As the white receipt fluttered to the floor and Ally took out the object, Gia didn't know whether to laugh or cry. Ally held a cheerful plastic handle that sprouted a bundle of pink and white cords, like the fluttering ribbons on Gia's first banana seat bike.

"But...you don't..." Gia shook her head. Ally hated toys. For seven years, Gia had nearly gotten carpal tunnel from Ally's demand to have "real" sex or none at all. *Toys are real. Aren't they?* And now Miss Ally herself had taken the plunge.

Ally blushed even brighter. "Lara uses a flogger. Why don't we?"

Gia's own blush must have matched Ally's. "I thought you didn't read my books!"

Ally twirled the pink flogger in her hands. "I thought if I'm a book widow, I might as well learn about the other women in your life." She grinned, all irritation gone. Good old Ally, never one to hold a grudge. "I didn't know what kind to get, and some cost more than our monthly grocery bill. I got this flogger for a few dollars on Etsy. It will be okay, don't you think? Lara's was purple, but color shouldn't matter. Right?"

Gia's head spun. "It's dangerous," she protested. How would she know about technique? She'd never used spanking toys in real life, but her tireless research had brought up enough information to write convincingly. Come to think of it, she had never admitted her lack of experience to Ally. There was no need when they never discussed the bestselling books that paid their monthly mortgage.

"How do you use it?" Ally held out the flogger, and Gia couldn't think how to reply without admitting her ignorance. Ally gave her a hopeful grin. "Lara has her women touch their toes. Should I do that?"

Her Ally, bent over in submission? Stunned, Gia nodded. As much as the kink scene didn't appeal to her, she had always been curious. Her first girlfriend had insisted on vanilla sex on scheduled days of the week, and Ally was her second. Ever since a mommy porn book had taken the publishing world by storm, Gia had incorporated kinky elements to her stories for business purposes rather than pleasure. It was smart marketing to follow the trends, not a sign of her own perverted desires. At least, that's what she told herself as she spent hours scouring online fetish sites and chat rooms.

The flogger felt more like a child's toy than a real implement. She'd had a ribbon streamer as a child, a plastic handle with a long ribbon she could twirl. This felt much the same but shorter. What harm could an innocent plaything cause? As far as Gia could tell, the worst a flogger could do was brush limply against the buttocks when not given the correct flick of the wrist. She might embarrass herself, but she wasn't likely to hurt her Ally.

Ally bent at the waist, grunted, and spread her feet apart. "How about if I touch my knees? I don't think this thing about touching my toes will work. Maybe I should start yoga again."

Gia had to remember safety above all else. She had read exhortations to maintain safety protocol. What were they, again? *Safe, sane, and consensual?* Ally asking for it meant the flogging would be consensual, but safe? Gia had no idea what she was doing. Sane? No way.

"Maybe this isn't such a good idea," she began, but Ally bounced on her feet.

"Bet you're too chicken. You can write kink, but you can't do it for real."

What could Gia say in rebuttal? Nothing. She opened her mouth to agree, but instead Lusty Lara's voice came out. "That will cost you extra. Bare your bottom and spread those cheeks."

Shocked, Gia bit her tongue. Ally would run away screaming. Maybe she'd file for a divorce and cite spousal battery. She'd out Gia to their neighborhood, and all of their mutual friends would shun her as a wife-beater.

Then Ally lowered her shorts and panties, and Gia forgot everything else. How long had she lived with this gorgeous woman? How long had they had relegated sex as something to squeeze in between oil changes and dental appointments? She stepped forward and ran her hand over the sweet, cool flesh. Ally trembled beneath her touch.

"You never talked to me like that before," she whispered. "Like you own me."

Were those tears in her voice?

Ally wanted an alpha lover, did she? Lusty Lara's book exploits would be hard to match, but Gia would do her best. What would Lara say to put a woman in the mood? Oh, yes. "This will hurt," Gia warned. She felt like a fraud, but Ally gasped and bounced in response. *Keep going.* "Hold still, or I'll flog that naughty ass until you remember to whom you belong."

It was corny. Ridiculous. They didn't use coarse language with each other. But Ally moaned, and the scent of her arousal matched Gia's own. "Hurry up," Ally begged.

Gia raised the silly child's toy, took aim, and flicked the flogger backward to gain downward momentum. That much she remembered from reading. What she hadn't remembered was the gilt-plated wall sconce right above her head. *Clunk.* The falls of the flogger snarled around the fixture and brought it clear off the mounting. *Crash.* Oops. Lusty Lara never mis-aimed, and she certainly didn't destroy home furnishings. Well, not unless a villain needed to be decimated. "Sorry!"

"Are you okay?" Ally jumped up. "Did you—"

"I guess we shouldn't be so close to the wall." Determined not to let Ally down, Gia shoved the sconce toward its mounting. "Bend over. Now," she growled, trying to channel Lara once more. *Does Lara ever feel this stupid? I should give her self-doubt sometime. Humanize... Stop it! This is what got you in trouble in the first place! See, now you waited too long and Ally's going to argue. What would Lara say? Quick!* "Take the licking," she offered. "Or I'll lick you."

Ally dove to rest her hands on her knees, sticking her bottom out like a lascivious baseball catcher. "If you don't take down all the decorations first."

"Silence, mortal!" Lara's superhuman powers came in handy when she had to taunt her foes. "I'll teach you a lesson." Gia glanced behind her to make sure she had clearance and brought down the flogger with all her force. She almost closed her eyes, praying she would hit the right spot.

The pink and white cords hit the edge of Ally's right hip before collapsing on impact. Tufts of nylon cord rained onto the carpet, and Gia clutched the bereft handle. A thick blob of glue sported a few nylon hairs where the falls had been attached.

"Ouch!" Ally cried, rubbing the faint mark on her skin. "That wasn't sexy."

"No." Gia stared from the broken handle to her lover's bottom. "Not at all."

How come Lara's floggers never break?

Gia tried to give me what I wanted. Why am I sulking? Ally didn't know whether to pout or laugh. What would Gia's quilting circle friends say if they knew she had taken a flogger to her wife? Would they gasp in horror, or would they pretend not to understand and show off their newest rectangular-fabric cutting tools? She could never understand how her unassuming wife had turned into the kinky phenomenon of literature. At first, Ally had objected, stunned and horrified. Porn objectified women! But she relented when Gia explained that the stories, although explicit, were about women needing connection. After that, they both agreed not to speak of Violetta Beauregard, Gia's over-sexed alter ego. For a while, Ally had been afraid every night of sex would become fodder for Violetta's next book.

Ally puttered into the kitchen, where she took a slab of bacon from the fridge and some tomatoes from the counter. She was trying yet another anti-grain diet, but the cholesterol of red meat probably canceled the benefit of reducing processed carbohydrates. She dropped a pat of butter into the small cast-iron skillet they had received as a wedding present and then paused. The unnecessary fat bubbled and hissed against the black bottom of the pan. Too late now. She laid a few slices of bacon in the butter, curling the ends where they were too long for the pan. Fatty meat. Since she'd eliminated cookies, cakes, scones, and all her other favorites, it was her new treat. Some days, she would kill for a fresh blueberry muffin.

She washed and quartered the tomatoes Gia had picked from their garden earlier that morning and then pressed the serrated edge of her steak knife against the ripe flesh. Yellow seeds and pulpy goodness spilled from her knife into the sizzling pan. Her mouth watered.

Gia had retreated to the desk she kept in the living room. As much as she liked quiet, she had yielded to Ally's demand not to set up a private office. Writers put in eighteen-hour days with little to no vacation time, and Ally wanted to see at least the back of the woman to whom she had dedicated her life.

"Are you hungry?" Ally flipped the bacon with her tongs and cut the strips into bite-sized pieces with her favorite green-handled kitchen shears. Should she add some avocado, or would the creamy fruit disintegrate into the bacon grease?

A grunt could have meant Gia heard, or it could have signaled annoyance at a sentence gone wrong. Lara, Gia's heroine who linked together all of her books, had occasionally violated their rule about keeping kinky books private. Gia often exclaimed after a particularly good episode in bed, "*That's* how Lara should do it!" Lusty Lara's newest love interest, Sex Kitten Kate, defied her ability to seduce any red-blooded woman with a functioning hormone. Kate played Gabrielle to Lara's Xena, if Xena and Gabby had ever gotten it on.

They *should* have gotten it on.

It had been embarrassing but titillating to read Gia's books. Ally's favorite, by far, was Sex Kitten Kate and her ability to reduce Lusty Lara to a quivering, speechless mess. The best episode depicted Kate locking Lara to an iron bedframe with real police handcuffs and then using Lara's own toys against her. Kate had wielded nipple clamps, talons, and even vampire gloves until Lara's hoarse moans dwindled into one word. *Kate.* She had left the vanquished heroine unsatisfied for hours, taunting for each time Lara had done the same to a conquest. By the end of the book, Kate unfastened the cuffs and instructed the chastened lover in how to pleasure a woman instead of conquering her. Ally couldn't wait to see whether Sex Kitten Kate's dominance would continue, or if Lusty Lara would teach her a lesson. Who would wield the hairbrush next?

"No!" Gia pounded the desk. Had Sex Kitten Kate foiled her plans? How could Gia become so absorbed in fake women when her real woman stood beside her, offering homemade food and all the kink a suburban housewife could muster?

Then again, Ally couldn't muster much. She speared a piece of bacon and a triangle of fried tomato with a fork, blew on the steaming mouthful, and held it out. Gia reached for it, but Ally shook her head. "Open your mouth."

"That's what Kate just said to Lara." Obediently, Gia accepted the fruit and meat. "Yum! What did you put in it this time?"

"Not much. The bacon is so fresh it didn't need more than light seasoning."

Gia swiveled her chair around to face Ally. "Look, I'm sorry. I don't know how to use a flogger."

"No shirt, Sherlock." Ally grinned, using their favorite PG adaptation of the catchphrase. Ally put a forkful of bacon and tomato into her own mouth and savored the unlikely combination of flavors. She swallowed. "Why do you write about it, then? I wanted to be..." She blushed.

Gia's dark eyes lit up. "Lara? You wanted to be Lara?"

Ally shook her head. "No, I wanted you to be Lara. I wanted to..."

Gia named a few of Lara's lovers, and Ally blushed even more. Finally, she squeaked out the embarrassing truth.

"I wanted to be Sex Kitten Kate. Not—"

"Kate!" Gia's eyes shone like birthday candles. "You as Kate! *You!*"

Ally giggled. "Thanks for nothing, wifey. You saying I can't seduce you? You're the one who broke my flogger."

"You're the one who can't manage a lap dance." Gia scooted her chair backward, patting her legs. Ally hopped onto it, curling her arms around her wife's neck. "It was a terrible flogger. London Tanners or Adam and Gillian have far better—"

"Shush, wifey, or I'll take out the other toy I got." Ally traced the outline of Gia's lips and sucked on her forefinger. Gia's breath quickened. "And I didn't cheap out on this one, either. Sara let me borrow hers." Having a police officer for a friend had its uses other than feeling safe at night.

Gia shuddered, licking her lips. "How did you get her to share?"

"Easy." Ally slid off her wife's lap to retrieve the gleaming brushed steel handcuffs. "I promised to give her your tulip pattern."

"Ally! No!"

Gia's pride and joy was her famous tulip quilt, impossibly intricate and baffling even to experienced quilters. The trick was to sew the pieces together in the right order so the folds would lie flat. She guarded the secret more jealously than Ally's fidelity.

Ally held out the handcuffs, unsympathetic. After all, Gia could have wrestled herself away from her writing and set up the scene on her own terms. "That's what I expect you to say in a few minutes, but with a lot more desperation." *And moaning.*

Gia raised an eyebrow. "Haven't we broken enough things for today? Maybe we should just accept that we're boring old women who can't get it on."

"Speak for yourself, granny. Do you want Sex Kitten Kate to spank you or not?"

"Spank?" Gia's eyes grew round. "The flogger—"

Ally wiggled the fingers on her hand. "This won't break. Stop stalling."

As if in a dream, Gia held out her hands. Ally started to cuff them and stopped, looking puzzled.

"Thought you were the big bad Kate." Gia couldn't help the gentle taunt. Really, it was a treat to discover this new side to Ally. She had almost hyperventilated at discovering the smutty nature of Gia's books. How much had changed in a few years! "If I were Lara, I'd take the handcuffs and shackle you. Oh, and throw you over my shoulder to—"

Ally pulled Gia out of the chair, and she was startled enough to follow. "Silence, mortal!" They both giggled at the line.

"That's what *Lara* says," Gia stage-whispered. "Not Kate."

"Kate can say whatever she wants," Ally corrected. "She's badass like that."

"So, are you going to seduce me, or should I take a nap?" Gia gave a polite yawn. "Perhaps I should pretend to be afraid?"

"That does it." Ally scanned the living room before shrugging and pushing Gia over the back of the chair. The rollers squeaked, but she wedged the chair against the desk. "Uh, how do I get these open?"

Gia giggled into the cushion of the chair back. "That is the worst pickup line I've ever heard."

Slap!

Gia jumped as Ally dropped the handcuffs and tugged the linen capris to her ankles. "I'm going to lick you like a popsicle."

"Not a cherry one. I've already lost that—"

Smack! "I'll spank you as red as a cherry and suck on—"

"Where'd my sweet, cute Ally go?" Gia wriggled against the chair, struggling to keep her legs pressed together. They were a comfortable married couple, not sex-crazed rabbits humping in the wild. She should not quiver with desire like a teenage boy hoping to get laid.

Swat! "Ouch. My hand hurts!"

"Now you see why Lara has so many toys." It took all of Gia's self-control to speak in a semi-normal tone. While she had written many a spanking into Lusty Lara's exploits, she'd never dreamed that a few mild spanks could send her into such a tizzy. She'd do a better job of writing the aftermath in her next—

Ally gave another noisy, open-handed slap. "Stop thinking how you'll put this into your next book!"

Oh, she was good! Gia melted into a puddle, kneeling while hanging on to the back of the chair. "Ally-kazam," she murmured, using her long-ago pet name for the girl who turned her world upside down. "Take me now!"

"Not until I'm good and ready." Ally cupped Gia's buttocks, kissing the skin that longed for contact. "Okay, I'm ready. Turn over."

"Are we going to break the chair this time?" Gia rotated to face the unexpected lust in her usually complacent wife. "Uh, Ally. The neighbors will hear..."

Ally knelt before her, luscious pink tongue at the ready. "I'm not Ally," she insisted. "I'm Sex Kitten Kate."

At that, Gia entangled her hands in Ally's still-damp hair. "No." She bent down for a kiss, both frantic and assured. "You are my Ally. Better than any woman I put onto paper."

They stared at each other for a moment, Ally's eyes blurring with tears.

Gia! What were you doing! How could you let Ally think, for one second, that she had to measure up to your characters? Gia had to look at the floor, her hands, or anywhere but at Ally. "I don't deserve you."

"No. You don't." Ally spread Gia's legs farther apart and fondled her inner thighs. "Take notes, because it's my turn next, and I expect nothing less than brilliance."

"So, uh…" Gia blushed. "Could you make a mistake? I'm not sure if I can live up to this new sex-kitten you."

"Nope." Ally gave a long, luxurious stroke of her tongue that sent Gia into paroxysms of tingles. "We've had enough faux pas for today, haven't we?"

ABOUT THE AUTHORS

ELAINE BURNES

Elaine Burnes grew up and lives in Massachusetts. She works full-time and writes fiction when she can, publishing her first story, "A Perfect Life," in *Skulls and Crossbones* in 2010. Since then, she has had several more stories published, including "A Certain Moon," in the Goldie-winning anthology *Wicked Things* from Ylva in 2014. A collection of short stories, *A Perfect Life,* will be published 2016. Her first novel, *Wishbone*, came out in 2015.

Connect with this author:

Website: elaineburnes.com

Facebook: facebook.com/elaine.burnes

JOVE BELLE

Jove Belle is the author of several novels, novellas, and short stories. The novella *Cake* is her most recent release and is the first installment of the *Bitterroot Saga*. She also works as the operations director US for Ylva Publishing, an international publisher based out of Germany.

Connect with this author:

Website: jovebelle.com

MELISSA GRACE

Melissa Grace is the author of *Tainted Elite*, *Aspen's Stunt*, and several other lesfic titles emphasizing strong female characters. The joy of completing a book tends to inspire her to spontaneously break out in ninja moves. An engineer, avid motorcyclist (both on and off road), devoted martial artist, and passionate violinist, she grew up in Hanover, NH, believing she would someday become a stuntwoman. While she enjoys many opportunities for exploration of the world around her, her most treasured journey has been building a life with her family in Texas.

Connect with this author:
E-mail: melissa.grace@att.net
Website: inthebardroom.wordpress.com/
Twitter: @melissagraceitb

LEA DALEY

Lea Daley has written fiction and poetry while raising children, claiming a lesbian identity, earning a BFA in painting, teaching preschoolers and college students, surviving the death of her only daughter, and heading a nonprofit agency that serves low-income working families. Her debut novel, *Waiting for Harper Lee,* was a Golden Crown Awards finalist and received a Lavender Certificate from the Alice B Readers Appreciation Committee. Her second book, *FutureDyke,* won a Goldie Award and was a Lambda Literary finalist.

Connect with this author:
Website: leadaley.com

A.L. BROOKS

A.L. Brooks currently resides in London, although over the years she has lived in places as far afield as Aberdeen and Australia. She works 9-5 in corporate financial systems, and spends many a lunchtime in the gym attempting to achieve some semblance of those firm abs she likes to write about so much. And then promptly negates all that with a couple of glasses of red wine and half a slab of dark chocolate in the evenings. When not writing she likes doing a bit of Latin dancing, cooking, travelling both at home and abroad, reading lots of other writers' les-fic, and listening to mellow jazz.

Connect with this author:
E-mail: albrookswriter@gmail.com
Facebook: facebook.com/albrookswriter

CHRIS ZETT

Chris Zett lives in Berlin, Germany, with her partner. TV inspired her to study medicine, but she found out soon enough that real life in a hospital consists more of working long hours than performing heroic rescues. The part about finding a workplace romance turned out to be true, though.

She uses any opportunity to escape the routine by reading, writing, or traveling. Her favorite destinations include penguin colonies in Patagonia and stone circles in Scotland.

Connect with this author:
E-mail: chris-zett@web.de

CORI KANE

Cori Kane has an addiction: stories. Whether they come as books, movies, TV shows, or even song lyrics, she wants them—and uses them as inspiration for her own work. She started writing at fourteen when her first crush inspired her to write some "seriously lovely, seriously naive poetry."

Many years later, Cori Kane still hasn't given up on entertaining herself and others with her less lovely and—hopefully—less naive fiction. When not writing she indulges in all the other ways to feed her addiction and loves to take strolls in her hometown by the sea.

Connect with this author:
E-mail: cori.kane@web.de
Website: seriouswriterdude.wordpress.com/
Facebook: facebook.com/pages/
Cori-Kane/268830173306877
Twitter: @corikane

KATHY BRODLAND

Kathy Brodland is a seventy-eight-year-old retiree, living in Langley, British Columbia. She has been writing most of her adult life, but it is only recently that she realized there might actually be a market for the kind of stories she likes to write. She loves speculative fiction, along with stories that involve the paranormal and things that go bump in the night.

She acquired a taste for lesbian fiction after her wife introduced her to Radclyffe's writings. She has been hooked ever since.

Connect with this author:
E-mail: brodlandk@gmail.com

HAZEL YEATS

Hazel Yeats resides in the Netherlands, the country of flat polders, green pastures, and lots of water. She knew from an early age that she wanted to write, but it wasn't until decades later that she finally wrote a novel. Once she had, there was no going back—she was hooked.

When she's not slaving away at her day job, she's cycling, sipping cappuccinos, or getting her hands dirty by growing her own veggies. And she sings, in a very unambitious choir. You wouldn't peg her for a soprano, but she is.

Connect with this author:
E-mail: hazelyeats@outlook.com
Facebook: facebook.com/Hazel-Yeats-1041782659197796/

JACELLE SCOTT

Jacelle Scott is the pseudonym of lovers, bound to one another for over forty years, who live in the northeastern United States. Scholars, writers, and each a parent, they work as historian and researcher respectively and have published books, articles, essays, and many academic papers. At last, they are planning their wedding and searching for a new house, replete with studio space where they will continue to write, learn to paint, and drink afternoon tea or whatever strikes their fancy.

JAE

Jae grew up amidst the vineyards of southern Germany. She spent her childhood with her nose buried in a book, earning her the nickname *professor*. The writing bug bit her at the age of eleven. For the last eight years, she has been writing mostly in English.

She used to work as a psychologist but gave up her day job in December 2013 to become a full-time writer and a part-time editor. As far as she's concerned, it's the best job in the world.

When she's not writing, she likes to spend her time reading, indulging her ice cream and office supply addictions, and watching way too many crime shows.

Connect with this author:
E-mail: jae@jae-fiction.com
Website: jae-fiction.com
Facebook: facebook.com/JaeAuthor
Twitter: @jaefiction

ANASTASIA VITSKY

Cookie queen, wooden spoon lady, and champion of carbs, Anastasia Vitsky specializes in F/F fiction. She hates shoes and is allergic to leather. When not writing about women who live spankily ever after, she coordinates reader and author events such as Ana's Advent Calendar, a month-long celebration of books, community, and making a difference.

Her notable works include *Taliasman*, *Mira's Desire*, *Simple Gifts*, *Love Spanks 2015*, *The Way Home*, and *Lighting the Way*.

Connect with this author:
Website: governingana.wordpress.com
Facebook: facebook.com/anastasiavitsky
Twitter: @AnastasiaVitsky

OTHER BOOKS FROM
YLVA PUBLISHING

www.ylva-publishing.com

SHAKEN TO THE CORE
Jae

ISBN: 978-3-95533-662-2
Length: 368 pages (126,000 words)

Kate Winthrop, daughter of a shipping magnate, is expected to marry a respectable man. But her true passion lies with photography—and with women.

Much to the dismay of her parents, she becomes friends with their maid Giuliana.

Then an earthquake hits San Francisco. Will the disaster shatter their tentative feelings? Or will they be able to save each other's lives and hearts?

BUNNY FINDS A FRIEND
Hazel Yeats

ISBN: 978-3-95533-499-4
Length: 204 pages (55,000 words)

Cara Jong's bad day doesn't improve after a run-in with Jude Donovan, who's playing Santa in a department store in Amsterdam. When Cara finds out that the woman beneath the Santa suit is a children's book writer, she's intrigued. But she doesn't trust her luck in love. Can Cara's meddling sisters and a hilarious road trip convince her to go after her happily-ever-after with the writer?

CAKE
Jove Belle

ISBN: 978-3-95533-612-7 (mobi),
978-3-95533-613-4 (epub)
Length: 23,000 words

Together, Kelly and Elana are a recipe for disaster. They meet at the church where Elana's ex-lover is marrying Kelly's brother. Then, without even tasting it, Elana insults the wedding cake Kelly made.

Despite the reasons they shouldn't be together, there's still an undeniable something between them. All they need is a chance to enjoy their slice of the cake.

THE AFFAIR
Cori Kane

ISBN: 978-3-95533-404-8 (mobi),
978-3-95533-405-5 (epub)
Length: 22,000 words

A close working relationship turns into a passionate affair for Linda and Robin, but they never counted on falling in love, since they're both married.

While Linda struggles with her husband's attempts to save their marriage, Robin feels guilty because her wife is dying of cancer. A night away together deepens their connection, but can love grow out of the ashes of shattered lives?

COMING FROM YLVA
PUBLISHING IN SUMMER 2016

www.ylva-publishing.com

THE CLUB
A.L. Brooks

Welcome to The Club—leave your inhibitions and your everyday cares at the door and indulge yourself in an evening of anonymous, no-strings, woman-on-woman action. For many visitors to The Club, this is exactly what they are looking for and what they get. For others, however, the emotions run high, and one night of sex changes their lives in ways they couldn't have imagined.

HEARTWOOD
Catherine Lane

When the law firm she works for sends Nikka to the Springs, home of lesbian author Beth Walker, she jumps at the chance to prove herself to her boss, Lea.

But nothing is as it seems. Beth is hiding her past with a film star. Lea may be keeping Beth prisoner in her own home. The only person who knows the truth is adorably impulsive Maggie.

Will Nikka dare look into the mystery—and into her own heart?

Finding Ms. Write
© 2016

"Consignment" © 2016 Elaine Burnes
"Cherry Park Pulp" © 2016 Jove Belle
"Books, Renovations, and a Vespa" © 2016 Melissa Grace
"Kindred Spirits" © 2016 Lea Daley
"Between the Lines" © 2016 A.L. Brooks
"Romance on a Side Note" © 2016 Chris Zett
"Wrote Trip" © 2016 Cori Kane
"Orphans' Christmas" © 2016 Kathy Brodland
"Vegan Delights" © 2016 Hazel Yeats
"Cruise" © 2016 Jacelle Scott
"Sex Sells" © 2016 Jae
"Faux Pas" © 2016 Anastasia Vitsky

ISBN: 978-3-95533-670-7

Also available as e-book.

Published by Ylva Publishing, legal entity of Ylva Verlag, e.Kfr.
Ylva Verlag, e.Kfr.
Owner: Astrid Ohletz
Am Kirschgarten 2
65830 Kriftel
Germany

www.ylva-publishing.com
info@ylva-publishing.com

First edition: June 2016

No part of this book may be reproduced, scanned, or distributed in any printed or electronic form without permission. Please do not participate in or encourage piracy of copyrighted materials in violation of the author's rights. Thank you for respecting the hard work of this author.

This is a work of fiction. Names, characters, places, and incidents either are a product of the author's imagination or are used fictitiously, and any resemblance to locales, events, business establishments, or actual persons—living or dead—is entirely coincidental.

Credits
Edited by Jae & Jove Belle
Proofread by Blu
Cover Design by Jove Belle
Cover Photo by BillionPhotos.com
Print Layout by Streetlight Graphics

www.ingramcontent.com/pod-product-compliance
Lightning Source LLC
Chambersburg PA
CBHW020557260626
47157CB00003B/749